ONE BEHIND THE EAR

ONE BEHIND THE EAR

WENSLEY CLARKSON

Published by

MAXCRIME

an imprint of John Blake Publishing Ltd,
3 Bramber Court, 2 Bramber Road,
London W14 9PB, England

www.johnblakepublishing.co.uk

First published in paperback as Hitman
by John Blake Publishing in 2002.
This edition published 2010.

ISBN: 978 1 84454 909 2

British Library Cataloguing-in-Publication Data:

A catalogue record for this book is available from the British Library.

Design by www.envydesign.co.uk

Printed in Great Britain by CPI Bookmarque, Croydon CR0 4TD

1 3 5 7 9 10 8 6 4 2

Papers used by John Blake Publishing are natural, recyclable products
made from wood grown in sustainable forests. The manufacturing processes
conform to the environmental regulations of the country of origin.

MAXCRIME series commissioning editor: Maxim Jakubowski

When I was in Northern Ireland the Provos used to call it givin' someone the O.B.E. – One Behind the Ear. It's got a neat ring to it, don't you think.

Author's note

Naturally, all the characters described here are fictional. But to all the faces that I've met over the years and all the clubs I've crashed in to, I say, "Thank you".

Chapter One

My eyes were everywhere. The buzz had kicked in. Fuck, I felt horny. Even my dick was tingling.

You see, pulling the trigger wasn't the really exciting bit. The biggest hard-on was walking calmly into your killing zone. The anticipation. Knowing that you're the only one who knows some poor bastard's about to cop it.

Inside myself I knew I was playing judge, jury, executioner and fucking God Almighty. And it was turning me on. I was floating ten feet off the ground it felt so good.

I tried to control it, to keep my senses sharp and alert. But it wasn't easy. I was almost too aware of being this poor bastard's ultimate provider. Heaven and hell all rolled up into one.

The adrenalin pumped through my body. My stomach was rumbling like I was hatching a huge crap. I was tuned into every sound and sight around me, every smell, every slight movement.

Even a yellowing gob of spit on the pavement caught my eye. I was picking up sounds that your average punter wouldn't notice and that even I wouldn't normally hear.

Felt like I'd had a big line of Charlie – but I hadn't. Never use it during a job. That's how you can lose it. Best kept just for special occasions.

I was on hit number 12 at the time. I suppose you'd call it a public execution.

It took place in a crowded, noisy transport caff on the Old Kent Road. The caff was the last resort because my target knew he was on a hit list and he'd been ducking and diving for weeks.

His bosses, and mine as well, solved the problem by getting him into the greasy spoon for a slap-up breakfast and then telling me to turn his brain to scrambled eggs.

At the time I had no idea what he'd done wrong, but I did later hear he'd been fingered for thieving the produce.

1

I reckon Number 12 was a perfect hit. I drifted into that caff nice and casual about a quarter past eight and headed straight for the gents.

I was more worried about the bulge in my trousers than the bulge under my jacket. On my way through I had a butchers around and spotted where my man was sitting.

He was parked near the back of the caff, facing the door. I'd approach from the gents, which was on the side and in the rear. It would all fall together very nicely.

Once I was safely in the toilet, I locked myself in and checked my .38. Then I put it back in my belt and headed out into the caff once more.

That buzz was growing by the millisecond. It got even better when I felt that cold steel of the shooter rubbing against my bare skin.

He never even saw me coming.

I strolled up right behind him and popped him three times in the back of the head and neck. Bits of his brain flew into his breakfast plate, blood mingling with his bacon and eggs.

As usual, the sudden loud noise of the .38 going off sent everyone diving under tables.

I stood there for a second or two and let the sweet smell of cordite waft up my nostrils.

No doubt many of the punters in the caff got a good look at me, but I'm certain that seeing my man's head sprawled in his breakfast would help cloud their memories.

Frightened witnesses always get so confused, and I'd just created a caff full of frightened witnesses. If the cozzers tried to get a photofit from the descriptions provided by those punters, they'd have ended up searching for the Elephant Man.

I left that caff by the front door, naturally. But I didn't run. Just casually hopped on the nicked Suzuki 500 I'd left parked up outside.

Then I drove half a mile, slung the bike up on a perfectly legal spot and dumped it.

As I walked down the road I ripped the see-through latex gloves off my hands. They felt hot and clammy but at least my hard-on was going down.

Then I strolled into a tube station and jumped a Northern Line train. By the time I picked up my own motor, dropped the shooter and got home, it was a few minutes past midday. Just in time for lunch.

Hit number 12 earned me a modest bit of news coverage; a small piece on page 9 of the *London Evening Standard*, a few paragraphs in the dailies – and 20 grand in hard cash. I liked the cash the best.

There was no comeback. I was never pulled by the law, never questioned, never given any bother. In a nutshell, it was a perfect, professional hit. Looking back it was too easy, which is where my problems began.

Usually, after doing a job, I keep well away from any other action for at least three months. That way, if plod has sussed anything, it gives them plenty of time to track me down and speak to me about it. If I've done everything right, they won't be able to pin anything on me – but you don't want them sniffing around when you're planning your next job.

Also, if you start knocking 'em out too quick you can get careless. And this is a profession in which anything less than perfection just ain't tolerated.

It only takes one mistake and you're fucked. So if I'm to be entirely honest about it, I never should have gone near job number 13.

Of all the hits I've done, number 13 was the most problematical. Lot of it was down to me. But 12 had been so cushy and 13 had come to me through a mate of mine.

Then there were these gee-gees that took a few seconds longer than I thought to get to the finishing line. I didn't owe big bucks, but I wasn't exactly rolling in it, either.

So I took the contract on 13. I knew I'd broken my normal pattern, a stupid thing to do for a hired gun.

I prided myself on being careful, super-fucking-careful. I saw problems ahead when they didn't exist, but on this job I didn't even notice the most obvious ones.

That's what made number 13 so dangerous, and the strangest of my career. It's a lesson to any would-be hitman on how not to carry out a job.

Chapter Two

My biggest problem in life is that, even though I do know the difference between right and wrong, I don't give a toss about it.

That's why it didn't bother me that I'd made a small fortune from popping 12 hoods on the streets of London.

Sure I was a bit superstitious about job number 13, who wouldn't be? But that just kept me on my toes.

The fact I'd knocked off 12 people and never been convicted of anything didn't guarantee I wouldn't fuck up the 13th hit and end up in Parkhurst watching my toenails grow.

As it happens, one of the biggest drawbacks of having done so many jobs is that you get to think you might be invincible. Now that is fucking dangerous.

Trickiest moment in any shootist's career is pulling the trigger on number one. It's more of a mental thing than a physical thing. Doesn't take much actual strength to squeeze the trigger. Anyone can do it. Kids, women, old dears, every fucking one of us.

But planning how you're going to point it at someone's head and then pull your finger back is a different kettle of fish. There aren't many who'll do it. (Of course, I'm not including the really sick ones who knock off their old ladies and kids and stuff like that.) But once you've done it, once you've seen a bullet ripping through someone's skull and watched as the whole pineapple splits open, once you've seen how quick and easy it is, then it's not so tricky.

My first "paid for" job was exactly like that. The hit itself couldn't have been simpler, but the build-up nearly did my head in. I kept planning it for a specific time and place and then cancelling it at the last minute.

In the end, I plugged this old bloke in a boozer in New Cross. As luck would have it, he was so pissed he was taking forty winks in a booth in the corner when I wandered up.

I pressed the cold steel barrel of my .38 snubnose up to his right eyelid, and squeezed tight.

The kickback nearly knocked the gun up above his head. I re-aimed, held it rock steady this time and let rip with bullets two and three. But I needn't have bothered.

Poor bastard didn't even have time to wake up. If he had, he would have known his time had come.

That first bullet entered the left corner of his eye, travelled through his brain, exited the right side of the back of his head, and embedded itself in the base of the armrest of his seat.

His life was snuffed out in a split second. Too easy by half, if you know what I mean.

Then I pointed the .38 towards the ground so no one else would get hit and walked straight out through the double doors of the boozer.

No one raised an eyelid and they all went out of their way to avoid eye contact. I don't blame them, d'you?

That's the problem, it can be too fucking easy. You start thinking of yourself in a different way. You reckon you're safe, that nothing can go wrong. That you're above everyone else. It's that word again – *invincible*. Must be how some of those life-saving surgeons feel. Nothing can touch you. You're in charge. You're master of the fucking universe.

It's a good feeling if you know how to control it, but a lot of people don't. They get too cocky. They really do believe they're untouchable. Then they get stupid and they get touched.

But real pros like me who treat the work as nothing more than a job don't usually lose it like that. We stay alert. That's how we survive. Before any job I cover all the angles, all potential problems. I plan it down to the last second. I make pages of notes and I make standby plans.

Must be a bit like being a fighter pilot on a mission. Everything builds to the moment you let that missile go. And you better be very careful you hit the right target.

Having said all that, I've got to admit that even I've dropped some right clangers in my time.

I've been spotted pulling the trigger. I've been fingered in areas where bodies have turned up.

These things happen. They're part of the luggage if you work regularly. But I've never been convicted by plod for anything because I'm always on the lookout for those sort of problems.

I play by my own special rules. I always make sure I'm working for proper firms who'd back me if there was a bit of bother. And they have.

The witnesses who spotted me weren't sure they really saw me, and the people who said they'd seen me in a specific location decided maybe I wasn't there, after all.

The firms I work for can make sure that so-called witnesses tell the truth: first we agree on the truth, and then they tell it.

None of this was going through my head on the day I knocked off number 12 and then got home for lunch to find the missus was out.

She's quite a character is my old lady. She knows how to handle everything, including me.

Because of my profession I keep very strange working hours. Sometimes I'll be home for dinner, sometimes not. Sometimes I leave the manor for a day or two with no more than a couple of hours' notice. But the old lady takes it all in her stride. She's got a life of her own – but she still manages to slot my life into it.

I'm not really superstitious or anything but I've got to point out here and now that we're both Virgos and my old aunt Mary warned me that could be a big problem when we first got spliced. I know I'm the typical Virgo – selfish, obsessional, solitary – but luckily she's the bloody opposite. And you know what they say about opposites.

Anyway, I hadn't a clue where the old lady was that day when I got home from number 12. She could have been out shopping in Bromley, at her golf classes or round a mate's house.

But I didn't reckon she was off seeing another bloke. I wouldn't want to know about any of that.

I've treated her like a princess. I've given her more readies than there's sand on Southend beach. And I've given her the respect she deserves. Well, I think I have.

You see, my first missus was knocked off when I got deep in the shit with a heavy team of Turkish Cypriot nutters. I was shipping heroin through Kent and south east London for them. It was all pretty easy at first. I was taping the packages to the rims of the wheels of my motor.

Customs at Dover, Ramsgate and Newhaven would often inspect the tyre, but they'd never take it off the rim.

I'd done enough trips to be owed more than £30,000, but this mad Turkish smack merchant thought it'd be cheaper to have me blown away. Which it would have been, had he got the job done properly.

He rented three ugly gorillas to plug me, and they turned up at my house when I wasn't home. My missus, who was very pregnant at the time, let them in. Instead of pulling out when they saw I wasn't there, they kicked the life out of her and our baby, and then left her lying in the hall. She haemorrhaged and died.

That ignited something inside me. I was gutted, heartbroken, confused, guilty – all wrapped up in a grenade of fury.

Some people reckon disasters strengthen your life by changing the entire course of things. In my experience that's a load of old bollocks.

My mum lost my kid brother when he was 18 months old. He caught his head between the bars of his cot and choked to death. I found his body the next morning. Poor old thing took to her bed for five years after that and started popping more Tuinal sleeping pills than Marilyn fucking Monroe. (I know because I used to nick a few of them and flog them down my local boozer.) Didn't do her life much good, did it?

Then there was this schoolgirl who lived a few doors away from where I was brought up. She was raped by some noncie neighbour git. Her dad had this geezer knee-capped but he never stopped blaming himself for what happened. Poor bastard ended up driving off Beachy Head one day. Call that a blessing in disguise, do you?

It's made me realise there's only one way to cope – and that's not to care any more.

So my first missus gets murdered and that sends me off in the direction of the local hitman job centre.

Eventually I tracked down each of those arseholes who forced their way into my house and killed the lot of them. It didn't make her come alive again but it made me feel a little better.

That Turkish bastard who commissioned them was nicked and sent to jail. If he ever gets out I'll have him over, too.

Suppose all this makes me sound like a bit of a psycho. But what they did to my old lady was totally out of order, you know what I mean? Eye for an eye, tooth for a fucking tooth. It's what gets us through life, ain't it?

Chapter Three

I've been able to knock off all these bastards without feeling too bad about it, but I have to get myself in the right state to do it. I didn't really understand that until recently when I started getting a bit heavier about my feelings. That's when I began to realise what type of person I really am.

You do a lot of thinking when you're stuck outside your next victim's house waiting for them to come out.

I know the work I do might seem fucking strange to most people. But the reason I can do this sort of thing is, I reckon, because there's a lot of hatred inside me for the tossers I have to deal with. It's the truth, I swear.

I might have to knock round with them, even have a laugh with them, but deep inside I fucking hate them. I hate them not because of anything they've done to me, but because of what they did to my first missus.

Most people wouldn't get it but, although in some ways I must be a bad person, I'm not sure that I'm truly evil. I do care about certain things and I get on with people as long as they don't cross me or my family.

My dopey brother-in-law Ray is always telling me, "Malcolm, you think about things too fuckin' much. You're goin' to do your head in, mate."

Shame I've never been able to tell him how I earn a crust out of doing other people's heads in, so to speak.

Anyway, enough of this psycho-babble, as my missus would call it. Job number 13, from start to finish, took place mostly in and around south east London between the months of September, October and November 1998.

Obviously I wasn't there for every second of it, but I can fill in the blanks because I know how the system works. And I know people who know people, so I can keep track of what's happening when I have to.

On this job, I was so convinced there were other forces at work, that I felt the need to be on top of things throughout. The whole business kicked off with a simple blagging which it transpired was not so simple after all. And by a complete coincidence, it started the day I finished number 12.

Danny "The Downer" Urquart is a face in Southwark and Bermondsey. He's one of the biggest coke, puff and E controllers on the manor.

For those not in the know, E, coke and puff are the biggest profit-making drugs on the street today.

To be a major player like The Downer you've got to have contacts ranging from the local youth to the cozzers. They've all got to be in your pocket somehow. It ain't easy. Then you've got to run a vast distribution network of street dealers. They're known as runners. The man in charge of these runners, the man who collects for the collector, is the controller.

Danny "The Downer" Urquart had worked south east London, first as a smalltime dealer, then as controller, for maybe 20 years and everyone knows him and everyone respects him. I've been aware of him since I was a youngster just getting started in the business.

I know he's got a wife and some kids, and I know basically he's all right. He got the nickname "Downer" because he's so fucking happy all the time, like a tall geezer who's called "shorty", or a skinny git becomes "muscles".

At one time he was probably well hard – he had to be to get himself into this very powerful position. But by this time he relied more on the reputation of the main collector we will call the "MD".

Now the MD, a heavyweight character who still controls most of the gear from Bermondsey through to Bexleyheath, has a deadly reputation. It's been said he's put more people underground than London Transport.

In other words, it's better not to bother any of his chaps.

Danny "The Downer" Urquart usually finishes his day on the northern end of a sprawling high-rise estate on the edge of

Peckham. He has a street dealer who lives in one of the flats there. By the end of his day he's seen all his team and can have as much as five grand in cash on him.

One night in mid-September, cash in pocket, he left his street dealer's one-bedroom flat on the second floor and began walking down the piss-drenched concrete staircase that all those sort of places seem to have.

He must have seen two blokes standing there, hanging about, but he obviously didn't think anything of it. That was a big error.

These two geezers – both white, one tall and one medium – were waiting for only one thing. They had goatee beards and wore shell suits, but then so does just about everyone under the age of 40 on a highrise estate.

They didn't wear masks or anything stupid but they had tea cozies on their heads and those wrap-round sunglasses which was a bit odd since they weren't black and it was raining outside.

Anyhow, the tall one pulled out a shooter and pointed it right at Urquart's head.

"Ya diss me, man. I kill ya."

They both spoke like black men, which was also well out of order. The Downer didn't panic, but he wasn't exactly thrilled about the situation, either. He knew exactly what they were after.

"Look," he said, still smiling, "take the fuckin' lot. I don't want no grief."

You can't blame him, can you? Urquart's job doesn't normally involve any violence. There are guys in this line of business who are nutters, or have a reputation for being nutters, but they're the exception. Most street dealers or runners are pretty normal blokes. Many of them are married with kids. They might talk funny and act like hard men, but they're usually sweet as a nut. They don't hurt anyone. And they don't like to get hurt, either.

Urquart's attitude went down OK with these two armed white rastaboys.

"Ya giss us respect, man, den der's na problem," the tall one told him. "Now stop de fuckin' smilin' and giss us de bread, man."

They took him down to the basement and made him lean up against the central heating boiler. Then they dropped his mobile in the furnace.

The cash really was all they were after. They didn't even nick the puff he'd picked up for a later dropoff – or give him a whack because he looked so fucking happy all the time.

"Stay cool," the medium-sized one told Downer after his partner had pocketed the cash.

I'm told that particular rastaboy was slurping on a carton of Ribena at the time, which must have been fucking irritating for anyone he came across.

Anyhow, he says to Downer, " 'Ang loose 'ere, 'cos if I see ya head we gonna 'ave ta shoot it off."

At that moment there was a loud popping noise. All three turned in the direction of the gas furnace where The Downer's mobile was exploding with a well weird mix of ringing tones in the flames.

Then the smaller one sucked his Ribena carton dry, chucked it on the floor and they disappeared.

Urquart didn't move a muscle at first, then he started to shake. Until this moment, the worst thing that had ever happened to him was a few collars for dealing in nicked fags and booze. The Downer waited about 15 minutes and then, very slowly and very carefully, walked upstairs to his runner's maisonette and called the office.

"I been fuckin' robbed," he said.

The outfit Urquart worked for was located in the basement of a funeral parlour just round the corner from the old Millwall Football Club stadium, in New Cross.

I'd worked for them a few years back and I never forgot how they used to lay all the cash out on body slabs. Piles and piles of readies, and on occasions, a stiff would be laid out there waiting for the embalmer or cosmetician or his funeral.

I didn't mind killing them, but I wasn't keen on looking at them.

Anyway, the office told The Downer not to move and they sent two of their soldiers over to bring him back. By the time he arrived at the parlour, the MD had been contacted and had come over.

They sat Urquart down, gave him a good stiff drink to relax him, and then started firing questions at him. For six and a half hours they grilled him and regrilled him, over and over. If he was telling them porkies, he would have coughed at some point. But he didn't.

It wasn't that they didn't believe him – The Downer had been with the firm for a long time and they'd never had any problems with him before. Street dealers and controllers have been known to hold themselves up, but they knew Urquart wasn't messing about. He was still shaking like a leaf. And he wasn't smiling any more, either.

Two days later a second controller was held up.

This time it was a little old fellow called Harry working up in the Camberwell New Road section. Again, as I found out was true for all these blaggings, the old boy had just seen his last street dealer of the day. This particular runner also lived in a high-rise maisonette from where he flogged all the gear for the entire estate.

Old Harry walked out of the building and towards the car park at the back. Before he'd got to his motor, two fellows, the same two who'd blagged Urquart, wander up to him and stick a shooter in his ribs.

The old boy said nothing and did nothing.

"Hey, lit'l fella," the big one commanded. "Don' be foolin' wi' us. Giss us all de bread, or we gonna shoot ya in de feet."

They took his cash, his simcard and his car keys. The cash was a fucking healthy day's payout – ten grand. The keys were worth about a nicker and they dropped his simcard down a drain hole. They even told Harry they'd leave the keys under a brick on a wall two hundred yards away. And they did.

By now the firm knew something was up, but they weren't

sure if it was an inside job. They still thought it might just be a run of bad luck.

Then the luck got worse.

Up at the Elephant and Castle end of the Old Kent Road there's an estate of neat little modern private houses and a small park. The street dealer worked in the park, flogging gear to yuppies and schoolkids in the neighbourhood.

Usually, the controller didn't even get out of his motor. He showed up at about 6.30 in the evening, hooted twice and waited. The street dealer came out, handed him an envelope, and disappeared. Hey presto.

This time the controller – a fellow called Bigs – collected his envelope and started pulling out of a parking space next to the entrance to the park as normal.

But before he'd moved five yards another motor cut him up. The tall fellow in the shell suit jumped out and pointed a shooter at the controller's head.

"Keep de foot off de pedal, or I kill ya," he said. "Ya dig?"

"Fuck off," screamed Bigs.

"Win' down de window, man, and giss up de cash."

"Fuck off," said Bigs, not noted for his good manners.

"I mean it," said the tall, white rastaboy.

Bigs wound down the window.

Knowing what I know now, that these were part-timers, I doubt if they'd have had the bottle to pull the trigger. Of course, I could be wrong. But Bigs had sensibly decided not to put them to the test.

"Absa-fuckin-lootly," he shrugged and handed over what he had, which was about six grand.

The tall fellow then reached into the motor, took out the keys and heaved them over the railings into the park. Then he was gone.

By this time they were screaming blue fucking murder at the funeral parlour.

Obviously the controllers were being fingered by someone on the inside who had definite information, because robbing a controller isn't that simple. First, you have to know who the controller is. That in itself is not that difficult.

But then you have to establish where he's going to be, when he's loaded with cash, and what time he'll be there.

This can be tricky because a good, pro controller makes between 30 and 50 pick-ups a day, and he never stays in any one place too long. Even if you know his schedule, you've still got to isolate him, and since the job requires the controller to be around people, that is not as easy it sounds.

But these two cowboys were doing it, and doing it fucking perfectly, so they had to have a connection with someone inside the firm.

The firm tried everything except bell the nearest copshop. They had controllers change their schedule. They started using armed muscle to ride shotgun with their employees. None of it made any fucking difference. The two white rastaboys were always too quick. Before any of the muscle could pull a shooter out they were on to him.

These two fellows took the firm to the cleaners during September and early October. Sometimes they had the bottle to hit the same controllers two or three times, and still the firm had no fucking idea who they were or who was grassing them up. These two blaggers had picked up nearly 100 grand in swag. It was fucking outrageous.

Then, unfortunately for certain parties, they got themselves picked up.

Since it was obvious that someone inside the firm (it had to be a controller rather than a street dealer or some other dipshit) was feeding the dynamic duo with their info, the MD and his top brass took some action without bothering to tell the men on the ground. They went outside the firm and hired some even heavier muscle. They started using backup cars with those two-way Motorolas you can pick up in Toys R Us.

Even the controllers didn't know they were being followed. It took a few more days but the two rastaboys eventually met their match.

This particular controller had changed his run so he ended up at the park in front of the Peabody Estate, on Southwark Bridge Road.

He usually made a point of getting to the park during daylight, because you never know who's going to be in there after dark. All a controller needs is to get mugged and lose his day's takings, but he was running a bit late, so he went after dark which made him extra jumpy. He pulled up next to a bus stop, parked, and then walked into the park.

His street dealer was waiting on a bench. After taking the cash the controller strolled back to his motor. Our two friends were waiting for him.

"Fuckin' hell," he said, "not you two again," or something along those lines. At that moment I bet he wished a mugger had shown up instead.

The two blaggers relieved him of his daily bread. Then they told him that for his own safety he should take a walk in the park before they headed off to their own motor.

The medium-sized one was driving. I'm told he had his customary carton of Ribena hanging out of his mouth at the time. He didn't get very far. He'd just put the key in the ignition when he looked up to find a very large Remington sawnoff pointing directly at his head.

All that Ribena made a right mess of his white T-shirt.

The tall one had a similar experience.

"Game's over, gentlemen," said one of the muscle merchants who'd been shadowing the controller.

The two white rastaboys were called Dave Hedley and Pat Tucker. Hedley was the medium-sized one and Tucker was the tall one.

Hedley lived on what they call the armpit of Bermondsey and Tucker came from Eltham. No one in any of the old firms had even heard of them.

The heavy mob delivered them to the funeral parlour and

they were taken down into the basement. From there the buttonmen took over. They chatted about all the usual subjects: football, New Labour, the United Nations, Stephen Lawrence.

At first Hedley and Tucker were mightily reluctant to voice their own opinions on such far-ranging topics, but they soon realised that the firm did care about their opinions on world affairs.

It's not that Hedley and Tucker wanted to play the hard men and protect their silent partner, it's just that they took a butcher's around, saw the empty coffins, and decided they'd be brown bread as soon as they coughed. So they were in no particular hurry to talk.

In a nutshell, it was up to the buttonmen to, number one, convince these two rastaboys they wouldn't be rubbed out if they coughed to everything or, number two, convince them that being brown bread could actually be better than staying alive.

The buttonmen took the second option. They used some very subtle techniques.

It's a well-known fact that in the basements of funeral parlours you can really hurt someone by prodding his balls with a meat skewer.

Pins inserted directly under the fingernails can also do the trick.

This was demonstrated to Hedley and Tucker and they showed an immediate willingness to co-operate. So, as soon as they stopped screeching, they started singing. By the time the MD turned up, the two boys were so eager to have a friendly chinwag they would have owned up to the last time their old mums got a shagging.

I'm told it all went something like this:

"Right, let's 'ave it," the MD said, snapping into heavy business mode.

"Few month back," Hedley said, "dis cat, he come ta us and say he want some 'elp. He giss us respect so we went wid him."

"What the fuck you on about? Speak fuckin' English," spat the MD.

Hedley had been speaking rasta-style for so long he didn't know any other way.

"Dis cat …"

"Oi!!!" interrupted the MD. "If I want a fuckin' Yardies impersonator I'll call up fuckin' Lenny Henry."

The MD might have been the wrong side of 60 but he was still a bloody scary sight. I understand Hedley then took a long gulp and tried again.

"Dis Kenny Marshall come to us …"

"Kenny fuckin' Marshall!" The MD couldn't believe it.

Kenny Marshall had been working for the firm for donkey's years. He'd been a controller for eight years and there'd never been a single problem with him or his street dealers. The MD was gobsmacked. This was more than just biting the hand that fed you, it was chopping it off with a fucking meat cleaver.

"Bollocks!" the MD spat out his words. "Marshall got turned over himself."

Now you might rightly expect the MD to be the first person to suspect one of his team would pull such a double bluff. But such was the bond of their friendship that he'd never once doubted Marshall's loyalty. He was in for a shock.

"He did dat so no cat wud rumble it was 'im," Tucker said in a virtual whisper. " 'Im giss us da money, dat was it. He giss us all de info 'bout dem other dudes. Kenny Marshall."

"Why would he give you his real name?" the MD, who still wasn't in the least bit convinced, snapped back.

The two boy-blaggers shrugged their shoulders.

"We'ad some jobs through a dude we knew who 'angs at a boozer next to Eltham nick and …" Hedley started to explain.

"What sorta jobs?" interrupted the MD.

"Little collectin' from de shops and de bars and stuff. Droppin' off ganja at de fat cats' houses in Bromley, bit of de muscle work, shooter jobs now and again …"

"Only de stick-ups," Tucker said, interrupting his mate. "We never shot no dudes. No fuckin' way, man. Never fire de gun."

The MD was well pissed off. A couple of wannabe rastas with

stick-on goatees who sucked on cartons of Ribena had turned his firm upside down.

Just then, so I'm told, Hedley looked at his partner almost in disgust.

"Don't diss yourself, bruvver. We 'ad respect …" he continued, "… so dis pub manager, he tell us he know dis man might 'ave work for us. 'Im meet us and he say his name is Kenny Marshall. Dat's it. Ya dig?"

"I don't fuckin' dig you two for starters," snapped the MD. "What'd this Kenny Marshall look like?"

The MD obviously thought someone else might have been using Marshall's name.

But Tucker went on to describe him perfectly.

"Medium size, five nine, ten. He weigh maybe 12 stone. De beer gut comin' on a bit …" he paused and looked up at the MD in the hope he might live a bit longer.

The MD didn't even glance back.

"… Dude combed de hair back 'cross his head like muvver fuckin' Bobby Charlton. Some time he be wearin' wicked hats, know wot I mean?"

Tucker paused and eyeballed his interrogators again in the hope of some kind of reaction. But still no one said a word. Then he scratched his ear poking out from under his tea-cozy.

"Yeah, I fink bit of his ear missin'.'"

"That's Marshall," was the MD's conclusion.

Meanwhile Hedley continued his tale. "… So we meet cat who says he Marshall, and he say dese dudes we can easy stick-up. Said he cut deal so he get sixty per cent and de other forty, we split."

"Forty fuckin' per cent?" spat out the MD. "You were takin' all the risks for just forty lousy per cent? You're more fuckin' stupid than you look."

"Was more dan we was gettin' any place else," Tucker said truthfully.

After all, they had ended up making 20 grand apiece.

The MD just couldn't swallow it. You gotta remember, this

is a hood whose whole life revolved around the deal. He was baffled as to how these two rastaboys could cut such a onesided deal and he certainly couldn't understand why Kenny Marshall was turning him over.

It all deeply offended him. He turned to the bloke who told me this story and asked, "What the fuck is Kenny Marshall playin' at? He makes five grand a week."

Nobody had an answer. All Hedley and Tucker knew was that Marshall had fed them top quality info and never fucked them over when it came to splitting the money.

The MD didn't ask any more questions. Instead, he took his buttonmen upstairs and held a meeting.

Pinky and Perky were left just sitting there. I'm sure the spent their time praying hard and clutching the chunky gold crosses that dangled from the chunky gold chains around their necks.

But if they thought their time was up, they were wrong. As they would no doubt say: "De MD, he needed dem."

He just couldn't believe that Kenny Marshall had done the dirty on him. He knew Marshall, he knew his missus. They'd even been to one of the MD's kid's weddings.

Upstairs, the MD kept saying how much he'd trusted Marshall, and believed in the man, knew him so well. Then he said he wouldn't knock off the two rasta cowboys until he was sure Marshall was his man.

So he trotted downstairs and told them that if they followed his instructions to the letter, there was every chance they might live to become fathers ... if their bollocks were still up to it.

They were all ears.

A hit is always bad for business so the MD had to be sure he had the right man. He told Hedley and Tucker they were to act like nothing had happened. Like they hadn't been picked up and they hadn't grassed on Marshall.

The MD told them they were going to be given the readies they'd got from the controller they'd held up that evening. They were to hand the cash over to Marshall. But they had to inform the firm before every meet they had with him. And when Marshall outlined the next blag, they were to let the firm know all the details.

In return they'd be permitted to live.

The two white rastaboys conceded that this was a very agreeable plan.

Then the firm started looking into Marshall. Even though he'd been with them near to 20 years, nobody could claim to know him very well except the MD. They knew he was married, where he lived, and that he kept his activities almost exclusively confined to puff, coke and E.

He didn't even have liver problems. And there was no posh motor or fancy detached mansion. He didn't even pull crumpet in nightclubs. True, he had one long-term bird tucked away but she didn't require much upkeep as she was the wife of one of his old schoolmates.

So, what really fucked everyone off was, what was he doing with all the money he was making? Where the bleedin' hell was he stashing it?

It took them a couple of days, but they got their answer: Marshall was deep in the shit with at least five bookies. He was losing at a rate of knots and it wasn't getting any better.

The story went that he'd started out by betting a grand a week. Then he went up to two grand and he was still losing the lot. So he went for five grand. Eventually he went into the pit for more than one hundred and fifty big ones, which is a very large pit.

Marshall was locked in. He was hooked and there was no way out. No one seemed to know the full story of why or how come, but all of a sudden he was picking up the phone and betting on the length of his own nose hairs.

As I've already stated, he was making at least five grand a week. But that didn't get near helping him clear his debts. Marshall reckoned the only way he could survive was to go into business for himself. Unfortunately, he chose the wrong business.

His staff recruitment drive led him to a pub landlord in Eltham who found him two local dickheads, who wished they'd been born a different colour. Marshall offered them this golden opportunity and they jumped at it. He was stealing to pay off the bookies.

Hedley and Tucker did exactly what the MD required and, just as they said, it was Kenny Marshall who met them for the payoff and Kenny Marshall who gave them the details of the next blagging.

It was then the MD decided Marshall had to be permanently fired. Or, as it is known within the business, plugged.

That's when I got a message that somebody wanted to see me.

This was the story I was told after finding out Kenny Marshall was my target. It didn't sound like the Kenny Marshall I'd grown up with.

Chapter Four

One thing about people who work the way I do, hit and run, on and off, is that you end up with a lot of free time to fill. I think that's why a lot of us get stuck on the gee-gees.

Betting can get like a second job. You've got to prep it by carefully studying the form, then you've got the excitement of the event itself and then there's the results.

It can take fucking hours but, if you do it right, it's bloody magic.

I was in the middle of some serious horse speculation on a grey, windless Wednesday afternoon when I was approached for job number 13.

At the centre of that speculation was an age-old question: How long would it take a certain four-year-old to cover some prime turf at Windsor Race Course?

I was convinced I'd picked a really good investment, and I was checking my financial status to see how much I wanted to invest. Unfortunately, I'd made a number of similar investments earlier in the afternoon and my luck was as low as my bank account, if I'd had one.

Then I decided to put a final score on one more of my four-legged friends. As I finished making what would soon prove to be yet another one-way trip to the pitch of my number one bookie Scotch Johnny, this bloke I'd known since my days as a runner for one of the biggest firms came up to me.

"How you keepin', Malcolm ?" he asked.

"Not bad, and you?"

"Careful Craig" is easy to spot at any time of the day or night. He's got a habit of keeping his right hand inside his coat pocket, when he's wearing a coat (and I've never seen him not wearing a coat, whatever the weather).

Careful Craig is a buttonman. He controls a certain territory for the MD, which means he gets a piece of all the action going down in that area, from gear to tarts.

He and I go back a long way, back even to before the time I returned to the manor to hunt down the last of those three bastards who killed my first missus.

During that time Careful helped me out by getting me a few jobs where I could earn good money without much hassle. More importantly, he's one of only a handful of people alive today who knows my real name and what I do for a living. He knows I'm a hitman. And he knows I do good work.

Unfortunately, he also knew he could find me at the geegees, which is a bad habit I've got caught up in, but I knew if Careful was carrying the message, there had to be some genuine work in it. And I'll always consider any offers.

Anyway, Careful and I spoke about old times for a minute or two.

"How's your old lady?"

"Fine, how's your old lady, Careful?"

"Fine. When we gonna have a night out together?"

"Whenever you want, my old son. We'll really hit the town."

"Definitely, where you want to go?"

And so on.

Finally he said, "I think I've got a contract for you."

A contract is simply a verbal agreement to have something done. It does not, necessarily, involve an actual hit. But I knew if Careful came alongside me at Windsor it had to be some decent work.

"All right," I said. "What's the score?"

"Haven't got a fuckin' clue, old son. I'm just the messenger boy. Sunday night, be at the Fusilier. When you walk in the door you'll recognise someone you know ..."

"Hang about," I interrupted. "That's that fuckin' Nazi pub in Eltham ain't it?"

Careful nodded slowly. "That's where he wants the meet."

I wasn't happy, but a job's a job.

Careful continued, "You go up there, you talk to him, see what the score is."

"What time's that then?"

" 'Bout nine-thirty, ten. He'll probably buy you a plate o' nosh 'cause he'll want to rabbit for a while."

"Lucky me. Microwaved chicken korma? I don't think so."

Careful was just passing on a message, but he knew it would mean curtains for some poor fucker.

I left Windsor after the seventh race and hit my Nokia to find out when I had to do the next pick-up of wacky-backy from Rotterdam.

You see, at this time, besides knocking off people for cash, I was running the odd stash of puff from Holland. I was also doing a little wheeler-dealing and picking up bits and pieces here and there.

I could do a puff run each and every week if I wanted. It was a piece of cake, really. I'd just whip across to Ostend, hammer up the motorway and then meet a couple of Dutchmen in a service station where they'd hand over the merchandise.

But there was a problem today because I'd been beaten to the job by someone else and that pissed me off.

"I thought I always got first shout," I told my controller.

"You shoulda called earlier," came the icy reply.

I was convinced this cunt had it in for me. He was one of those people who, if you gave him a bit of lip, he'd take your whole head off.

Having sorted out all my other bits and pieces I found myself with an entire evening to kill. The only other business that needed attention was organising a meet with two new booze and fags customers.

I've been in and out of the bootlegging game for nearly 15 years. The operation is simple; by bringing lorryloads of fags and booze directly from France to Kent and south east London, you avoid paying any British taxes and sell the stuff on at a handsome profit.

It's a very tidy little earner. All it takes is a rented Artic, couple of drivers, a good-sized lock-up and customers. A mate of mine had called me a few nights earlier and said he had two blokes who were fags and booze wholesalers who needed a supplier. I agreed to meet them and this third party set up the meet.

We linked up in a boozer called the Admiral Nelson in Tooley Street, Peckham Rye, so I could combine business with my real pleasure, which is eating. This place is something special when it comes to grub.

I sat down, examined the menu, and we started rabbiting. Actually they started rabbiting and I listened. I learned a long time ago that listening is much safer than rabbiting, especially when you don't know who you're talking to.

It turned out that their previous supplier had been nicked and they were desperate for a lot of merchandise. They wanted as many as 2,000 cartons of fags a week plus crates of spirits, mainly vodka and whisky.

It sounded like a decent proposition. I still hadn't said a word.

Finally, without ever admitting to actually being in the business, I asked these geezers to tell me the names of some people they knew who could vouch for them. One knew a few faces in Bexleyheath, the other one named a couple of characters in Dulwich.

"All right," I said after writing down the names, "I need your drivin' licences."

They didn't like that one fucking bit.

"You the Old Bill?" one of them asked as the steak and kidney pie arrived.

"What the fuck is your problem.?" I asked in my hardest voice. "You came here, I didn't go looking for you. You want to do business with me, you give me what I fuckin' ask for. Right? If not, fuck off outta here. I don't need you."

You've got to put on a good show with these type of people.

"Hold up. Hold up," his mate tried to cool things down.

Truth is, I wasn't even pissed off. It was all an act. I just didn't want my steak and kidney pie getting cold while these geezers dicked me about.

Finally, the diplomat handed me his licence. The lippy one then did the same.

"Now we're speakin' the same language."

I wrote down their names and addresses from their licences and returned them. They looked kosher, so I asked them for their phone numbers.

"All right …" I finally told them, "… I'm not saying I'm in the business or anythin' like that, but if I can help you out I'll be in touch."

I didn't even want to talk money with these two until I was sure they weren't the law. And I couldn't really be certain of that until I'd checked them out.

All of that would have to wait until Friday anyway, because Careful Craig and my meet in that Nazi pub were very much on my mind.

The booze and fags boys and I discussed finest pub grub and fillies for the rest of the meal. They picked up the tab, which is traditional when you've asked for a meeting; and we parted at the door of the boozer.

I've never been able to understand what a sixth sense really is. But I can assure you it definitely exists. When something's up, when something is about to happen, you can feel it. You know it.

As I've said, I don't usually take jobs too soon after having completed one so I reckoned I probably wouldn't take this one for that very reason. But it's only common courtesy to speak to people who want to speak to you.

In any case, I was fucking curious – and I could use the readies for my property speculations, which lately I'd not been getting a good return on. A helicopter whizzed noisily overhead through the cold, clear night sky as I walked from the boozer to my motor. I looked up and felt a sudden shiver.

"Someone just walked over your grave, son," my mum used to say.

As the helicopter circled around with its spotlight panning the rooftops nearby, I stood there watching just watching and thinking.

My old mum was always right.

Obviously, carrying out hits is more enticing than booze and fags, and more profitable. But it's not as steady.

If you're going to work within organised crime, you've got to make sure you have some sort of steady income. That's why I always have a few bits and pieces on the side.

Sure, fags and booze are profitable but they take up a lot of your time. The same kind of caution that leads up to pulling the trigger goes into hammering out a deal. Justice is indeed blind, she'd just as soon bang you up for bootlegging fags and booze as wiping out some psycho toe-rag.

And it's a lot easier to prove. If they nab you with a lorryload of gear, your only hope is to stack the jury with alcoholics and chain-smokers.

So I spent a good portion of Friday checking up on those two new wholesalers who wanted to leave an order with me. They proved clean as a whistle. The bloke from Bexleyheath had a reputation as a ducker and diver who always came up smelling of roses and, as far as anyone knew, was honourable with his commitments. It was the same story with the one from Dulwich. So I set up a second meet at a little caff on Northridge Row, just off the Duckworth Estate.

I laid it all out nice and careful for them. I told them the price, which depended on how large their order was.

"And," I told them, "I get paid on delivery and in cash. There's no credit available."

I told them I'd let them know when I wanted their order and how soon I could deliver. Dirtbrain from Dulwich chipped in that they'd done some calculations and needed about two and half thousand cartons for starters, plus twenty crates of booze. "How do we get hold of you?" he asked. "You don't," I told him.

Chapter Five

The Fusilier is a boozer that should have been fire bombed years ago. It's known as "The Sawn Off" on account of its popularity with certain Eltham armed robbers in the 70s when Securicor lorries were the number one source of income.

The Guinness in The Sawn Off is watered down and the customers are mainly skinhead scum off the local white-trash estates.

Meetings of the type I was attending are usually held in certain boozers, mainly off the Old Kent Road or out in the open for safety's sake, unless there is a specific reason why two people should not be seen together.

I had no idea who I was meeting or why I was having to meet him at this Third Reich branch office. But as I strolled in, some of the familiar faces made my stomach turn.

Sitting at a table with a couple of other boneheads I recognised was a well-known pratt called Bobby "Half Pint" Bucknell.

The "Half Pint" bit came because he was renowned in these parts for threading half-pint mugs on to his prick (it had the cross of St George tattooed on it, apparently).

It was supposed to be 12 inches long and strong as iron. I'd heard that him and some of his mates were planning to start a dance troop of blonde Neo Nazis called the Full Arians, which they thought was really witty.

I was getting a couple of nasty looks from their direction when Ron "Twiggy" Sharkey lumbered in.

He'd worked as a bookie, a money launderer and now a buttonman for the MD. Some said he'd knocked off a couple of people, but I never saw anything in his character that even suggested that.

As a front "Twiggy" ran a second-hand car business in Peckham Rye, and I don't need to mention what some of his motors were used for.

Now you're probably presuming that he's called Twiggy because he's a bit on the large side as per my previous reference to villains' nicknames. But as it happens the name came about because Sharkey had no arms and was the proud possessor of these two plastic limbs that looked like ... twigs.

He could even pick stuff up with two hooks on the end of each plastic arm. They were powered by a pressure pump strapped under his shirt. He even got away with driving a motor by using a specially adapted steering wheel – although I heard he had a lot of prangs.

Twiggy. What a nonce. Lost his arms when he was a teenager – lay down on a railway track for a bet, passed out pissed, woke up with no arms. But then Twiggy was the sort of character who never saw anything coming.

Back in the Nazi tavern I took one look at him, saw his pink plastic arms dangling down by his side and looked no further: I knew he was the man I was supposed to see.

I'd known Twiggy on and off for at least ten years but we hadn't been close for years, not since I plugged some bloke known as Little Legs.

Legs turned out to be Twiggy's best mate. I later heard they'd grown up together, and went into the profession side by side.

I never did find out exactly what Legs had done. I was just hired to do my job and I did it. But what I didn't know was that friend Twiggy was trying to get the contract cancelled. In fact, he thought he'd just sorted it when I hit Legs with three bullets from my .38.

So, a few weeks later, I heard a rumour that Twiggy is going to "ice" me. (That's when "ice" was a very popular word.) I didn't know then and I never discovered how he found out I was the shootist. That is one piece of info he had no reason to know about.

I only heard he was looking for me when people started asking me what I'd done to him, because he wouldn't tell anyone why he was so fucked off with me.

For a long while I didn't know the reason, either. Then I

heard that Twiggy had asked somebody to see me and get me to give Legs an extra week, so that Twiggy could put the job straight. I never got the message. Mind you, it wouldn't have made any difference if I had – unless it came from the man who hired me but I really never got it.

Twiggy didn't believe that. He reckoned I'd got the message and ignored it, so he was out to settle the score. This is considered highly unprofessional. Organised crime has certain rules and regulations, and getting even is outlawed except under very special circumstances.

It never bothered me at all.

"Let him try," I said.

But he never did. Never. And there he was, lumbering through The Sawn Off with his plastic arms dangling by his side, looking for me. I thought it was well out of order, and I began to wonder why the fuck I'd been asked to do the job.

Twiggy looked just as narked to see me as I was to see him, especially in this skinhead dosshouse.

It's just possible he was a bit confused. I've gone under so many names that Twiggy might never have worked out the connection between me and the name the person who hired me to hit Little Legs knew me by. Possible, but not probable.

More likely, my name had been brought up at a meeting and the MD gave it the nod. When the MD says something will be done, it's Twiggy's job to make sure it happens, no matter how unpleasant he might personally find it. Anyhow, I was only there because of Careful Craig.

Far as I was concerned, Twiggy was one tool short of a box. This fellow doesn't like me and I don't like him, so why wind each other up? But I trusted Careful. The only way I do this sort of work is through someone who knows me and knows what I do, and who I trust. And that is Careful. After all, there are lives at stake here.

All this stuff was running through my mind as he sat down at the table next to me.

"This shithole winds me up," I said.

Twiggy shrugged his shoulders.

"Yeah, well."

Just then I heard this hissing noise coming from him as he moved his fake arms. When I first met Twiggy I reckoned he was farting the whole time. As a result, people tended to sit well away from him.

"How're those dodgy old cars you're sellin', Twigs?"

I knew he hated his nickname.

"Yeah, all right," he said before letting out another hiss.

So far, as you can see, this is not such a perfect chin-wag. But then neither of us is 100 per cent positive we are talking to the right party, so there is no sense in jumping the gun, so to speak.

"What else is new?" I asked him.

"Not a lot."

He wasn't even putting on a half-decent show of being pally.

"Still ridin' those gee-gees?"

"Yeah, now and again," I said in the sort of upbeat voice I knew would get on his tits. "Got shares in a few bookies. What 'bout you?"

"Bit of firm puff out on the street. Those spliffheads up on the Maldon Road go through it like fuckin' water."

He was loosening up a little bit.

I would guess Twiggy probably had a large stash of cash, not all his own, out on the streets. Besides his second-hand car business, he was the backbone for a number of other dealers in the area.

Suddenly, there was a ruckus at the bar. We both turned round.

"That Half Pint's a right tosser," I said.

"He hangs half-pint glasses off his dick for money. Strong as iron," said Twiggy, almost admiringly.

"This pub. What you doin' here?" I said, shaking my head.

Then he asked me if I'd eaten anything that night and I lied and told him I had. He ordered some microwaved Shepherd's Pie.

"So what you doin' on the manor?" he asked as we waited.

"Gotta see a mate of a mate 'bout some business." I made a point of panning my eyes round this fucking Ku Klux Klan tavern.

34

"Yeah?" he says. "Small fuckin' world. I'm here to meet a mate of a mate as well."

"Whose mate you s'pposed to meet?" I asked, as if I didn't know.

He hesitated for a split second. Then he hit the spot. "Careful?"

I nodded slowly with a grim expression on my face. I didn't have to be greasy any more, just get down to business.

"So, Twigs, what's so important that you bring me into this shithole?"

His tongue came shooting out of his mouth and smacked across his lips. This was his other irritating habit. He was either about to say something important or he was getting well narked at me calling him Twigs.

"Gotta job for you. You interested?"

"I'm here, ain't I?"

He nodded as if this all made sense.

"It's a special contract this one."

Remembering Little Legs, I didn't want any cock-ups. I wanted to be sure we was talking the same language.

"What kinda contract?"

"Want a certain person plugged."

"*You* want someone *plugged*?" I said, emphasising the *you* and the *plugged*.

"No," he corrected, "the MD wants him done."

I tried to pick up on something in his voice or his face that would tell me what he thought of me ... but there was nothing.

He tried to look me straight in the eye as he talked so I wouldn't think there was anything personal about what he was saying. The first few times I sat in on meets like this I felt a sort of buzz, a sort of excitement. Not any more. Now it's business. How much? How quickly? And who? The only answer that usually made any difference was the first one.

"What's the score, then?"

"It's one of our controllers," wheezed Twiggy. "He's been settin' up other controllers to get fuckin' jammed."

35

I didn't exactly understand what he meant by that. Telly and films always show hoods talking in slang words that everybody understands. In the real world it doesn't work that way. Not everybody understands everything.

Of course, there are certain words that we all use, but when a contract is being discussed there is very little flash language. It's cut and dried and laid out on the table.

"Jammed?" I asked him.

"Yeah, jammed," said Twiggy impatiently.

"Don't take this the wrong way, Twigs. But what the fuck you on about?"

To have a communications breakdown this early in a job was a bad sign that should have made me sit up and take notice.

"He's got a crew out robbin' our other boys."

Robbing I understood.

"You're fuckin' jokin'? What sorta pratt would do somethin' like that?"

He laughed. "A stupid one."

The conversation was getting a whole lot easier now. As much as he might have disliked me, he obviously liked the twat we were discussing a fuck of a lot less.

I laughed too.

"You sure 'bout this?-" I asked.

I didn't want to know about the job if there was anything iffy about it. But then again I wasn't *that* bothered. I knew the firm wouldn't commission me unless everything had been carefully checked out. Organised crime thrives because it's organised. Everything is checked and double checked.

Back to Twiggy's briefing.

"We nabbed the two muppets doin' the stick-ups. They told us everythin'. Then we set up our man and watched him take a payoff ..." He paused. "Yeah. We fuckin' know."

It was certainly an interesting story.

"Has he sussed you're on to him?"

Twiggy shook his head slowly.

"No way. He's a sittin' duck."

At this point I had to make the all-important decision – commit myself or go walkies. Nine times out of ten I would have said thanks but no thanks because I don't do such heavyweight work too often. Like I said, you can get careless.

But this job seemed like a piece of piss. I could smell the greenbacks and see my gee-gees surging ahead of the field.

And there hadn't been any comebacks on number 12.

The only thing that would have made me turn it down was if I'd thought the designated target was somebody I knew and liked, or somebody that I owed something to. I'm not close to many in this business, so when he said "controller" I instantly knew there was no one I cared about working that kind of job, and I went for it.

So I asked the one question that binds me to the job.

"Sounds all right. Who's the target?"

"Kenny Marshall."

I started laughing.

"You know him?" Twiggy asked.

"Yeah," I said. "We was raised in the same street."

Twiggy's tongue came darting out of his mouth again. Friendships have a habit of causing complications. It was, after all, Twiggy's friendship with Little Legs that got him so bitter and twisted about me.

"Got a problem with that?"

"Leave it out," I said. "If I've had three pints with him then that's three more than I remember."

To be honest about it, I knew him a lot better than that, but I didn't think it was worth mentioning. Kenny Marshall and I were raised on Kenton Avenue, in Bexleyheath. We lived about ten prefab bungalows away from each other.

We were close in age so we played football on the green round the corner, we nicked sweets out of the corner shop together, we both leaned on the smaller kids at school for protection money. Kenny Marshall wasn't my best mate or anything but he was always around. Our dads were both dockers rehoused out in the sticks after Hitler bombed the shit out of Bermondsey.

If it hadn't been for the Jerries all the villains would have stayed close to the river. Instead they were spread right through south east London out into Kent. Then we came along on the crest of that fucking baby boom wave in the fifties. As I said, Kenny and me weren't that close but I was with him the day a bull terrier took a chunk out of his ear when we were running out the back of an off- licence in Bexley Village.

If it hadn't been for Kenny challenging that hound to a spot of hand-to-paw combat, I would have been ID'd by the manager. But all he saw of me was my backside as I scrambled over his fence.

I got a right bollocking from my mum for that little caper. I'll never forget the way she stood over me with her hands on her hips after our local bobby informed her that next time I'd be nicked.

Women have been standing over me like that since the first time I dropped my dummy over the side of my high chair. Summer 1957.

The old man was out and about as usual at the time. I was lucky because he'd have beaten the crap out of me if he'd known. He died not long after. I didn't miss him much. My mum brought me up with a lot of help from her two sisters, my aunts. They lived just up the street.

In some ways I owed Kenny Marshall a favour for losing a bit of his ear to that dog. They might say one good turn deserves another, but my old man knocked that sort of crap out of me when I was three foot tall.

But I couldn't help wondering how the fuck Kenny Marshall had landed himself in such deep shit. He was never what I'd call a stroppy type, much more a follower than a leader.

When I worked briefly as a stick-up merchant at the age of 15, Kenny did a bit of part-time thieving like the rest of us. I never kept track of him. I didn't go round asking, "What's old Kenny Marshall up to these days?"

However, his name would crop up in conversation now and again. I'd hear of him on the manor or I would cross paths with him occasionally and we'd catch up on old times. I didn't have any problem with him.

I was well surprised he got to be such a big fish. A chap who works hard at this business can do well. They go out, they work, they earn. That's what Kenny Marshall did. And he kept his head down. Think he even got five or six 'O' levels at Bexley Secondary Modern. Then he went on and did some time at the London College of Printing, up at the Elephant.

I knew Kenny's mum and dad by sight, but I didn't know them to go into their home. And he certainly didn't come into mine because my mum kept it so clean and tidy that teenage boys were not top of her invitation list.

I did know the bird he married but I wasn't asked to the wedding. Didn't bother me much because there's nothing worse than a bunch of squiffy villains trying to be greasy to each other.

Me and my second missus married in Vegas so we didn't have to ask one criminal to the ceremony. Best fucking way, I can tell you.

Anyways, one day my missus and I were out shopping in Bromley and there is Kenny Marshall with his new wife, Brenda. She came from Erith. Brenda was a tasty-looking bird which didn't surprise me because Marshall had been a bit of an operator in his youth. He was tall and well built and the girls certainly gave him a second glance.

In those days he had longish, dark wavy hair which hid that bitten-up ear of his. Looked a bit like the cozzer who drove John Thaw's Granada in *The Sweeney*.

Then Marshall's barnet started thinning out, which can happen to the best of us. He went from George Best to Bobby Charlton.

Marshall even lived near me before moving out to Bromley. They stayed there a while and, after Brenda had a couple of kids, they moved over to one of the best streets on the manor, just round the back of the tennis club. Very posh.

Twiggy didn't say anything while I was thinking about all this. "If you're not up for it we'll just pull someone else in," he said hopefully.

"Not up for it? You must be fuckin' jokin'. I know him, that's all."

And that was all. He really didn't mean bollocks to me. Nothing. But I just couldn't understand how he'd got himself in such a mess. It didn't make sense.

Marshall was a minor puff merchant who'd worked his way up three rungs of a five-step ladder. He probably had all the usual run-ins, but he was not what you'd call a nutter.

He had about 50 street dealers working for him. Now, if each of them is making 150 quid a day, he's getting ten per cent of 150 quid times 50, which is 750 quid a day.

Plus he's got his own customers where he's getting 35 per cent. That probably means he's getting another 250 quid a day with his own punters. Every fucking day except Sunday. That's one thousand a day, six thousand a week.

What the fuck is he doing bothering to rip off his own firm? I was right curious, so I asked the man who knew.

"Twigs. What's he doin' it for? He's making a fuckin' good livin' as it is."

"He's gone mental. For the last eight months he's been bettin' on everything that moves," wheezed Twiggy. "We even got hold of some of his bookies and they say Marshall is in deep shit. It's only since the blaggings that he's started paying his dues."

"How much is he down?"

"More than two hundred big ones."

"Poor bastard. Should 'ave stuck to print."

Twiggy shook his head slowly.

"Bollocks. He's a slag who should 'ave kept his hands off our fuckin' wedge."

"Dead right," I agreed, although I didn't really give a toss about it.

Then he changed the subject.

"So what's all this gonna cost us, then?"

There is a going rate for this level of heavyweight work. The only time the price varies is when somebody really big is going down. But Marshall wasn't even in the Premiership.

"Twenty grand."

Twiggy reached into the inside pocket of his jacket and pulled out an envelope. I always get paid in full, in advance, in cash. How else could I handle it, take a cheque? There are other unwritten clauses that go into every hit contract. Twiggy and I didn't bother discussing them because we both knew what they were.

If I got nicked the MD would take care of all my legal costs plus my bail if I managed to get it. He would also make sure I was comfortable in the clink, that my missus was comfortable at home, as well as do everything to try and get me out. Finally, when I did finish my bird, he would have a bundle of cash waiting for me.

This is done to guarantee silence. As long as all obligations are taken care of, I'm not going to say a word to anyone.

I'm certainly not going to land Careful, Twiggy or the MD in the shit – unless I want a one-way ticket over the edge of Blackfriars Bridge.

I glanced at the envelope and shoved it into my inside jacket pocket.

"I need everythin' you got on him," I said. "Every street dealer he's got and where he meets 'em. I need the name and address of his bit on the side. Every-fuckin'-thing."

"It'll be in your hands by tomorrow afternoon," said the breathless Twiggy. "We been putting it together for the last few days."

"Good," I said, giving the envelope one last squeeze.

"I'm at Epsom tomorrow at the fifth gate before the last race …" I knew I'd be there because there were a number of favourite fillies on display. "And make sure whoever turns up is known to me," I added.

Twiggy said, "He will be, 'cos it's me."

I looked at him and nodded my head slowly. I'd hoped this was the last I'd see of Twiggy, but business is business.

"Any chance Marshall will do a runner?" I asked.

"Absolutely not. He thinks he's sittin' on a fuckin' gold mine."

"But he must know you'll catch up with him one day," I said.

"He doesn't know fuck all. We told his two toyboys to say they couldn't do no more jobs for two weeks. They agreed."

"How nice of them."

"Ain't it just," he agreed.

I looked over at the skinheads standing by the bar in their cross of St George T-shirts slagging off everyone for queen and country and felt fucking irritated.

Just before I got up I asked Twiggy the one question that, in view of what he thought of me and what I thought of him, was really bothering me.

"Why did I get the contract?"

Twiggy shrugged his shoulders.

"Careful told the MD you're a good operator. The MD told me to get you on board."

I nodded and got up to leave.

"See you tomorrow."

"Definitely," he said.

As I began walking away he said one more thing.

"Malcolm?"

I turned.

"Yeah?"

"This time," he said, "do what the fuck I tell you, all right?"

I didn't say a word, I just walked out. Twiggy obviously had a long memory. He also knew my real name.

That was when the paranoia started to take hold.

Chapter Six

On the face of it, the Kenny Marshall job didn't look that tricky. I had the full back-up of the team who'd hired me, including all the background info I needed. The target had no idea he was in the frame. And I had as much time as I wanted to honour the contract.

But, the more I thought about it, the more suspicious I became.

Why should the MD and Twiggy put Marshall on a plate for me? I hadn't worked for them in years. Twigs fucking hated me and there were other pros available.

I reckoned it might have been because I knew Marshall. It's not such a bad thing to know the man you're after because then you can get close to him easily.

But none of them could have known I knew Marshall, so that didn't make any bloody sense.

And, of course, Twiggy was a *real* mate of mine.

I tried to push all these niggly doubts into the back of my mind but I had to properly nail Twiggy down about what had been said at the meeting where my name came up. I was also going to watch my back. At the end of the day there wasn't much point in losing any sleep over it. I had a job to do.

By my reckoning, Kenny Marshall had about two weeks left to live.

Watching the gee-gees at Epsom helped me forget about work for a few hours, although it didn't help my finances as I can blow money at one track just as easily as I can at any other.

Wasn't a bad afternoon, though. The sun came out and you could see across the Downs for miles. I even copped a couple of winners early on. By the end of the fifth race I was still a few bob up.

I loitered near Scotch Frank's pitch and waited.

Twiggy was dead on time. He strolled up to me with a large yellow envelope clutched between his two right plastic claws and then let out one of his prosthetic farts.

HISSSS!

"Gotta present for you," he said.

HISSSS!

"Well done, mate," I told him and dropped the envelope into my inside jacket pocket. No harm in being a little nicer to him, I thought.

"You stickin' around?"

He shook his head.

"No way. Only thing I'd put my money on is the number of wheels on your motor."

I let out a loud laugh. Not at his joke but in surprise at the quickness of his humour. Reckon he'd been practising that line all day.

"Pity I haven't still got my Reliant three-wheeler."

Twiggy stopped in his tracks and looked puzzled. I could hear his brain turning over so I gave him a clue.

"Remember? Del Boy?"

He still looked blankly at me.

"*Only Fools And …*"

"Oh yeah …"

So this was the man commissioning me for a hit.

Then he gave me a squinting glance that felt as cold as a copper's truncheon and wandered off without even waving goodbye.

I took a few steps in the direction of Scotch Frank and slapped down a monkey on Irish Velvet in the 4.30.

If I'd been a bit wiser I would done what Twiggy didn't – wave goodbye.

This was my last trip to the races before getting properly down to work. When I'm on a job it has to take priority.

As I've said, it's not the only thing I do – you've got to keep your other business interests simmering but I do try and stay away from the gee-gees. Planning a job properly doesn't leave much time for studying form.

I pulled out of Epsom almost evens for the day which wasn't a bad result for me. I then called my main bookie and got hold of the entire week's results.

At that time I was working half a sheet which means that I had to split the profits with my main man, but he then covered all my losses and took whatever I was down out of my future winnings.

My bookie reckoned I was five grand ahead for the week. They called that a "black sheet".

Of that five grand, I kept £2,500 and the bookie got the other half. All I had to do was collect it. I never have to even go near the bookie himself.

As I headed back into south east London to see a few booze and fags clients, I stopped off at my accountant's office in Lewisham and handed him £10,000 cash from the money Twiggy had slung me.

He put that in a safety-deposit box, and held on to the key. The only people in the world who know about that box are my missus, my brother-in-law, my accountant and me. And my brother-in-law, Ray, *is* my accountant, even if he's a half-asleep spliffhead most of the time.

If anything happens to me that cash goes to my old lady. Her brother will see to that. You gotta trust somebody.

I spent the rest of that afternoon visiting customers from my other business interests. I met them in their shops or in boozers. With some it was to finalise shipments. Others just wanted a preliminary chat to see if we could do business together.

I always began with the ones who owed me cash. I'm used to them.

A fellow who owes money is usually well chippy and says things like, "I'll have you over if you lean on me too much" or "You're a lucky man this week."

Or the one I hear all the fucking time, "If only I'd listened to my brother-in-law who had a mate who knew this bloke who knew this bigtime ciggie merchant ..."

But most of my debtors pay up on the spot. Only

occasionally, like, d'you get someone who's way over their heads and can't pay – like Kenny Marshall.

No one I know is as deep in the shit as Marshall, although I've had a few mugs owe me upwards of 50 grand for a shipment.

I let it go on for a bit if they've got a reputation for coughing up in the end, because I know they'll find some way of paying me back, if not in cash, in special services.

I'd had free use of a '92 BMW 5 series M3 all that year thanks to a supermarket chain owner who fell behind. Instead of letting the interest stack up each week, he let me have the motor while he got together the readies. That motor is life insurance in a sense.

That afternoon I got to everyone on my list with just one exception.

Suddenly I find it's 6.30 and Marty from Peckham Rye is nowhere to be found. He's always ducking and diving whenever I turn up for my wedge.

He was only locked in for about two grand. I knew his business was doing all right so he had the cash back-up.

But Marty had been taking the piss for weeks so I wasn't surprised he was a no show.

I don't get angry with wankers like Marty. I just make a mental note to have a word with them and let them know they can't just keep taking the piss.

After collecting those debts I usually ensure that most of my clients feel I am indispensable. That means making it clear that I would not appreciate it if they tried to buy their booze and fags from other sources.

I've been trying to win round this Indian doctor geezer who owns three all-night supermarkets in New Cross. He keeps telling me he'll soon be up for a huge shipment. Apparently he works out of the casualty department at Deptford Hospital.

But every time I see him in his tatty little office behind his biggest shop he's surrounded by his relatives and waves me away because he doesn't want them to know what he's up to.

If I was sick I wouldn't go near him with a cold.

So, I'd ticked off my list with the exception of Marty from Peckham Rye which was pretty good going. I was home by 10.30pm.

I appreciate my second missus. I appreciate what she does for me. I appreciate the fact she's not a typical fussy Virgo git like me. And I appreciated the fact she wasn't home on this particular night.

I sank into in my Parker Knoll TV recliner, took advantage of the old lady's absence by whacking on a James Brown CD (she hates music) and opened the envelope Twiggy had given me.

There, on a piece of paper neatly typed, was everything I always wanted to know about Kenny Marshall but never bothered to ask. There were six pages filled with stuff about Marshall: where he lives, background about his family life, where they went on their holiday the previous summer (Disneyworld in Orlando, Florida), even his middle name (Winston, his runners would have split their sides if they'd known!).

Then there was his motor, the type, colour, number plate and even the fact that someone had keyed it down one side.

The firm also provided the name and address of Marshall's bit on the side and his best mate, an advertising salesman who had nothing to do with the business. There was even a list of info about his favourite haunts and habits. But the thing that most caught my eye was the line that said:

"*Marshall does not carry a gun. No one has ever seen him handling one.*"

The last couple of pages outlined his daily schedule and info about his runners/street dealers: where they lived, their phone numbers (mobiles and landlines) and where Marshall picked up from them.

The firm had instant access to all this info in case something happened to Marshall and someone had to fill in for him. When what was going to happen to Marshall happened, somebody, probably one of those runners, would be in line for promotion.

The names on the list weren't listed in any particular order, they were just chucked together in location terms.

There was even a little note alongside each name, indicating if they were early or late pick-ups.

The firm knew all this was because Marshall would call or stop at the funeral parlour before finishing most days and say, "I'll be back in half an hour 'cause I've got to stop and do a pick-up from such and such."

The notes said Marshall began meeting his runners by 8am at the latest. This was a right pain because I'd have to get up bloody early to keep track of him.

The list did not say where the runners were picking up their produce, but they would meet him at various predetermined locations.

By 10.30 he'd have picked up about 10 envelopes and then drive over to Millwall with the cash where he'd drop everything off. Then he'd go back and meet the next batch of runners.

Twice a week, at least, he wouldn't even get over to Millwall halfway through the morning. Instead, he'd hold on to the money and go to his bird's place in Sydenham. The file made it sound like she was quite a looker. Not one of those young bimbos but an older woman who'd seen a bit of life.

It also said she'd been married to one of Marshall's old schoolmates who was now a well-known estate agent on the manor. They even had a couple of kids. I vaguely remembered her old man when we were kids at Bexleyheath Secondary Modern. Think he was a right tosser.

The info clearly stated that Marshall finished all his pickups by 6.30pm – earlier if it was already dark.

I checked out the sunset times in the *Telegraph* and calculated that at this time of year he'd be done by six at the latest.

That meant he would then head back over to Millwall to drop off the cash at the undertakers.

But the one thing all this info didn't tell me about Kenny Marshall was how the fuck he got himself in such deep shit to the bookies. He owed around £200,000!

That meant he'd probably spunked another £50,000-300,000 before that and paid it off. It baffled me and I don't like mysteries. I mean, Kenny Marshall must have known what a sucker's game he was caught up in. He knew no one ever came out ahead, surely. Marshall had more taxfree loot than he ever dreamed of, yet he let it all get out of control. I make good money. I gamble. I lose, and I blow a lot of dosh but I never bet more than is in my pocket (well, not very often). I've never yet made a bet I couldn't cover (well, not very often). I never sub money unless I know I can pay it back pronto (well, not very often).

Seems fucking outrageous that someone in this business can leave themselves wide open to be shafted. Or that they get greedy and start nicking. Marshall was supposed to be doing both. It didn't make a lot of sense.

I tried to finish the file before my missus got home and found me sitting there reading it.

She's clocked me doing a lot of hooky things in the time we've been together, but if I had anything besides the racing form or the *Telegraph* in my hand she'd know something was up.

And I didn't need that sort of grief.

She finally pitched up about 12.30. By then I'd swapped James Brown for a spot of cable channel-hopping between topless darts, soft porn and a re-run of *Minder*.

The old lady was full of herself because she'd just won a score off her mates during a game of bridge.

But I had an even bigger surprise for her.

"How about a cuppa?" I asked her.

"Good idea," she agreed. "You know where the kettle is."

"Tell you what," I bargained, "you make it and I'll give you a little surprise."

She looked directly at me. "You goin' away again?"

There were times when I wasn't too keen on her sense of humour.

"Ha, ha. Very funny," I answered. "Just whack the kettle on, darlin'."

This time she did exactly as I suggested.

Few minutes later she served up a pot of tea in the lounge.

"Where's my surprise then?"

I handed her the envelope. It had £5,000 in it.

"Here you go," I said. "If you made a better cuppa you could have had more."

I laughed. I make a point of regularly chucking a wedge of my cash at my missus. It keeps her happy, and when she's happy she doesn't give me earache, so I'm happy.

It also keeps her loyal. And she deserves it. So, £5,000 was left for me and the gee-gees to share.

She smiled as she counted it up. I don't really know what she does with her money. I never ask, but she must have a fucking huge stash somewhere.

She kissed me on the forehead. She never gives me the third degree about where it comes from. She's got an idea of what I do, but I don't reckon she actually knows I'm a triggerman. That's how I like it. And that's the way she likes it, too.

I'm not so sure she'd have taken the cash if she'd known it was a downpayment on the murder of Kenny Marshall. Anyway, by blowing that money on the missus I knew I'd be a dead man if I didn't go ahead with the hit.

Sometimes you need that sort of pressure to get a job done.

Chapter Seven

From the age of ten I had to get up at 5am every day to work a two-hour turn on my aunt's stall flogging hotdogs and hot drinks to punters and traders at Bermondsey antiques market. Always seemed to be fucking cold and I was well knackered by the time I got to school. Used to nod off during half the classes.

So when I started earning some decent wedge, I began sleeping in most mornings. Nowadays, if I do have to get up early, my brain doesn't kick into gear until about half an hour later.

Early mornings are bad enough, but freezing cold mornings are even worse. The chill cuts right through you. It doesn't matter how many clothes you've got on. This particular Tuesday morning was brass monkey weather so I wasn't exactly thrilled to be up and about at 6am chasing Kenny Marshall around south east London.

But business is business. I had a job to do so I got up and got on with it.

I left the house and got into my highly polished BMW – funny how so many villains in south east London prefer Beemers and Mercs. Not only did the Germans bomb us out of our homes but now we're supporting their fucking economy.

The only accessories I had on me in the motor that morning were an extra-large colour print version of the London A–Z, a couple of pens, a notebook, a walkman, a wristwatch and an old blanket.

I wasn't even tooled up, although I did have a reserve piece tucked under the dash.

I don't like carrying a shooter on me unless I have to. Obviously I wouldn't go to a meet without a loaded weapon, but shadowing Marshall didn't make it a requirement. The piece under the dashboard is for emergencies. And I haven't had one of them yet.

51

The reason for the A–Z is obvious. Although I know most of the streets like I know every wrinkle on my missus, I knew I'd need to pinpoint my movements in terms of one-way streets, traffic lights, roadworks, stop signs, mini-roundabouts and those bloody annoying sleeping policemen.

I planned to mark all these things off as I went along. I'd use the pad to make notes about certain locations – what made them good, reasonable or fucking useless.

The walkman was to preserve my car battery when I was just sitting there waiting and watching. The wristwatch was because that Beemer might have been worth 25 grand but its clock never kept the correct time.

The blanket was obvious – it gets cold sitting in a stationary motor for hours on end. The car's heater is all right but it works better when the engine's switched on which you cannot do when you're sitting outside someone's house. Anyway, I don't want to run down my petrol supply in case I suddenly have to tail someone for a long distance.

To check out Kenny Marshall's movements I needed to be outside his house before he took off for work. I got there, just off Seymour Road in Bromley, about a quarter to seven.

Marshall was just walking out of his four-bed mock-Tudor semi as I rolled up. It wasn't much different from my own gaff except he'd knocked the front garden wall down to build a car port which niggled me because my missus refused to have it done at our place. She reckoned it would ruin the look of the front of the house. I can't fucking stand not being able to park outside my own home.

Anyway, if I'd been five minutes later that day I'd have had to start again the next day.

Marshall was dressed for the cold with a leather coat that looked to be lined and a golfing hat. The hat I expected because he was one of the few hat people in this game.

You see, Marshall was a bit sensitive about his thinning hair, so hiding it under a hat made total sense. This particular hat was the sort of thing you'd find old codgers wearing at the

Arnold Palmer Driving Range on the old A2 at Chislehurst; Black watch tartan, brim bending slightly over his forehead and one little multi-coloured feather sticking out of the side.

If you didn't know he was about to start picking up the proceeds from drug deals you'd think he was on his way to a Butlins pitch 'n' putt.

Marshall drove a J-reg Ford Scorpio. Nothing flash, but reliable enough. Not many geezers making a lot of dosh from the big firms drive brand new limos or live expensively. Gone are the days when mohair-suited spivs in bright red Rollers would sweep up and down the Old Kent Road doing a milk round, which is what they used to call collecting protection money.

These days you'd be asking for a pull from the Inland Revenue as well as Old Bill. There's just no need to attract that sort of attention.

Marshall pulled out of his car port and headed off towards Bexleyheath. I waited a few ticks, then took off after him.

The name of the game is not to let them out of your sight, but to stay out of their sight as much as possible. There aren't many ways to do this. You can drive to the rear left of the fellow you're trailing. That way he won't see you the whole time in his rear-view.

The number one rule is never spend too long trailing someone because in the end he's going to spot you. I'd already decided I'd stick with him for two hours, top whack. I only wanted to get a feel for the job that first day.

Kenny Marshall's first stop was at a caff on Rankin Road next to Bexleyheath station. He parked his motor on a double yellow line, strolled in and sat down with what looked like a mug of coffee.

I was parked up across the road and couldn't see too clearly. As he walked out two blokes in puffa jackets came up to him and handed him envelopes. From the caff he took off down Rankin Road, then on to the old A2 before cutting across into Faraday Avenue. He then headed to the crossroads with Tyburn Street.

Marshall stopped by a subway that ran directly under the A2, met some geezer on the corner and picked up another envelope. Then he drove to Eltham Green and picked up another envelope.

After that he headed south on the A2 until he reached Eltham High Road where three black geezers were standing outside a boozer waiting to meet him. He took their envelopes as well. He was like a fucking machine. Bim-bamboom. He's on a tight schedule: his runners are always already there to meet him, he never hangs about for more than a few seconds.

Reckon he had a timetable taped to his sun visor.

A lot of them must have been selling gear through the night to their customers. The day action, from pubs, restaurants, spliff-heads and rockheads, would come later in the morning and through the afternoon.

From Eltham High Road Marshall travelled to Wilton Avenue and Digby Road where he met what looked like a couple of gypsies.

Then he parked up on a double yellow line where Wilton Avenue crossed Aberdeen Place. He got out of the motor and walked briskly on to the council estate with a brown envelope under his arm. I reckoned that big envelope was where he kept his records of payments and collections.

He went into the entrance to one of the buildings and was there about 30 seconds, then came out and walked across the playground back into another building. Another 30 seconds later and he's out again with at least six envelopes in his hand which he's stuffing into the bigger brown job.

Marshall then headed for Eltham station, got out of the Scorpio and hopped a train to New Cross station, where he walked into a nearby restaurant called The Pancho Grill and saw two geezers.

Minute or two later he's walking 100 yards to another restaurant where he meets three blokes, although I couldn't see clearly if he collected from them as well.

Marshall was floating by now. From that restaurant he went into a boozer where two more geezers were waiting for him.

Then he took the train back to his motor and headed off towards Bromley. All this time I've followed him by car and then on foot, keeping well back in case he spotted anything. But I knew he didn't have a clue I was there.

At the same time, I'm trying to take notes, which ain't easy. I haven't got to thinking yet in terms of each location as a potential spot to carry out the hit. I'm just following and scribbling, following and scribbling.

Next, Marshall stopped on Bromley High Street. Another motor pulled up next to him and a bloke leaned over and handed him a whole stack of envelopes.

Then Marshall drove south along Stanley Road to where it met the Bexley Village turn-off. There was a big supermarket there and he slung the Scorpio up in the car park and went inside. Suppose he saw someone in there.

Then he headed north again towards Bromley. He stopped in Dorchester Road and met a geezer. Next came Eltham Green, a tough area with more villains per square foot than B wing at Belmarsh. Stopped in front of the old bingo hall on the high street, there were four real rastas waiting for him. They reached into Marshall's car and dropped envelopes on to his passenger seat.

Then he nipped off up Fraser Road back towards Bromley where he pulled up outside a Chinese takeaway near a set of lights. In the entrance, a short Chinese bloke in a blue and white apron handed him an envelope.

Must have been flogging gear with the takeaways. Clever way to punt out the produce, come to think of it.

Marshall parked 200 yards further up that same road next to the entrance to a small industrial estate, again on a double yellow. The man had absolutely no respect for the law.

He headed into four small factories in quick succession. They are highly profitable markets for the runners because all these places have loads of powderheads who want to score a bit of Charlie before work to break up the boredom of their jobs. A lot of them also want some more gear before they head off home.

Ten years back, nose gear was considered the yuppie drug of choice. Now, every-fucking-one is after a gram of yours truly. Supply cannot keep up with demand and the price is the same as when I was a teenager; around £50–£60 for a gee. It's almost cheaper than a session down your local boozer followed by a slap-up curry – and it certainly helps keep your weight down.

Anyhow, from that industrial estate, Marshall went back towards Bexleyheath where he stopped at a brewery and met three more runners.

By this time it was after 10am and I was knackered and bored. Not careless, though. I never forget I'm on a job – one mistake and I'm fucked for life.

I followed Marshall into another caff on Belfrew Road near either Montgomery Avenue or Stoneleigh Road, I can't remember which because they both look the same.

He sat there and started reading the paper and making a few calls on his mobile. Maybe he was calling his bookie but I doubted it as he hadn't even had time to study the form. None of it mattered because it was time for me to pull out.

Enough for one day. I'd already gone way over my two-hour limit. Having worked in the same business I knew that controllers were creatures of habit, so I was certain that Marshall's morning schedule wasn't likely to change much from day to day. I'd pick him up at this same caff late Wednesday morning.

I needed a cuppa and a spot of grub so I drove inland to a transport caff near Blackfriars owned and operated by a mate of mine called Donny Moyle. Donny's the sort of guy who's got the bottle to say anything to anyone, particularly his customers.

I once heard him tell some old blonde who was giving him grief to "go and dye your fuckin' roots and get your teeth done while you're at it."

Donny didn't give a fuck about repeat business.

His caff was a lunch and breakfast place with a little bookmaking on the side. He had a direct line to six of the bestknown bookies in south east London and maybe 20 punters who were after him at any one time.

Donny did all right. A lot of those customers preferred landline calls because there's still a lot of paranoia about mobile phone lines being insecure. They also didn't want to lose brownie points from their old ladies when their Cellnet bills came in the post.

Meanwhile, the charming Donny Moyle didn't give a flying fuck if my eggs were black or sunnyside up.

As I walked in he was taking down a round-robin. Donny was very serious when it came to booking bets. But that didn't stop him giving everyone lip.

"What you got that's not going to poison me?" I asked him as he hung up the phone.

"Welsh Rarebit in the 3.30 at Epsom," he said.

I put on a smile, even though it was a crap joke.

"So what's on the menu, then?"

"Chelsea and Man United, Chelsea and fuckin' Man United," he said. "All my punters want me to find someone who'll take their bet. What do I look like?"

"A bookie's middle man," I told him.

"Animals only," he corrected me. "I don't take bets on fuckin' football games. They're all fuckin' bent. Give me the gee-gees any day. Those fillies give you an honest day's work for a bale of fuckin' hay."

At the time we were a couple of months into the 1998–99 Premiership season. Chelsea were being tipped for the championship but Man United were the solid, reliable option with the previous season's champs Arsenal still the most hated team in the land.

"Who d'you reckon'll win it?" he asked me.

"Who cares?" I said. "What d'you reckon?"

He didn't give a fuck either, so I poured myself a cup of tea and repeated my earlier question, "So what's cookin'?"

He picked up a greasy menu and looked at it. "Not a lot."

I bravely stuck in an order for eggs and bacon with fried bread and retired to a booth in the back. I just hoped the old lady had kept up those private healthcare payments. Fucking NHS wouldn't save me from Donny's food.

I took out my pad and began checking the info I'd noted down. I cross-checked it with the material Twiggy had given me and calculated that Marshall had picked up at least 30 envelopes. A good, solid morning's work.

For the first time I started to think about when and where I might make my move. I'd deliberately avoided the issue until then.

The only time when that rule is broken is if you're working in an unfamiliar area and you're told by someone you trust that this location would be good, or this and that spot could work. But if you know your territory, you don't need to rely on anyone else.

I hadn't decided day or night yet. It's better when it's dark, although that's not always possible. If your target makes a habit of staying in watching the telly, you can forget it. No one's going to sit glued to the box and then wander outside so you can take a pop at him.

I went down my list very carefully and next to each possible location I'd written down "OK". That meant it was a place I'd come back to and look at again. The no-go areas got a predictable "No" and a thin line through the name.

The best location seemed to be Eltham Green.

Eltham Green is not as twee as it sounds. It's a dead, rundown collection of low-rise council estates and post-war, paint-peeling, three-bed semis.

Lots of families moved to the area from Bermondsey and Rotherhithe. Lucky them. Few residents go out on the streets of Eltham Green at night. People mind their own business except for the occasional glance through their net curtains, which meant I wouldn't even have to bother with a silencer in Eltham Green.

If I could catch my man on his todd it would be perfect. I already knew there were moments when he was out of sight of his runners.

I made a little cross alongside Eltham Green. It wasn't perfect but it wasn't bad by any means.

While I studied my research notes, Donny Moyle was yapping up a storm on the phone.

"Don't gimme that fuckin' bollocks ..." he yelled, "... I called you four days ago to get in here and fix the fuckin' khazi. I want it fuckin' done!"

"See you, Donny."

Donny looked up and put his hand over the receiver.

"You owe me two-ten."

"Two-ten?" I yelled back.

"One-fifty for the nosh and sixty for the cuppa."

"For a cup of cat's piss and a fuckin' slice of tuna-fed bacon? You got some bottle!"

I doshed him up. But no way was I going to leave him a tip, not that anyone ever did.

Chapter Eight

That afternoon, I started the ball rolling to get the equipment I needed. In other words, I lined myself up with a shooter. Getting a gun in south east London is about as tricky as getting a blowjob in King's Cross.

I can go anywhere on the manor and be tooled up inside 12 hours. But it's gotta be a totally clean weapon, one which can't be traced back to you, or to the geezer who supplied it in the first place.

The armoury network in south east London has been in place ever since sawn-off blaggers started going across the pavements in the late 60s. There are a couple of excellent gun dealers who make a packet supplying clean pieces and asking no questions. Probably the finest of them all is Stanley "Old Bill" Wink.

Old Bill and I have known each other since I was a kid. He was a copper once (hence his nickname), stands about six-foot-three and weighs at least 18 stone.

He collared me for nicking lead when I was 11 but let me off with a clip round the ear, which was fair enough.

Old Bill was drummed out of the Met 15 years later when he half-inched a shooter from a pavement artist and flogged it to a rival face.

He was just two years off a decent retirement pension and lost the lot. You could say that's what pushed him into the game full time, so to speak. After he left the Old Bill, people kept saying, "Can't trust him, he's Old Bill," so they hung the name on him.

But I never had a problem with him. I reckon he's more trustworthy than other gun fences because he knows that a lot of faces think he's up to no good on account of his police background – and his old cozzer mates would love to pull him in. All told that makes him a very careful person.

Old Bill has even done some freelance work in his time.

A few years back him and I did a muscle job for a bookie mate of mine. We paid a visit to this businessman who wasn't paying his bills like he should have been. First time we dropped in on this twat his secretary told us he was in a meeting and couldn't be disturbed.

Next day we came back and his secretary gave us the runaround again.

This time I opened the door to this blokes office with a good, swift kick and we went straight in. He was sitting behind his desk and turned as white as a fucking ghost – like he'd just seen Reggie Kray walk in with Ronnie in tow.

"What's your game, then?" I asked.

He didn't respond so I continued.

"If you're gonna fuck us about, it's always more polite to tell us first."

Cheeky bastard answered back, "I'll pay up when I'm ready to."

Finally, Old Bill opened his mouth.

"You will?" he asked casually.

This punter then looked at Old Bill, very puzzled. We were in an old office building with windows that opened. It wasn't that high up, but high enough to make a right mess of anyone who fell out.

"It's fuckin' stuffy in here, ain't it?" asked Old Bill.

Without bothering to wait for a reply, he sauntered across the room and opened the window.

"That's better, ain't it?" he said.

Then he moved towards this bloke's posh, high-back chair and stood right behind him.

We had no more intention of throwing him out than we did of mugging his granny, but he wasn't to know that. I moved round to the back of the dickhead's desk and we picked him up, still in his chair, and carried him towards the open window.

That's when he started screaming like a fucking St Trinian's schoolgirl and clasping at his chest.

"My heart, my heart. I've got a bad heart!"

"A dodgy ticker, eh?" Old Bill grunted as we stood with the geezer's chair balancing on the window edge.

"That's not gonna matter no more, my friend."

"I'll pay! I'll pay!"

We put him down and pushed the chair back to his desk. He wrote out a cheque there and then. The three of us then held hands all the way down to the bank and cashed it.

Old Bill's brother had been a docker with my old man just after the war. Everyone on the docks had known them. His brother's reputation certainly helped Old Bill when he got drummed out of the local constabulary.

Like most of the villains nearer the river, Old Bill had shifted his operation from a council flat in Catford to the suburbs a long time back. So I hit my mobile and called up a contact of mine who always knows where Old Bill is.

"Tell him I'll be at The Bull and I need to see him."

I didn't know or care precisely where Old Bill operated from. Much better that way.

My contact did me proud. By the time I'd walked into The Bull, ordered a pint of Guinness and flipped through the *Racing Post*, Old Bill Wink appeared at the door.

He crossed the entire bar in probably about five long strides, nearly knocking over some kid with a bottle of coke in his hand in the process.

"Fuckin' kids. Shouldn't be allowed in boozers," said Old Bill in his finest tooth-wobbling, smoker's voice.

I nodded.

"It's all this fuckin' satellite telly that does it ..."

I didn't know what the fuck he was on about so I just nodded.

"My grandson gives me nonstop earache to take him to my local to see the football on Sky. In my day you left a kid outside with a bottle of pop and a packet a crisps. Now you got ten-year-olds naggin' to go to the boozer. It's fuckin' out of order."

Old Bill looked to me for a response. I nodded again politely but he knew I wanted to get down to business.

"So, what you after?"

"A decent bow 'n' arrow," I said.

He knew exactly what I meant.

"No problem," he said and lowered his voice. "Piece will be a grand and three hundred for the silencer."

"You takin' the piss?" I said.

I couldn't resist a bit of haggling, even though I knew Old Bill was fast and reliable.

"Give you a grand top whack."

Old Bill looked well miffed and got up.

"Forget it."

I looked up at him and he looked back down at me. He might have been five years into a state pension, but I knew he could flatten me with one punch.

I winked at him.

"Sounds like a fuckin' bargain to me. When can I have it?"

He smiled back. We always go through the same wind-up every time.

"Gimme a couple of hours. Where you gonna be?"

"Out and about. Call me on the mobile."

The whole meet took five minutes flat, and I had myself a top quality piece and silencer on the way. There are some characters around who'd take you for two grand for that sort of package and you might not even end up using the silencer. A muffler cuts the sound of a gun from the moment it discharges but there are times when you don't need to use them. And it doesn't half attract attention sticking out your pocket.

But at this early stage I didn't even know if I'd need one for the Kenny Marshall job.

Old Bill was as good as his word, as usual. Less than two hours later, I was out in Peckham seeing a booze and fags customer when my Nokia started singing.

"You all right, then?" asked Old Bill.

"Still shittin' bricks," I replied.

That was my little pre-agreed response when he wanted to make sure it was me on the other end of the line.

"Fuckin' glad to hear it," he said. "Your bird has landed."

"Domestic or imported?"

"Domestic. Only the finest ..."

I said, "Fuckin' marvellous," emphasising the marvellous.

When I first got going in this game I ended up with whatever my supplier could nick. Sometimes he'd sling me some poxy little .22. They don't call them Saturday Night Specials for nothing. They're for kids and they're rubbish.

Then Old Bill came on the scene and educated me to always stick to a .38 because it didn't spit out bullet casings which could be traced back to me later.

Those 9mm semi-automatics favoured by many villains and coppers are the worst shooters a true pro can use. Too easy to trace.

Old Bill taught me a lot. He also told me to respect every piece I ever came across.

"A gun's no different from any tool," he said to me when we first linked up, "but remember that any tool is dangerous if it's not handled properly ..." He paused for a moment to make sure I was nodding in agreement. "If you put a hammer down on this table it ain't gonna go off and bang a nail in the fuckin' wall by itself, is it? But it's lethal the moment you put it in your hand. Always remember that, son."

Just listening to Old Bill's patter was a pleasure. It was like poetry.

"It's the same with a piece," he'd say. "If it just sits there and nobody ever picks it up then obviously it'll never go off. It takes a human being, either intentionally or by mistake, to turn it into a killing machine."

He looked at me really hard in the eyes as he said "killing machine".

"Never forget that."

Despite all this chit-chat, we never once discussed how I knocked people off with the weapons he supplied. That would have been crossing the line.

A lot of Old Bill's supplies are lifted from crates at Tilbury Docks. I think he's still got a couple of nephews who work down that way.

You wouldn't get rubbish in crates full of weapons heading for the IRA or UDA, would you?

That day Old Bill said he'd got me precisely what he always recommended – a .38. He said to meet him at an allotment near the A2 turnoff at Bexley.

Old Bill's a bit of a pigeon fancier but his missus got the hump about his hobby so he'd had to move his birds out of his back garden to a hut on an allotment. He was digging away on his cabbage patch when I strolled up. His shed looked like it would blow over in a 5 mph gale.

He nodded in the direction of the hut, so I followed him in. There must have been about 40 or 50 fat, coo-cooing pigeons, each in its own cage, if that's what you call them.

I kept my head down just in case the pigeons did a mass breakout. One fat, evil creature caught my attention. I pictured him pecking my eyeball out.

Meanwhile, Old Bill was cooing at them through the wire and smoking a pipe.

"Shush-shush, my darlings, it's only little Malcolm.'

"Oi, steady on," I said.

"You're not scared of the birdies, are you? Anyway, your little birdie has landed," said Old Bill, handing me a brown paper bag. I looked inside and there was my shooter.

"I'll have the muffler either tonight or in the morning. Give us a call at that number I wrote on the bag."

"Top man …" I said, backing out of Old Bill's pigeon motel at top speed. "Gotta run. I'm cookin' for the missus tonight."

Usually at about this time of the week I'm starting to put all my booze and fags deals together. I'd been thinking about sending a lorry across the water to pick up a shipment but I knew the Marshall job would take up a lot of my time.

I also needed to sub the cash to finance the deal and then hire the geezers to deliver it all.

It was a lot to handle on top of the Marshall job so I knew I had to drop it for the week – although my two new punters would be well pissed off. But there was no point in damaging both operations by splitting my time.

On top of of all this, I hadn't spent much time with the missus. We didn't do enough sitting down and talking, so I decided to beat her home and cook a nice surprise dinner for us.

Cooking is one of my true pleasures. My mum used to say that any man who was a dab hand in the kitchen would have the birds queuing up for him. She had me cooking homemade spaghetti bolognese at the age of eight. She also made a point of saying what a useless git my old man was because he couldn't boil an egg.

Even the missus admitted it was one of the horniest things about me. Mind you, she might have been taking the piss. I've even got an apron my brother-in-law gave me which says, "If You Fuck With The Chef He'll 'Ave You." My brother-in-law thinks he knows.

Anyway, the biggest decision of that day would be what I'd rustle up. The winner was what I knew was her favourite – Penne Carbonara with my special riccota, cream and bacon sauce. It was guaranteed to put her in a good mood. On the way home I stopped at the massive Asda just outside Bromley and picked up all the ingredients – riccota cheese, double cream, parmesan, eggs, penne pasta, a pack of prime back.

You never know – I might even get a bonk on the strength of it.

But then my missus walked in – and she had a surprise of her own.

"Tonight, I want to go to Harrods!"

That £5,000 I'd given her was burning a hole the size of Whitstable Bay in her handbag. Naturally, I got the hump because I'd already cracked the eggs into the cabonara mix.

Then she began reeling off a shopping list of presents we owed to relatives and mates and how she was so embarrassed we hadn't kept up with them all.

I smelt an opportunity for some much-needed brownie points so I dumped the pasta and off we went up west to London's poshest department store. I'm not a big shopper, and I hate crowds. But I've got a soft spot for Harrods.

It all started when I was a kid in Bexleyheath. Sometimes on a Saturday I'd go up west with a load of mates and we'd take a wander through the place, eyeing up the produce trying to nick anything that looked as if it was worth a tug.

One time I went in the men's changing rooms, stuck a pair of £100 strides under my own jeans and walked out without anyone being the wiser.

But stealing wasn't the only reason we went down Harrods. We wanted to see how the other half lived. These days I've noticed loads of villains show up with their birds at Harrods. That's what I call a true seal of approval.

That night me and the missus headed first for the electrical department. One of her nephews was about to turn 18 and she wanted to buy him a CD player. Seemed a bit steep at £150, but it was her dosh and her relative.

Then it was up to linens to get a wedding present for the daughter of one old-time blagger I'd known for years. £85.00.

Then the missus chips in, "Now I want to get some stuff for myself."

Like a good husband, I followed her into the women's department. And like a good husband, I sat myself on a ledge in the corner near the lingerie and watched all these housewives inspecting the latest thongs.

There's a game I sometimes play where I imagine what each bird would look like if they were wearing the lingerie they were showing so much interest in. Of course, they have to be up to a certain standard before they qualify for this game but in a place like Harrods you can't really go wrong.

One brassy brunette walked past me a couple of times after I first noticed her.

Wiggle. Wiggle.

She started handling a see-through body stocking on a hanger.

Wiggle. Wiggle.

I snapped a brain photo of her covered head to toe in black panty hose for my collection.

Wiggle. Wiggle.

Hopefully that full-colour image would develop in time for my next hand-shandy.

Wiggle. Wiggle.

It was while I was sitting there, lost in my own fantasies, that I met another obedient husband, Kenny fucking Marshall.

I didn't see him coming. Then all of a sudden I heard my name being called out. I swung round and there was the entire fucking family: the target-to-be, his missus and their three kids.

I swallowed and turned on my widest smile.

"Hello, Kenny, how's things?"

"Can't complain," he said.

As usual he was well dressed.

As usual he had a hat on.

And Brenda, his missus, looked better than ever. I could have sworn her tits had grown upwards, and her waist was still as trim as a 20-year-old's.

"What you up to?" he asked.

I nodded over in the direction of my old lady. "Spending my hard-earned cash. How 'bout you?"

"Join the club," said Marshall.

My missus had spotted us talking and was fast approaching. She'd met them before a long time back but I didn't think she'd really remember them. That didn't stop her immediately bonding with Brenda. Before I could take avoiding action, she and Brenda were on their way to the toy department with the three Marshall kids.

So Kenny and I sat down for a pint just across the street in an overpriced little boozer full of suits and Knightsbridge hookers.

We were both a bit quiet at first. That's what often happens when two pros get together. They don't like to give too much away.

"You still going to Gillingham games?" asked Kenny Marshall.

When we were kids nearly everyone on the manor supported Millwall – except for me.

I'd bet on a Gillingham versus Millwall game when we were all at school and copped a fiver when they won. It was a right turn-up for the books. From that day on for years I went to all Gillingham's home games. But when I hit 15, other priorities kicked in. Also, I got well fed up with all the aggro amongst the supporters at the time.

So, when Kenny Marshall jumped 25 years to ask me about Gillingham FC, it didn't exactly get the conversation flowing.

"Don't get down there much any more," I said. "Last time I went some poor bastard got sliced up by a Fulham fan."

"Oh," replied Marshall. There wasn't much else he could say, was there?

Then we moved on to all our old schoolmates. It was easier to handle than football. He told me Frank Wilson was a doctor, Billy Chittenden in the rag trade, Duggie Page a copper and Dave Wright had just come up for sentencing for assault.

I informed him that Mike Campbell was an accountant, Silly Bollocks we-couldn't-remember-his-name got killed in a nasty prang on the M20 and Tom Deans owned a sports shop in Eltham.

"I'll tell you what, Kenny," I said to him. "All things considered, we didn't do so bad."

He agreed.

"What about you?" he asked me. "What you up to these days?"

Marshall knew I'd been in the puff game and the cigs and booze shipments and everything else I could get a piece of. He might well have even heard I was into more heavy duty work but I wasn't going to tell him about it.

"Bit of this, bit of that. You know what it's like, Kenny. I keep busy." I paused. "You still with the MD?"

He smiled. "Yeah. Got promoted to controller a few years back."

He made it sound like he'd been made up to manager of the local supermarket.

"Yeah," I said. "Think I heard that from someone. So you're doin' all right, then?"

"Can't complain."

It wasn't that strange sitting there talking with him once I'd got over the initial shock of bumping into him. I'd sat alongside targets who were about to cop it a few times before. The big difference with Kenny Marshall was that I was the triggerman.

After our little chat I didn't know what else to say. A brief, slightly awkward silence followed. Then I decided to use the occasion for a little research.

"Never see you at the gee-gees no more. You used to be the first bloke on the starting block."

Marshall laughed. He had a big smile. I'd forgotten what a big smile.

"What you up to? Punting for business?"

I laughed.

"Dead fuckin' right!"

"I'm well out of the gee-gees these days," he said. "Ain't got the time. Haven't got the dosh for it. Mind you, I used to ..."

I stopped listening. This fellow was saying he never went near the horses! It made no sense at all. Here was a bloke allegedly 200 grand in debt from gambling and he's telling me he never goes near the gee-gees.

I got a queasy feeling in the pit of my stomach. Something wasn't right.

Meanwhile, Kenny Marshall was still rambling on.

"... learnt me lesson. No more. No fuckin' way."

I chuckled uneasily.

"Wish I could say the same."

We finished our beers and strolled back over to Harrods' toy department to meet the wives.

My old lady and Brenda had become best mates, which was OK by me because I had a bit of a soft spot for Brenda.

They even swapped phone numbers and talked about meeting up. I said I'd be on for it, lying through my teeth. This wasn't going the way I wanted it to go.

Then, as we said our goodbyes I'll swear I saw Kenny Marshall giving my missus a strange sort of look.

I didn't say much on the way home.

"What's your problem?" my missus asked.

"I'm not sure yet," I told her.

Then she buttoned it and left me to my thoughts. I remembered something a bent copper once told me about how the filth run murder inquiries.

"We always start from the centre of the circle," she said. "That means spouses, lovers, relatives, friends, workmates. 95 per cent of all murders are committed by someone from within that circle."

Every fucking person involved in my 13th hit came from within that circle.

Chapter Nine

As you get older you start thinking everyone's out to plug you. When that happens you know you're in fucking trouble. All that point-of-the-circle business had got me well wound up. As I drove over to the caff to pick up on Marshall the next morning, I ran through the entire job in my mind.

It was giving me a right fucking headache, like someone had cracked my head open with an ice pick and left it lodged in my brain.

What it boiled down to was, I'd been hired to do away with a man I knew, for doing something he said he didn't do, by a man who hated me and who'd threatened to kill me.

On top of all that, my missus seemed to have a dose of hot pants for my target. So now I'm thinking – am I the one being set up for the kill?

It's happened before. I heard about one hitman from Stepney who was hired to knock off a geezer out at Romney Marshes. He hung about there for a couple of hours. Then his intended victim turned up – with three muscle merchants and a fucking shitload of ammunition. They left that hitman face down in the mud.

Maybe Twiggy was setting me up in a similar fashion to even the score over his mate Little Legs. I couldn't believe Careful Craig would get involved in such a bent operation but he might not have known about it.

Or perhaps I was just getting right fucking paranoid.

Then I wondered if both me and Marshall were for the chop, but I couldn't exactly front up Twiggy or the MD about it. They weren't going to sit me down with a nice cuppa tea and tell me I was the real target.

In any case, there was no question of turning the job down now because I'd taken the money. So I'd steam on and follow Marshall, get the job done pronto, and watch my back every which way I turned.

I also began carrying a loaded .38 tucked into my belt.

I got to the caff and stayed outside in my motor waiting. I thought about going in to get a coffee and bringing it back outside, but I couldn't take a chance Marshall would walk in.

If this job was on the level, I reckoned Marshall would get well wound up if he bumped into me twice in two days.

I didn't want him getting twitchy this early on in the game. When a bloke gets nervous he gets unpredictable and erratic, and that is precisely what I didn't need. So I stayed put in my motor.

Marshall turned up a few minutes later. I watched him sit down in the caff, knock back a couple of coffees and chat to the old dear who ran the place. I was just starting to get irritated with him for taking so long when he got up and left.

He drove directly to the funeral home near Millwall Football Club to drop off all the envelopes he had on him.

Didn't make a lot of sense because he still had more collections to make but it had been mentioned in the background info that Twiggy had given me. So far all that info had been spot on. Maybe a bit too spot on for my liking. But I carried on making notes on my pad.

Marshall didn't stay at the undertakers for long and then headed back towards Peckham. His first stop was at a minicab office on the High Road. I reckoned the dispatcher was supplying his drivers with produce and they, in turn, were doing deals with passengers.

Clever, that; customers have to hire the cab to get the gear. Great earner for the dispatcher – they can pull in £300 a night just sitting in a minicab office while their drivers are out doing the hustling.

Marshall then took off for another minicab office on Talfourd Road, Peckham before heading over to Camberwell to the third and final minicab office that day. There were three blokes waiting for him with envelopes.

Then he drove back to the undertakers again.

While he was in there I checked off my list and read through Twiggy's background info before concluding that Marshall had completed all his collections for that day. The tricky part would be trying to work out some sort of pattern for the rest of his day.

People who work exclusively for a firm tend to lead chaotic lives once they've done their work for the day.

It's not easy predicting what a bloke is going to do in three days' time if he doesn't know himself.

The key is a location he keeps going back to: a bird, a card game, a mate's house, a club. And once you've nailed that, all you have to do is try and work out when he'll be there. But it ain't easy.

Marshall stayed at the undertakers for about 20 minutes while he sorted out the takings for the day. Then he headed back towards the suburbs, to a little modern redbrick house in Sydenham where his bit on the side lived.

He rolled up there about two and slung his motor up in front of her garage. She had a fluffy pink teddy in the front window and I later worked out it was a signal to tell Marshall he could come in without worrying about meeting anyone else.

I needed to know how long he spent shagging, so I slung my motor up across the street. There's no way of telling about a man and his mistress. Some guys turn up at their bird's home once a day, stay for ten minutes, just a quickie to keep the batteries charged, and then piss off again. Others like to make a big song and dance about it and spend the whole day bonking away.

I reckoned Kenny Marshall would be in there a while because he fancied himself as a bit of a swordsman. Being a hit and run merchant just wasn't his style.

So I hung about. And hung about. And hung about some more.

Waiting is the worst part of every job. You can compensate for everything except sheer fucking boredom. You start by tuning into the radio to pass the time … but the news gets fucking boring after a while.

Often I put a few sounds on. As I've mentioned, my old lady

hates me playing music at home. She thinks it'll upset the neighbours. So I end up listening to it in the motor, except when she's out at the shops or with her cronies.

I'm a bit of a soul man myself – James Brown, Stevie Wonder, The Temptations, Chaka Khan, Barry White, The Blue Notes, War, all that sort of thing. Outside Kenny Marshall's mistress's house I whacked Inner City into the walkman and sat back.

Great thing about decent music is that it helps clear your mind.

I needed to get rid of all that paranoid shit and start thinking properly about Kenny Marshall. To start with, why was he flying around the manor like he didn't have a care in the world when he was supposed to be a quarter of a mill in the shit? He didn't act like someone with a price on his head. This was a bloke who was supposed to have hired two cowboys to rip off his employers but he wasn't even glancing over his shoulder. He was making my job too easy. Much too fucking easy.

This is supposed to be a bright bloke, a year at printing college, a respected controller. How could he ever think he'd get away with it? Didn't make much sense.

Then it hit me that during all the time I'd been keeping an eye on him he never once looked like he'd placed a bet. Not one bet. He could have been phoning them in from his bird's house, but I couldn't see him diving into the Racing Post between bunk-ups.

And there was no way he'd quit the betting game because I've never known anyone quit when they were so far behind.

People like Marshall always think they can pay everything back with one good win. Problem was, I hadn't seen him even place one bet.

And that further convinced me I was the one getting the bullet.

Sitting there in my motor outside his mistress's house I never once took my eyes off her front door. I even began wondering which room they were in. Lucky bastard. I was going to have a look round the side to see if there was a back gate or something. But I gave up on that idea fast – I couldn't risk bumping into Marshall again, no way.

So I sat there and waited.

He eventually came out, looking well pleased with himself. He'd had a pleasant afternoon while I'd been sitting there freezing my bollocks off. I followed Marshall back to his family house in Bromley but it was a nightmare finding a place to park. I couldn't risk a parking ticket putting me near his home a week before he copped it.

Eventually I found a spot just past a bus stop, next to a lamp post, but just as I was parking up he took off again in his motor.

This time he headed for an after-hours drinking club in Erith which was located in the basement of Erith's only surviving pie and eel shop. I'd been there a few times myself. It was a bit like the Winchester club they all used in Minder. They don't make TV like that any more.

This particular establishment had no windows, lots of red plastic and a damp fishy pong on account of the takeaway above. It also had a pool table, a bar, a few card tables, a telly and a lot of chairs, usually occupied by blokes not doing much. Marshall didn't hang about for long in the club. Ten minutes later I trailed him back to his home and decided to call it a day. I'd had enough.

And he still hadn't looked over his shoulder.

That evening I had to meet Old Bill Wink, to pick up the rest of my order.

He asked to meet me at the local dog track because he had some favoured hounds running.

Asking me to any race meet featuring four-legged animals is a bit like offering Liberace a year's supply of free rentboys. There's no way I'd ever turn it down. It's not often I get an opportunity to mix business and pleasure.

"Promise me one thing," Old Bill had told me when we arranged the meet. "This mutt goes in the sixth. Whatever happens don't give me the cash before then otherwise I'll piss it away."

"You'd better be on time then," I laughed, " 'cos if you're not I'll be the one pissing it away."

Not only was he there on time, he was early.

We linked up just before the fifth race and he handed me a green plastic Harrods bag. I told you; all the best villains shop there.

I could tell from the weight the silencer was in it.

I stuck it in my coat pocket and asked him, "You sure you don't want the cash now?"

Old Bill shrugged. I could tell he wouldn't hold out five minutes let alone half an hour till the sixth race.

"Go on, then," he nodded.

Betting does that to people. So I gave him the money I owed him and by the time the sixth race came along he'd already pissed half of it on the previous race.

Then Old Bill put the touch on me. His next three tips gave me an all-ways trio (first three dogs home in any order) and I copped £250 and some change.

Those winnings went towards the gun and silencer.

I don't watch a lot of films but there's this little cracker no one's ever heard of starring Dennis whatisname, that bloke from *Easy Rider*. Think it's called something like *Red Rock West*.

It's about a bloke who's mistaken for a hitman when he turns up in a small town in Texas. In one scene, he's trying to impress some bird when he gets into a conversation about guns.

"Guns? Guns?" he says in this stupid whisper. "Guns don't freak me out. I'm not scared of guns."

Then he pauses and sticks his index finger in the air to make his point.

"Bullets! Bullets are what freak me out."

My old lady's not much different. She knows I have to keep shooters around for business purposes although I don't think she knows what I use them for. I always keep a few new pieces around the house ready to be used if required.

So the old lady is used to shooters, not afraid of them. The only thing that bothers her is if I leave them lying around the house with bullets in them. Fair enough.

Shooters are both my salvation and my guarantee of success.

A decent gun is a piece of art and I've even got a couple of shooters I'll never use. I keep them because they're beautiful.

One is an original German Luger. The other is a hand-crafted .38 automatic built on a .45 frame. It's a classy weapon. A real turn-on.

Then I've got the guns I carry when I'm out on business. There are three of them.

One is a regular .38 that I only wear under heavy clothing 'cause it's not easy to keep hidden.

A second one is another .38 which, as I've already said, I keep under the dashboard.

And the third is more like a James Bond toy than a real shooter. It looks like a short metal tube, but it packs the punch of a small shotgun. I've got specially made cartridges that screw into it. By pulling back a black trigger underneath it I can blow someone away from 10 feet.

I keep at least three usable pieces for the same reasons there are supposed to be three candles on a birthday cake. One for good luck. One for good health. And one to grow older with.

But I never use any of them for a specific job.

The gun used on a job will only be used once and then disposed of as quickly as possible. Mind you, that doesn't mean I won't treat it with as much respect as my own pieces. That gun is my job, my protection, my survival, my life. It's the dog's bollocks.

If that weapon lets you down at the vital moment, you're fucked. So preparing and testing the gun is a vital part of the run-up to a hit.

After I left Old Bill at the dogs I went home for the first time that day. My missus was just about to put a bit of chicken under the grill when I steamed in and took over in the kitchen. She didn't mind. She hates cooking.

An hour later we sat down to softly broiled chicken with almonds and bulgarwheat care of the Delia Smith cookbook the old lady gave me for Christmas.

Afterwards we settled down for a quiet evening in front of the telly. She curled herself up on the corner of the couch, her reading glasses halfway down her nose, watching the box and knitting a woolly jumper with a "B" on the front for one of her nieces.

I sat on the settee and started unwrapping the weapon I was going to use on Kenny Marshall. It was a touching scene of almost perfect domestic bliss until she opened her mouth.

"Mind the covers, Malcolm." She said, peering over the top of her glasses. For a moment she reminded me of my mum.

I smiled back at her and winked. She rolled her eyes and went back to her knitting. Truth is she was more worried about her new, pristine settee covers than the .38 I was about to unpack. She never stays the g-word – gun – specifically, even if I get oil or grease on the furniture.

It's an unmentionable subject. I like it that way.

The g-word I had in my lap that night had come wrapped in cosmoline oil and grease paper. I took a dry Terry cloth and started wiping the oil off it. Then I dampened the cloth and wiped it harder. That got most of the oil, including the oil in the barrel, off the gun.

I then took another Terry cloth and went over it again, even more carefully. I got right into the barrel, the cylinders and down into the crook where the hammer is. I soon had it glistening.

"Where's that sewing machine oil, love?"

"In its usual place," she said without even looking up from her knitting.

"And where's that, then?"

"In the cupboard under the stairs."

"You sure?"

"That's where it was the last time I saw it."

"Bet it's not there."

She let out a big, long sigh.

"Why don't you go and look?"

" 'Cos it's probably missing, like half the other tools."

I went to the cupboard under the stairs and rustled around a bit. There was no sign of that little tin of oil.

"It's not fuckin' here," I yelled sticking my head out from the cupboard.

She flung her knitting down, sucked on her teeth and pushed past me into the cupboard. Seconds later she had it in her hand.

"You just can't be bothered, can you?"

I gave her a plastic smile and swiped the tin out of her hand. She was soon back watching me over her glasses as I squeezed a tiny droplet into the trigger housing to keep it lubricated. This stops it rusting up and jamming.

I then put a little oil on the cylinder so it would spin easily and another drop in the barrel, again to prevent rust.

I noticed the gun had been opened and then re-wrapped because there was no serial number on it.

It's always best if the serial number is filed off even before it gets to me. But it has to be done carefully otherwise the barrel can split open when you fire. Without a serial number I couldn't find out where the gun came from if I'd wanted to, which I never do.

Mind you, the cozzers can still take a gun into a lab and bring out the remnants of that number, even after it's been completely filed off.

Meanwhile, the missus continued with her knitting and we both watched the telly.

At 8.30 we found the only programme of the night we both liked – *Two Fat Ladies*.

They were in this fucking great big monastery in Scotland serving a load of old monks a dish of the tastiest stew I've ever seen. There was a brilliant moment when old Jennifer tells them it's called "Penis Stew". Straight up. That's what it had in it. Ram's dick and it looked fucking delicious.

After the *Two Fat Ladies* drove off into the sunset on their Harley I went back to cleaning my weapon and the missus started watching some rubbish film about a woman who ditches her hubby and kids to run off with a fisherman on a Greek island.

At ten I grabbed the remote and flicked it on to *Crimewatch* on BBC 1.

"I was watching that," snapped the missus.

She grabbed the remote and flicked it back to ITV.

"I gotta watch *Crimewatch*, love," I said, flicking it back to beeb 1.

"Why?"

"Because ..." I said trying to pull a pleasant smile.

"One of your mates starring in it?"

"It's better than that rubbish you've been watching."

"Want somethin' more *realistic*, do you?"

That tongue of hers could slice a brick in half sometimes.

"Tell you what," I said. "I'll toss you for it?"

She was well fucking irritated by now. But I ignored it and pulled out my favourite coin.

She lost but that didn't make it any better.

And *Crimewatch* wasn't really worth the aggro. They had a cheesy reconstruction of a murder on a towpath and a load of burglary appeals.

But I did have a laugh when Plod asked for witnesses to a lorry hijacking near Rochester. The villains made off with 2,000 burglar alarms but none of them had instructions in the boxes. Turned out the tentonner was on its way back to the manufacturer when some Robin Hood swooped. What sort of pratt nicks a load of useless burglar alarms?

I was knackered, as I'd been up since early and there was nothing else worth watching on the telly, so at 11 I packed it in for the night. My old lady couldn't believe it.

"What's the matter with you? You ill or something?" she muttered over the top of those annoying specs.

Sometimes she just didn't know when to give it a rest.

Chapter Ten

Thursday morning I picked up on Marshall again at the same caff as before. I needed to be certain there were no unusual breaks in his routine.

It was still too early to start making concrete plans, but Erith Green remained my favourite location for the moment.

I also wanted to take a closer look at that after-hours club in Erith in case he decided to visit it at night.

The prelims to the Marshall job had been smooth, but boring, and they looked set to get even more fucking tedious as I sat there outside his favourite caff.

I banged on the radio, which for me is rare. Everyone on my manor seems to listen to Capital Gold or some such shit.

I prefer swivelling the FM dial til I find something half decent. Eventually I stumbled on a low-budget station playing "Spill The Wine" by Eric Burdon and War. It was the highlight of my afternoon.

As it turned out, neither Kenny Marshall nor Eric Burdon let me down. Marshall made his usual three stops at the minicab offices and then zipped back to the undertakers near the old Millwall ground. Then he shot out towards the suburbs. I presumed he was going to his bird's place but he surprised me by going home.

I found a parking place just as he got to his front door and decided to sit it out for a bit. Of all the things I thought he'd get up to that afternoon, he did the one thing I never counted on. Nothing. Not a fucking thing. He stayed inside his house for seven and a half fucking hours.

A lot of rubbish goes through your head when you sit there watching a door because you can't take your eyes off it for one minute. I've had targets do a runner without me even noticing because I've turned my head at the wrong moment.

On one job I was parked outside this geezer's girlfriend's

home all day and got desperate for a Jimmy Riddle and some fresh air. At that moment he left. Only I didn't know he'd gone. It's not easy concentrating every second when you're watching fuck all. Waiting for any movement.

That's when you start thinking about things you don't really want to know about.

And the thing I think most about is my first missus. It happens all the time. Might sound a bit sentimental but I've got a heart like everyone else. I know I'm married to a fine woman today but this kid, my first wife, I can't get her out of my system.

When you find a lady, a really special lady, and she comes into your life, everything changes. That's what she did to me.

I might not even have carried on being a villain if she was alive today. We had plans to get away and open a little bed and breakfast in Scotland – that's where she came from.

I wasn't a triggerman then. In fact, I was going to make a clean break from the business.

But that all changed when she died. Every single time I hit one of those scumbags I feel like I've done away with more of the fucking vermin responsible for her murder.

Suppose that's the way I wind myself up for a hit. You can't blame me, can you? Trouble was, I hadn't yet got to that point with Kenny Marshall.

I knew him as a human being, walking, talking flesh-and-blood with a missus and three kids. But I was confident the psych-up would come.

I was already pissed off at him for having such a dull fucking life. I'd been sitting there for almost five hours. And he'd done nothing. I was getting into a bit of a daze just staring at his front door.

Suddenly there's a tapping on my window.

I snapped out of my trance and, before even turning around, I thought I'd been tumbled. And I had. This little old dear who must have been pushing 80 was tapping away and smiling in at me. I wound down the window, still trying to keep one eye on Marshall's front door.

"Yeah?" I said.

"Excuse me," she said, "but I was looking out of my window ... I live at number 49 ..." She pointed over at the house right next door to Marshall's place. "And I noticed you've been parked outside here an awfully long time."

"Yeah, well, 'er," I interrupted, "I've got to because ..."

Her ears perked up.

"Because, you know." I stopped because I knew I sounded like a right pratt.

She didn't say a word. She just shook her head from side to side with a very puzzled expression on her face.

"It's a long story ..." I finally blurted out. "My son's dog has gone walkabout and we used to live near here and ... and the dog used that lamp post ... over there ... and I'm hoping the dog might show up."

I was quite proud of myself. It was all completely off the cuff. I'm not even a great dog lover.

She didn't look too convinced.

"What kind of dog is it?" she asked.

I said the first thing I could think of. "German Shepherd." That seemed to calm her down a bit because then she said: "Well, my name is Mrs Curran and I live at number 49."

"The name's Randall. Billy Randall."

"Nice to meet you, Mister Randall. I will definitely keep an eye out for your dog."

"Thanks a lot, Mrs Curran."

"And where might I find you if he turns up?"

"Oh," I replied in quite a serious manner, "right here. I'll be coming back here every day until we find that dog. My kids are so worried about him."

She went a bit soppy at that last remark.

"What a nice father you must be."

Then she paused.

"You know, Mister Curran would have made a nice father, too, but he died in the war."

"Sorry to hear that," I said, still watching the door.

"Yes," she said, "he was in Burma. He fought against the Japanese, you know."

How the hell did I end up with some nutty old dear telling me about her dead husband? Trouble was, I couldn't budge. So I just sat there nodding politely for the next few seconds.

Then she announced, "Oh, well, I must be off."

"Take care," I said, meaning "Drop dead, you silly old dear." "You're a lucky man, Mister Randall, did you know that?" she said.

I asked her why.

"When I see a car just sitting here for so long I usually call the police."

She now had my full, undivided attention.

"How come you didn't bother this time?"

She knotted her bushy brow.

"Oh, I did," she replied flatly.

I was just about to reach down to turn my ignition on and scarper when she added, "But I think they've had enough of me calling them. They told me to come out and get the registration number and call them back so they could check it on their computer."

I eased back a bit.

"So now you don't have to bother, I s'ppose?"

She smiled.

"Of course not. There's obviously no need."

I shook my head in complete agreement.

"No need at all, Mrs Curran."

I glanced at her then and noticed a slightly quizzical look on her face. Maybe she hadn't fallen for it at all.

"By the way," she said. "What's his name?"

"Name?" I replied.

"Your son's dog?"

"Oh, it's Twiggy."

"What a delightful name," she said.

Then she trotted off back to her front window with its net curtains.

I saw it all as an extra bit of luck. There are some things you simply cannot plan for, and Mrs Curran was one of them. The key is to find a route over them, as I had. Or at least as I thought I had.

Meanwhile, Marshall hadn't budged from his house.

An hour later, I was about to pull out when my man emerged dressed to kill in a slinky mohair suit with all the matching accessories, even including a red silk hanky sticking out of his top pocket.

And he was on his own.

I presumed he was off to Sydenham to pick up his bird for a night on the town. That would probably mean an evening sitting across the street from a bunch of clubs up west.

But my old schoolmate fooled me yet again. He drove straight out to a hotel in Beckenham … to a wedding.

I couldn't believe it was a real wedding so I got the number of the place and called it on my mobile. A real wedding is exactly what it was. Only Kenny Marshall's mates would get married on a Thursday evening.

There was no point in hanging about, so I went over to Peckham to settle my bookmaking account for the week.

After sorting out my debt to the gee-gees I headed home to make myself some supper. The old lady was out and there was fuck all in the fridge.

I've got no objection to her going out, as long as she leaves me something I can cook up.

There's nothing worse than driving around looking for a parking space. Then having to go straight out again for a takeaway. If we had a car port like Kenny Marshall, then it wouldn't be such a problem, would it? In that sense he was, I suppose, a luckier guy than me.

Unable to find something to cook, I drove down the high street for a curry. I was a bit narked at the missus for not having any food in the house but it was Marshall who was really doing my head in. He was making things too fucking easy for me. Why wasn't a geezer as deep in the shit as he was a lot more careful? ,

I wanted him to shit a few bricks, and he wasn't. More importantly, I wanted him to lay a few bets. Even one bet would be encouraging – something to let me know he was doing what he was supposed to be doing.

I got back indoors about 11.30. My missus was there, bursting to tell me something, but before she got a chance I had a bit of a dig at her.

"Could've left me some grub."

"What you on about? There was some chicken and ham in the fridge …"

"That's not food. That's left-overs," I yelled.

"There's nothing stopping you doin' the shoppin'."

I interrupted *very* loudly.

"Don't fuckin' talk to me like that or I'll have that fuckin' money back …"

"You'll what?"

"You fuckin' heard me."

But that didn't exactly have the desired effect because she came back at me like a ton of hot bricks.

"Number one, keep your voice down or else the neighbours'll call the police and we wouldn't want that, would we?" she muttered, with a screaming note of sarcasm.

"Number two, I'm sick of you never telling me where you are or when you're coming home. I don't know whether you're even here for supper, or not at all. So why should I bother? Why?"

I didn't respond immediately. I felt bad about snapping at her.

"D'you hate me that much?" I said calmly.

That stopped her in her tracks, but she didn't try to answer back.

"Well, I love you," I said. "Whatever you think of me. I do."

"Really?" she said, far from convinced. "Could have fooled me."

She'd obviously had a bad day so I continued easing off.

"Sorry, love," I said very quietly and calmly. "That was well out of order."

She gave me another of those disbelieving looks. I walked

over to her and tried to give her a cuddle. At first she was stiff and awkward. Funny thing is, that I do love her. I'm just a bit of a selfish bastard sometimes.

After a minute or two she nuzzled into me. I could feel her body relaxing.

"You gotta stop punishing yourself because of what happened to her," she whispered to me.

All my missus knows about my first wife is that she died at the hands of people who were after me.

"We could still adopt a child," she said, looking up at me hopefully.

"That's not the answer, love."

"Why not?"

"I've told you a million times. This world ain't fit for human consumption. Easing my guilty conscience is a lousy reason to have a kid."

"But it would be so good for us."

"I had my chance to have a kid and fucked it up, didn't I?"

She looked up at me all funny again as I squeezed her harder to emphasise my point. I was heading down yet another dead-end road so I did a swift three-point turn.

"Look, you have to move on in life. Plan your next move. It's all about planning. The-man-with-the-plan is the one who survives." "Depends what your plan is," she replied. And she had a point.

I tried to give her a proper kiss on the lips then, but she turned her face away from me.

A few minutes later, just as we were about to get into bed, she dropped an even bigger one in my lap.

"Guess who I called today?"

Don't you hate it when people say that? Am I fucking Mystic Meg or what?

"No idea," I answered flatly.

I could tell she was bursting to tell me.

"Brenda Marshall. I've invited them all over for Sunday lunch next week."

As her words sank in, I felt that chicken vindaloo from earlier curdling in my stomach.

Chapter Eleven

On Friday morning I had a really nasty attack of the Delhi-bellies – and I couldn't tell if it was that vindaloo or the prospect of my target coming round for Sunday lunch with his wife and kids. When my missus first told me I felt like going fucking apeshit at her, but I caught myself just in time.

I wanted her to blow them out for the Sunday lunch, but I didn't have a decent excuse. It was too far ahead for me to say I didn't feel like having company that day. And she wouldn't have believed me if I'd told her I didn't like Kenny or Brenda Marshall.

Much easier to just let nature take its course, with a friendly hand from yours truly.

The bottom line was that Marshall was unlikely to live long enough to enjoy a helping of my succulent Moroccan lamb marinated in tandoori paste.

That Friday morning I picked Marshall up at the undertakers.

As I sat parked across the road waiting for him to come out, I wondered what was going on inside, what Twiggy was telling Marshall. They must have been planning what to do after Marshall took his last breath.

Of course, they didn't know exactly when that might be. I had no reason to tell them. One day there'd be no Kenny Marshall and a few lines in the *Evening Standard*. No doubt Twiggy and the rest of them would make out they were heartbroken. Then the MD would name a new controller. That's how it always works.

Then my eyelids started dropping ... and dropping.

Moments later I was dreaming about being laid out on one of those familiar slabs of marble in the basement of the MD's funeral parlour alongside wads of bank notes. Twiggy was standing over me with real arms, laughing his head off while he sliced my arms off at each elbow with a hacksaw. Then he dipped my limbs in a saucepan filled with my favourite peas and apple sauce.

Suddenly I shook my head violently and forced my eyes wide open. I blinked a couple of times in the sunlight. How the fuck could I rate myself as a top pro when I'd just fallen asleep doorstepping Marshall at the undertakers?

Luckily his motor was still there. When I looked at my watch I realised my heavy dreaming kip had lasted all of six minutes. It had seemed like hours.

Instinctively, I looked in my rear-view mirror. All I saw was a hearse and a funeral procession, which didn't exactly make me feel any better. I'm not keen on watching funerals or going to them.

I'd have sacrificed the winner in a daily double to know what the hell was going on inside that undertakers. Maybe they were talking about my funeral instead of Marshall's? I was sitting there on my todd and all these thoughts were jumping around inside my head.

When Marshall finally emerged he was running at least half an hour behind his usual schedule, which bothered me a lot. He began driving back over towards Erith. I kept well back from him but managed to keep him in view the entire time.

He popped into the club under the pie and eel shop, played a game of pool and downed a couple of pints. Within an hour he was back in his motor travelling up west. I didn't know where he was heading so I closed up on him a bit. He was up to something.

As we were motoring through Stockwell, I checked my .38 to make sure it was jacked up. Not that I was nervous, you understand. But you never can be too careful. Then I had a bit of bad luck, which happens from time to time.

In heavy traffic round The Oval he got through a couple of amber lights that I got caught at. He was soon pulling further and further ahead of me. So I took a left and got on a road running alongside the main road. I wanted to get ahead of him and then take a right and pull in close behind him again.

When I eventually spotted him again, though, it was already too late. He'd beaten me and parked his motor up on a double yellow.

When I saw him he was on foot, crossing the road right in front of me. I looked straight at him and he looked right back at me.

At least I thought he looked at me, but he didn't flicker an eyelid. He just kept on walking with a lady's fur coat over his arm, which explained why he'd come to Kennington.

I worked all that out later.

Meanwhile, I put my thinking cap on. If Marshall had spotted me, surely he would have walked over to me and said hello, how's the old lady?

Instead, he'd kept walking which meant he either genuinely didn't notice me because the sun was in his eyes or that he did spot me, but decided to deliberately blank me. If that was the case, there could only be two reasons:

First – maybe he knew I was a hitman. If he was guilty of these blaggings, then he'd have expected me, or one of my fellow professionals, to show up on his doorstep. This, however, meant that when he saw me parked in Kennington he should have panicked. He'd have known it was either a coincidence or he was being tailed. But he didn't panic.

On the other hand there was the second possibility – he'd been told by Twiggy that I was tailing him, which meant that this job was slowly being turned around on me. Knowing that I would be following Marshall, anyone could keep an eye on me.

When you start thinking like this everything makes logical sense, even though, if you took a step back, you'd realise it didn't.

All that paranoia shit starts kicking when you suspect you're being lined up to be plugged.

I fired the engine up and got the fuck out of Kennington as fast as my Beemer could carry me.

I'd intended to call in on a lady friend, but business definitely came before pleasure on this occasion.

When a job is going smoothly, hard-ons come with ease. But when it's not going so swimmingly it's a problem even focusing in on my memory bank for a wank.

The fact was that, if he did see me, he'd either try and talk his way out of it, or do a runner. If he was in on my demise, then he'd act as if sweet fuck all had happened.

It was time to pay a visit to Twiggy at his second-hand car emporium, on Willoughby Street, in Peckham Rye. The crumbling railway arches opposite his forecourt closely matched the crumbling vehicles that were supposed to be Twiggy's pride and joy. I walked into the garden shed that doubled up as his office and was about to say hello when Twiggy stumbled past me out of the only door.

"What's wrong with in here?" I asked.

"You never know who's earwiggin'," he said.

Twiggy was trying hard to be serious. Not easy with two plastic arms, women's white-rimmed sunglasses and that tongue of his shooting in all directions. I found myself staring at those sunglasses. They looked like something Brigitte Bardot might have worn at the 1965 Crufts poodle competition.

"Why the fuck you wearin' women's shades?"

"Migraine."

"What?

"Couldn't find mine so I nicked the old lady's."

"Oh."

There's not a lot you can say to that so we got back to business.

"Howz it goin'?" asked Twiggy.

"It's goin'," I said, acting casual and giving a better performance than him.

"I need to know a few things," I continued. "Is there any chance Marshall knows what's happening?"

As Twiggy shook his head his lobster pink plastic arms let out one of their customary hisses.

"No fuckin' way …"

HISS!

"No way in the fuckin' world."

HISS!

"If he knew what we was up to he wouldn't turn up at the parlour, and he ain't missed a delivery yet."

HISS!

"In any case, he's planning another stick-up next week."

HISS!

"Can't you turn that fuckin' thing off, Twigs?"

"What?"

HISS!

"The fuckin' fart machine."

"Got a leaky valve. Can't do nothin' about it."

HISS!

I leaned forward and pulled his shirt up.

"Oi! What's your game?"

HISS!

It sounded even louder when his air pressure canister was exposed, but I got an immediate fix on where the hole was.

I pulled a lump of wet, sticky Airwave gum out of my mouth and whacked it straight over the offending leak.

"Now, what were you sayin'?"

Twiggy tried to tuck his shirt back in which is not easy when you've got sticks for arms, I can tell you.

Still struggling, Twiggy said, "One of his two toyboys called me this morning and asked me how we wanted it handled."

"And what d'you say?"

"I told him to sit tight and I'd get back to him. I wanted to bend your ear first."

I caught him looking straight at me.

Then he said, "When's Marshall gonna be grounded?"

No way did I want Twiggy knowing my precise plans.

"Dunno. I haven't nailed down a day yet."

He then made a half-hearted attempt to apologise for putting me under pressure.

"Anyway, it's your fuckin' show, mate. We can set up a fake

stick-up or tell his rastaboys to put him off for another week. Whatever you want."

But we both knew Marshall would eventually get suspicious if his hired guns kept putting him off. I leaned on a 1989 shit brown Escort estate caked in so much dust some wag had scrawled "Deathmobile" on the bonnet. I brushed the dirt off my jacket.

"How the fuck d'you sell any motors when they're so dirty?"

He watched me brushing myself down.

"It's what's under the bonnet that counts."

"That's what they all say."

Then I enquired why Marshall had been so long at the undertakers.

"What was all that about?" I asked.

"It was just a show for him," Twiggy said ever so casually. "We don't want the controllers knowing we grabbed those two stick-up boys so every once in a while we hold one of them after work and pump them for info. Today it was Marshall's turn."

"And?"

"He didn't tell us a fuckin' thing."

Twiggy sounded like he was telling the truth.

"What a surprise," I answered, trying to make a joke of it all.

If I was the object of Twiggy's deadly desires then I didn't want him to get a whiff of my suspicions. I took a gamble and changed the subject to something even more potentially dangerous.

"Hey, Twigs, somethin' I been meanin' to ask you?"

"What?"

"Why did I get the nod?"

"What?" he said again.

"How come I got the commission? We're not exactly best mates. Why did the MD chose me?"

I watched for Twiggy's tongue, but it never shot out of his mouth.

Either he was a good actor or he was telling the truth.

"I haven't got a fuckin' clue," he answered. "We had a meet and Careful put you up for it so I was told to get in touch …"

"What did you think when Careful mentioned me?"

"I had another geezer in mind …" He paused. "But the MD doesn't take a lot of fuckin' notice of me. He just said you were the right man for the job. Like I've said, I only do what I'm told."

Then he looked me straight in the eye and spat a huge globe of snot on the ground. Couldn't get much more honest than that.

"Glad we got that little matter cleared up," I said. "You'd better get back to polishing your old bangers."

As we both turned to walk off on our separate ways I said, "See you about."

I headed to my motor across the street and Twiggy lumbered towards his garden shed, plastic arms whistling in the wind.

There was another explanation for Marshall's seemingly relaxed behaviour which I had previously chosen to ignore. Perhaps they simply had the wrong bloke in the frame. I turned back towards Twiggy.

"Hey, Twigs," I shouted.

He stopped in his tracks, turned and looked at me.

"You sure you got the right man?"

He looked irritated by the question.

"Ain't you seen him betting?" he bellowed back at me.

"Not yet," I lifted my voice across the second-hand jalopies. "Not one fuckin' time."

"Don't you worry, old son, you can have a wank on the strength of it," he said.

I thought about that for a second and then glanced down at Twigs' twigs.

"But could *you* have a wank on the strength of it?" I asked him.

"What?"

"Forget it."

He let off another *HISS!* and lumbered back into his garden shed scratching his head with one pink claw while he tried to work out what I was on about.

I was left wondering how any so-called heavy villain could wear women's Versace sunglasses on a cold, grey autumn day. Migraine or no fucking migraine.

Chapter Twelve

Twiggy had left me feeling far from reassured. At the end of the day I wouldn't really know the score until the final confrontation with Marshall. So I had to be certain I was the one with the upper hand.

After leaving Twiggy, I began driving back to Marshall's place. Then I changed my mind and decided to give him a rest.

I didn't want to risk Marshall seeing me twice in one day. If he had spotted me in Kennington, that would have firmed everything up from his point of view. I now felt even more uneasy about this fucking job and I was deeply regretting taking it.

All the recent aggro with the old lady didn't help, either. There were times when I wished I could tell her exactly what I was up to, but I knew that would spell curtains for our marriage.

And if that happened there was also the danger she might turn me in.

That would mean I'd have to consider popping her. Might sound a bit drastic but what choice would I have?

When your brain starts mulling over things like knocking off the old lady you know you've got problems. In reality, her survival depended on her not knowing about my secret life. That's gotta be something millions of husbands can relate to.

Going home that afternoon wasn't the answer. I'd just end up having a barney with the missus. On days like this, I like to get away from the manor and clear my head. Something about driving north of the Thames over Vauxhall Bridge and looking down at that murky water helps me feel like I've put everything behind me.

That's when the need for some stress relief kicks in, courtesy of my friend Catherine-with-the-plum-in-her-mouth.

Catherine – I call her Cat – lives just off Ladbroke Grove, up in Notting Hill, West London, on a posh tree-lined street filled with white-fronted mansions that go for upwards of a million quid.

This was good because it was a long way from the places where people knew me. As you've no doubt already worked out, I'm not averse to playing away from home, but I don't want the missus finding out. I'd never embarrass or humiliate her by parading some piece of skirt in her face.

So I do it quietly and carefully. In recent years I've gone out of my way to ensure all crumpet is from across the water. By this time I'd been knocking off Cat for about four or five months. Originally I met her in a villain's club in Chelsea of all places.

Now Chelsea might not sound like the sort of area to have such an establishment, but this particular hostelry has been there for donkey's years. I don't even know the name of the club but I could find it with a blindfold on.

It's run by a bunch of heavyweight South Americans and it's usually full of arms dealers, money launderers and women from all walks of life, although Cat wasn't what I would call a typical customer. I met her when she was on a night out with a couple of her fucking annoying, toffee-nosed friends.

Cat caught my attention because she seemed a lot like my first missus. I got talking to her and she told me she'd been married to some dodgy city stockbroker who'd died of cancer a couple of years earlier. I offered my condolences and then steamed in.

Her mates got well upset when we had a snog at the end of the evening and she slipped me her phone number.

Cat's a real laugh. She doesn't work and her two teenage kids are at some knobby boarding school so she's available in the daytime, which suits me perfectly.

It also made a pleasant change to have a bit on the side I didn't have to keep subbing cash to. Cat's house is done up like some Moroccan brothel. Masses of dark reds and greens – and lots of books on shelves, including dozens of grisly true crime paperbacks. She liked a good read did our Cat. Girl's got too much spare time on her hands, if you ask me.

I think it was the second time I went round her place I realised Cat was not one of your average peas-in-a-pod. We'd just screamed the house down and were about to start up again when she pulled a book off the shelf above her fourposter. It was about some woman serial killer in Florida.

"Want to play a little game with me, Malcolm?" she asked me.

"What you got in mind?"

Then Cat puts one forefinger to her lips and slides the other forefinger along an imaginary line down past her tummy button.

"Don't say a word. Just listen."

And she starts reading from the book:

"*Number one. Impulsivity or unpredictability in at least two areas that are self-damaging spending, sex, gambling, substance abuse, shoplifting, overeating, physically self-damaging acts.*

"*Number two. A pattern of unstable and intense interpersonal relationships – marked shifts of attitude, idealisation, devaluation, manipulation.*

"*Number three. Inappropriate, intense anger or lack of control of anger.*"

By now Cat was probing herself deeply with her left index finger and breathing unevenly.

She let out one long, deep breath and then continued:

"*Number four. Identity disturbance, manifested by uncertainty about … self-image, gender identification, long-term goals, friendship patterns, values, loyalties.*"

"What the fuck are you on about?" I said.

"Sssh," she replied, rubbing the tip of her finger along my lips. "Sssh … just listen."

Then she went back to the book and her finger continued working away between her legs.

"*Number five. Affective instability – marked shifts from normal mood to depression, irritability or anxiety, usually lasting only a few hours and only rarely a few days, with a return to a normal mood."*

Cat's breathing quickened again.

"Number six. Intolerance of being alone, frantic efforts to avoid being alone, depressed when alone.

"Number seven. Physically self-damaging acts – suicidal gestures, self-mutilation, recurrent accidents or physical fights.

"Number eight. Chronic feelings of emptiness or boredom."

Cat put the book down and turned to me as we sat up in the bed. Her finger was still working away at her clit but she managed a few breathless words.

"How many of those points apply to you?"

I looked down at her index finger as it slowed up a bit. Then I smiled. She speeded up.

"About six or seven."

"You only need five out of the eight and that means you are ..." She paused and her eye lids shut momentarily, then they opened again. "That means you are suffering from Antisocial Personality Disorder syndrome."

"Oh, dear," I said.

Then this broad smile zipped across her mouth. Her forefinger was working away furiously.

"That means ..." she breathed in and out heavily, "... you're capable of killing another human being."

I smiled at her and gently stroked her chin with the thumb and forefinger of my right hand. I looked directly into her.

Then, without taking my eyes off her, I snapped my hand around her throat and held it there tightly.

"Don't worry, Cat ..." I said, squeezing just a little harder. Her pupils flared with excitement. A sea of black treacle. Not a milligram of fear in them. "You're safe with me."

"What a shame," she replied.

Just like that.

From that moment Cat opened me up about myself. She called herself my mistress/ psychiatrist. With girls like her who needs a therapist?

102

I tended to see Cat once, maybe twice a week. The only rule I had was that I wouldn't see her too often on the same day of each week because you can never tell when someone's tracking you.

I'd already called her Thursday night and arranged to pop round at about 1.30. Thanks to Kenny Marshall's travels it was after three by the time I showed up.

"About time, too," Cat said in her clipped Home Counties accent as I strolled in.

Cat was in excellent nick for 38. She had short, dark hair and the neatest facial features I've ever seen. That day she was dressed in tight black leather trousers and a red silk blouse.

Leather definitely does something to the shape of a woman's arse. It certainly did something for me.

Cat's eyes were so dark I could never really tell what was going on behind them. She was a smart girl and the thing I liked best about her was her filthy mind. Just thinking about what might be going on in her head got me going.

Cat was also very proud of her small, but perfectly shaped tits. Her nipples were constantly erect always an interesting sign in any woman.

"I got tied up," I told her after her comment about me being late. It was our little injoke.

Cat had this very slight lisp when speaking certain words, almost like she had a brace in her mouth. I loved watching the action as her tongue hit the end of some words and a tiny speck of spittle frothed up in the corner of her mouth.

Obviously, a lot of our dialogue centred around sex. She loved hearing about what I'd been up to in the past and I was up for listening to any of her adventures. No doubt she had a few secrets she'd never shared with me but I had no right to get jealous. Cat's dark side really blossomed when she took over the rough and tumble.

She loved being in command. She'd stand over me, legs apart, hands on hips just the way my mum did.

I loved looking up at her as she crunched her heels into my

balls. Cat never really hurt me, but she certainly took me right to the edge. She's the only woman I've ever allowed to take over all that kind of stuff. I love it because I don't have to make the decisions. She does it all.

Cat even admitted she was partial to a bit of carpet munching. At first I thought it was just a horny windup line but I soon realised she was serious about liking girls. In some ways I think she preferred them to men. And I didn't blame her, either.

"That's why I'm into mummy's boys like you, Malcolm," she told me in bed one day.

Back at Cat Mansion that afternoon, I grabbed her in the hallway and planted a gentle smack on that black leather-clad arse. It echoed and the pleasant aroma of expensive hide wafted sharply up my nostrils.

The next two hours were spent playing sick and twisted games with Cat eventually rewarding me with a sweatdrenched fuck as I lay handcuffed to her cast iron bed.

I forgot about Marshall. I'd exorcised him from my mind. The next time I got my head round this job I wanted to start with a clean sheet. As we lay there puffing on a spliff, Cat proudly regaled me about her latest horny conquest – a middle-aged black girl she'd pulled in a bar the previous evening.

"You'd have adored her, Malcolm ..." she said. "She had the juiciest cunt I've ever tasted." Two more little specks of frothy spit bubbled away in each corner of her mouth as she said the words "cunt" and "tasted". Cat was gagging to spill more details and I encouraged her.

"How d'you pull her?" I asked.

"She pinched my bottom while I was getting a drink at the bar."

"So you knew you were goin' to fuck her from the moment you laid eyes on her," I pointed out in a matter-of-fact voice.

"Absolutely."

I took a long suck on her reefer and had another look inside those eyes.

Then I pulled her towards me and gave her a slow, wet blow-back, allowing all the dope smoke to swim into her mouth as our tongues slurped away at each other.

Then I sat back and shut my eyes.

When I opened them up again, Cat was staring right into me.

"What's up?" I asked casually.

She carried on staring for a couple more heartbeats. Then …
"I bet you've shot and killed people," she said.

"What you on about?" I replied coolly, letting just a slight smile come to my lips.

"You know. Murdered them …" She said it like others would say fucked.

"Don't be daft, girl," I said.

"You're a gangster, aren't you?" She said . the word gangster with such admiration in her voice.

The smile dropped from my face.

"You got a wire on you or somethin'?" I said quietly.

She giggled.

"You're the one who's wired, my dear," she said, tugging on her spliff.

Then I began sliding my hand up the inside of her thigh.

"That makes two of us …"

About an hour later Cat called up the Orient Express and got them to bike round a few cartons of their spiciest spare ribs. I was fucking starving. After we'd sucked the bones virtually dry I gave her a long, greasy snog. She tweaked my nipple hard and I was on my way.

I started driving home, then changed my mind and decided to head over to a drinking club I knew and sink a couple of pints and maybe play some cards.

But within a few more minutes I changed my mind again and decided to take a gander past Marshall's place and see what he was up to.

It was dark, so I wasn't so bothered about him spotting me.

105

Even with the best lights it's impossible to see inside a moving car after dark. Marshall's motor was slung up on his car port, a light was on in the front room and everything looked normal.

I parked in my favourite spot, near the lamp post, with the intention of only staying a few minutes just in case I got a lucky break. I don't really know what I expected to find. I just felt the need to sit outside there for a bit. After about twenty minutes the wrong front door opened.

Out of the corner of my eye, walking right towards me, I saw Mrs Curran.

I had no choice but to open my window. She smiled pleasantly at me.

"I saw you drive up and thought you might need some refreshment."

"Oh, that's kind of you," I replied, "but I'm not here for long."

Her face looked a little confused.

"Oh, no," she said. "I brought something out for you."

She held up a thermos flask and before I could say "German Shepherd" she'd poured me a cup of coffee.

"D'you take milk and sugar?"

I said I did.

She reached into a pocket and pulled out a container of milk. Then she conjured up a couple of cubes of sugar from another pocket.

As she stirred it all up she told me another bit of stop press news.

"I've put some notices up all over the neighbourhood for you. If anyone finds Twiggy I told them to call me."

I tried to look grateful.

"That's very nice of you, Mrs Curran."

I sat there sipping at her coffee as she rambled on. Then a thought crossed my mind.

For all I knew she could have been Marshall's best friend in the street, maybe a babysitter. Fuck knows what she might be saying to people in the neighbourhood. She might have described me. She certainly knew what I looked like. She was only six inches from my face at that very moment.

Then the old dear rudely interrupted my train of thought.

"Do you know why German Shepherds are called Alsatians?" she asked.

"What?" I said.

"I said, do you know why German Shepherds are called Alsatians?"

I didn't know or care.

"You tell me," I responded.

She looked very pleased with herself them.

"It's all because of the First World War. Anything German was deemed to be evil."

"That makes sense," I replied, shrugging my shoulders.

"My father had one, you know."

"What?" I was getting well confused.

"An Alsatian?"

"Oh, right," I replied with about as much interest as Lester Piggott shows for tax returns. I'd done my charm offensive but this meaningless rabbit was getting on my nerves. My business was carrying out contracts, not blasting little old ladies so there wasn't a lot I could do about it.

I've never knocked off an innocent punter in my life but and this is worth saying here and now – if an innocent person ID'd me making a hit I'd have to seriously consider it.

Thank God it's never happened to me yet. It has happened to others, though.

In one well-known recent case a villain was lured into bringing his perfectly innocent bird to a "business meeting", which was actually a set-up. They both copped it.

In another incident out in Epping this topless model was called to testify about her gangster boyfriend. They found her headless corpse floating down the Thames. Only reason I remember the story so well is the headlines in the newspapers the next day …

I finished my cup of Mrs Curran's coffee.

"I've got to be on my way, Mrs Curran. My little lady and the kids."

I poured it on a bit strong. She lapped up every word of it. And Kenny Marshall never showed his face.

I got fuck all sleep that night.

The demons were setting in again and they kept telling me that I was walking over glass eggshells. Every time I examined the elements of the Marshall job it bothered me big time. I know I told the missus that the-man-with-the-plan always survived. But if that plan went up in smoke he wouldn't stand a chance in hell.

The only sleep I eventually got that night wasn't worth the stress. I dreamt I was a copper in charge of solving the murder of Princess Di. I'd teamed up with this other detective who had exactly the same name as me.

Next thing I know I'm asleep at home with the missus when this same bastard creeps up behind me and shoots me up the arsehole with three bullets from my favourite .38.

It took 15 minutes for me to die as those bullets sliced like redhot razor blades through my gut tearing my insides to shreds. The corner of each blade ripped along the surface of my flesh like a shark's fin.

I woke up in a cold sweat and looked over at the missus who was out for the count as usual. I prayed that when my death finally came it would be over in a split second.

Chapter Thirteen

Saturday is no different from the rest of the week for a controller on a drugs firm. He's got to be up with the birds and at work as early as ever. In fact, weekend business is the liveliest of the entire week because that's when all recreational users come out of the woodwork looking for gear.

Druggies don't care about a five-day week. When they need to score you've got to keep the runners well stocked up and collect all that dosh.

Marshall left his house right on time that Saturday. I know because I was there waiting for him. I thought he might try a few strange turns to see if he had a tail. If that happened I'd drop out of sight for a day or two.

But he didn't seem to have a care in the world. Why the fuck wasn't he bricking it? It's pretty easy to check if you are being tailed; make four left turns in a row, or go right, left, right, left or some combination which makes no logical sense. If one particular motor is still behind you know the score.

I've no doubt been professionally trailed a few times but I've only picked up on it once or twice. It's the amateurs you got to watch out for because they're always after something.

Couple of years back me and my old lady had just been to see *Cats* up west. Fucking hated it and she's been back to see it 31 fucking times, can you believe it? Anyway, that night I'd parked the car just off Old Compton Street, in Soho, because I wasn't going to get taken to the cleaners by those £5-an-hour car parks.

The missus and I had polished off a bottle of vino and a bowl of pasta at a little spaghetti house after the show and she was in one of her good moods.

That meant *anything* could happen.

We were walking down an alleyway when suddenly she pushes me into a doorway and we have a brilliant snog-up. (This was back in the days when we really enjoyed our snogging). Our tongues are doing a sword fight and her right hand's on a one-way journey to my lower deck. Then I happen to glance over my shoulder, as one does in my sort of job.

I immediately spotted two bulky-looking blokes silhouetted by a flickering street light. They were walking slowly in our direction. I knew what they were up to.

I placed my hand over the old lady's which was in the middle of pulling down my flies and gently removed it.

"We got company ..." I whispered in her ear "... don't say another fuckin' word."

She zipped me up and stayed pressed against me.

I slowly pulled my gun out and covered it with my hand, still holding my old lady close to me.

That's when these two characters began running towards us. One of them had a long thin blade out, glistening in the moonlight.

"You got money, man?" he barked at me, in a weird sort of foreign accent. He looked eastern European.

I laughed in his face.

"How badly you want it, man?" I said, imitating the way he said "man".

He looked confused.

I pulled out my shooter.

"In the head or your bollocks?"

Seconds later I put these two bastards up against a wall and cleaned them out of every penny. One of them had £400 and the other £150. The first one had a tasty diamond ring, the other a pricey looking gold bracelet. They'd obviously had a profitable night.

I took the fucking lot.

"Hey, man, why you doin' this? We from the same place," one of them said to me.

"You know where Bexleyheath is?" I yelled at him.

He didn't know what the fuck I was talking about.

"Excuse me?"

"I said where's Bexleyheath?"

He looked at me blankly again.

"Wot is Bexleyheef?"

Pratt couldn't even pronounce it right.

"It's my hometown ..." I said, pointing the gun right at him and smiling. "Now fuck off."

He and his mate ran for their lives.

A few minutes later, as the missus and I drove across Waterloo Bridge I handed her most of the money.

"There you go, darling," I told her. "Little somethin' for being a good girl and doin' what I said."

Meanwhile, Kenny Marshall spent most of that Saturday acting like he didn't have a care in the world. So I started worrying for him.

He kept to his usual schedule, which wasn't that surprising. I ended up outside his bird's place in Sydenham wondering if it was feasible to plug him on her doorstep. So I sat there timing plod patrols because it's always important to know when they are in the neighbourhood.

Sometimes the boys in blue are inconsistent and don't stick to any schedule. Last thing I want is a panda car riding past when I'm parked up with a loaded .38 in my lap. The first panda drifted by 20 minutes after I'd arrived. It was a starting point. The same cop car reappeared 45 minutes later, and 45 minutes or so after that.

Marshall, of course, was still inside, pumping away at his best schoolmate's wife. Or so I reckoned. I wondered why he was wasting his time with his blonde bit on the side when he had a cracker like Brenda back at base.

Once Marshall's six feet under, I'll give Brenda a bell as any old and dear friend would, and maybe I'll pop by and see how the kids are coping.

And maybe I'll take her away for a few hours to help her forget about her dearly departed, and then maybe I'll take her home and give her one.

111

Somebody was going to. She was still young – late thirties – strong face, nice dark eyebrows, one of those lovely duck walks where their feet are just ever so slightly apart.

I don't like real blondes but when there's a hint of something darker beneath the surface it makes it all worthwhile. Some lucky bastard was going to have his evil way with her eventually. Why not me?

I gave it some serious thought as I sat there while Marshall biffed his mistress. I imagined me and Brenda giving it the light fantastic with her nice, strong thighs wrapped round my back, rounded off by a nice pair of heels.

Maybe she'd even be into a bit of the old rough and tumble as well? All I had to do was knock off Kenny Marshall, which was my job anyway.

Now that's what I call a perk.

I was off again; thinking careless thoughts. Killing is not a crime of passion, it's a job. When you do it for love – or a quick bonk for that matter – you get nicked. I did it for cash. It's a business. And I didn't want to cross that line.

But hang on a minute … I did know him and in many ways it was personal. That point-of-the-circle stuff kept running through my head. It still bothered the hell out of me.

But there was no denying that Brenda was well tasty. Maybe, I thought, maybe I will steam in there. Maybe. Looking back on it my head was all over the place, even at that early stage of the Marshall job.

When the time came around for the next panda to show up again in Sydenham, I left my motor to take a stroll round the block. I needed a bit of fresh air and I didn't want them checking me out because I'd been sitting there for three hours.

It wasn't one of my better decisions.

In the couple of minutes I was away from the car, I missed Marshall's departure.

Either that, or he'd slipped out the back door when I was daydreaming about giving his wife one. But none of this became apparent until much later.

After the panda had gone I returned to my motor and 45 minutes later I took another walk to avoid the next plod patrol. It's possible Marshall went awol at that point. I will never really know. It wasn't until six hours later I realised he'd done a runner.

Finally the front door opened and this elegant-looking blonde walks out.

I knew it had to be Marshall's bird because she looked a bit like his Brenda; smallish, shoulder length dyed blonde hair (Twiggy's background info said she had shortish hair, but it must have grown), good figure and, this was the clincher, she was wearing that fur coat Marshall had in Kennington.

Her appearance told me Marshall had done a bunk and that meant he must have been on to me.

I fired my engine up and headed down the road to check out his motor which was parked round the corner from the mistress's house. I tend not to watch an individual's car, I watch the individual. You never track a person by watching his transportation because they often use different motors, especially if they know you're on to them.

It's also dangerous to make any assumptions. That's something I picked up in the army during the Falklands War. Deal with facts. Deal with what you actually know.

None of that old bollocks got me anywhere that day. His motor was gone. I'd fucked up good and proper. Cock-ups don't help your reputation and, when people start slagging you off, the chances of being grassed up to the filth are much higher.

Anyway, Marshall had gone walkabout and I didn't know if that meant he was on to me or not.

A glance in my rear-view showed his blonde bird hopping in a cab. If he had deliberately given me the slip she'd have stayed in the house, surely?

I had to decide whether to follow the cab or go to the one location I was pretty certain he'd reappear at, his home?

I started following the cab. If it headed out towards Gatwick I'd have followed it in case Marshall was about to hop a plane.

But she went towards Swanley, so I took a chance and drove back towards Bromley.

Everyone has at least one location where they'll always show up eventually. Everyone.

I was looking for a geezer once and the only place I knew for sure I'd find him was at the races. The geegees were running at Goodwood, but that's too much of a trek from south east London. I reckoned, if he was going for the flat, he'd head for Epsom. I hit Epsom every weekday on the trot for two weeks to look for this fellow and, sure as blood is red, on the last day he turned up.

Mind you, it cost me a few bob. As long as I was at the races I couldn't help having a punt or two, but I got him in the end.

In Marshall's case, there were a few places he could turn up at: his home, the undertakers, his girlfriend's. I knew he wasn't at the girlfriend's. There was just no reason in the world for him to go to the undertakers at that hour. That left his home.

Unfortunately, he wasn't bloody there. No motor. Lights on in the lounge. I cruised round the block three or four times looking for his transportation. Not a fucking sign. Beads of sweat were sitting on my forehead and one of my ear-splitting headaches was coming on fast. It's like having a pneumatic drill roller-coastering through your brain pumping away at the inside of your head.

Cat says they're caused by tension and what I need is a bit of acupuncture. But I'm terrified of needles so I can't see that ever happening.

I reckon a lot of my headaches are down to guilt. As I've said, I'm not all bad. And that's why the guilt kicks in.

Sometimes it makes me stop and think and that's when I start to worry. My mum was just the same.

After I left home and joined the Army she set up camp at the local boozer, picking up punters when it took her fancy. Picking up a gin when it took her fancy. Picking up a foul mouth when it took her fancy. Picking up fifty Bensons a day when it took her fancy.

But my old mum always felt guilty after she'd been on one of her benders. She'd hide in her crummy little flat and not come out for days. Then she'd emerge and start all over again.

One day she was diagnosed with throat cancer, which would hardly have surprised me if I'd known about it, but she didn't tell a soul.

The guilt of not telling anyone did her brain in more than the actual cancer.

She went awol one day and tried to jump off the top of an NCP car park in Bromley. Old Bill eventually talked her down and she was locked up in the nutter's wing of the local hospital. If you hadn't been depressed before you got in there, you'd certainly get the blues within minutes of arriving – it was that grim.

I went to see her in there a few days after she'd been committed. As I recall, she was lying flat on her back sweating like a trooper, even though it was mid-December. Her ward was dimly lit and very dark, considering it was only about two in the afternoon. She had this grey, wet flannel over her forehead and she was breathing in loud huffs and puffs. I gave the flannel a rinse and carried on dabbing her head like any good son would do.

Suddenly, she opened her eyes and looked daggers right at me. Then she screams, "Nurse! Nurse!"

This middle-aged-matron-type walks over.

"Nurse! Nurse! This is my son Malcolm. You know, the one I told you about," she said proudly, eyes wide open.

I stood there and took a long gulp and gave the matron a weak smile. She looked right through me. Must have heard it all a million times before.

"His job is to murder people," said my mum, even more proudly.

My fake smile dropped instantly and I stared up at the ceiling where a big, fat black spider was scurrying towards the dusty neon strip light.

"That's his job. Killing people," said my mum. "But they deserve it, don't they, Malcolm?"

I didn't take my eyes off that spider for a second.

"That sounds exciting," said the nurse.

Then she just walked away. We were in a nutter's ward, after all. But my lovely old mum wasn't finished yet. Those eyes were still wide open.

"You knocked anyone off recently, son?" she asked me.

I could see a glint of watery excitement in those glazed, yellowing eyes. Then she pulled me towards her with a bony hand and whispered into my ear.

"Do me in if you want, Malcolm. I'd like that, I really would."

"Don't be bloody daft, Mum," I said.

But she wasn't listening.

"My time's up, Malcolm. Come on, you know how to do it. You're a real pro …"

Then she fell flat on her back in the bed. Her eyes were still open but she didn't utter another word.

I carried on dabbing her forehead with that damp flannel.

Then these tears began rolling down my cheeks. I couldn't even wipe them away because she'd start moaning if I stopped dabbing her head. It was the only way to keep her quiet. I stood there for ages just looking at her and trying to comfort her with that flannel. And I couldn't stop sobbing. I felt so fucking bad about what I'd become.

My mum never spoke another word and died a couple of days later.

The weird thing is that I'd never told her what I did for a living. She just knew it. Reckon she thought it was all her fault.

Well, it wasn't, Mum. I promise.

Back in the land of the living, I tried to put myself in the missing Kenny Marshall's shoes.

If someone was after me, where would I scarper to? How would I travel? Car? Plane? Train? Maybe even a coach from Victoria? There were too many options.

First thing I did was call Twiggy and have him put out the word that anyone seeing Marshall should get in touch.

I didn't like admitting I'd lost him because it was bad for my reputation, and I'm not good at coughing to anything, but I had to do something otherwise he'd get a head start on us.

I began driving towards Bromley shopping centre, picked up my mobile and punched out Twiggy's number.

At that precise moment I saw this fucking amazing sight – Kenny Marshall driving along the street coming from the opposite direction. As he drove by I turned my face away, made the first possible turn and headed back to his place.

I got there just in time to see him climbing out of his motor with at least four plastic carrier bags. He'd been out shopping!

He picked up the packages and walked inside. He didn't even have a glance about. I'm in the clear. I thought, he hasn't got a fucking clue.

I went straight home and had a big supper, prepared for a change by my beautiful, charming wife. I even made a point of not grumbling about her cooking which won me a few brownie points.

The best lies are the ones nearest to the truth, or so my old mum used to say.

Chapter Fourteen

There's a line you cross in life. I'd crossed it way back and now I was at the point of no return. But that didn't stop the Marshall job giving me a headache at every junction. Was Marshall really as guilty as they made out? Or was the entire operation set up to pop me?

Instead of fretting I should have been out and about finalising my plan.

I'd been on Marshall almost a full week and still hadn't decided on a definite location. I usually nail that down in the first couple of days. But here I was still arseholing around, not happy with any of the potential sites on my list.

If Marshall was really betting heavily then he must have been doing it on the sly. I hadn't seen him pick up a *Sporting Life* let alone go anywhere near the races. To be gambling such vast amounts of cash he'd have to be studying the form sheets with a fine-tooth comb.

It was possible he'd been betting from his girlfriend's house or even from his own front room, but I didn't reckon so.

His gambling was the key to the entire operation. If I caught him at it then I'd immediately know for sure he was the right target.

On Saturday night I decided to find out for certain.

I called a Brummie mate of mine called, a phone man I knew from my army days.

This geezer can do anything you want with telephones, from running a backstrap for a bookie scam that is two phones in different locations hooked together on one number – to putting in the poshest digital job complete with soft ringing tone for the missus.

"What you up to tomorrow morning?" I asked JJ after exchanging a few pleasantries.

"Prayin' in church. Like I do every Sunday."

The JJ was short for Jumpin' Jack and he could be a right jumpy little Brummie git when he wanted to be but his heart was in the right place, or so I reckoned.

"What you prayin' for?" I asked him.

"That my old lady will lose four stone," he answered deadpan.

"Don't hold your breath ..." I paused. "You interested in some consultancy work?"

"Depends how much."

"Two centuries for a couple of hours' work."

"What time and where?

"Good man. Bring your bag of tools and I'll see you at Donny Moyle's place at eleven."

"What you after?"

I don't like rabbiting about business on the dog under any circumstances and JJ was a notorious FBI (finest bugging individual). He was probably taping me at that very moment.

"Tell you all when I see you."

JJ didn't really get rattled, even when I gave him some gip. The jumpy act was a bit of a put-on.

"I gotta know what sized gaff we talkin' about so I bring the right gear," he asked in that dull, monotonous voice of his.

I told him, "Four-bed semi."

There was a short pause then he chipped in.

"There's only one condition." He took a long sniff. "Gotta be back at base in time for the footie on Sky."

"No problem, my old son," I lied.

I met JJ in front of Donny Moyle's place because I didn't want him knowing where we were heading. JJ lives in east London but, coming from Birmingham, he knows south of the river like I know Hounslow. At best, he's heard of it. As long as I was driving I knew he wouldn't concentrate on where we were going.

When he jumped in my motor he had his toolbox in one hand and the *News of the World* in the other.

"What's the newspaper for?" I asked him.

"To read," he said. Ask a stupid question ...

I was taking a big risk trying to tap Marshall's house, but I reckoned the odds against him spotting my man up a telephone pole were about the same as Red Rum coming down from the heavens and winning the next Derby.

And if anyone came asking, JJ was carrying more British Telecom ID than Alexander fucking Graham Bell.

Besides, this was a case of the ends justifying the means. I had to find out what the fuck was going on.

JJ made me clamber up a telephone pole 200 yards from Marshall's house. He even gave me a yellow BT hard hat which made me look a right plonker but at least old Mrs Curran the dog spotter wouldn't recognise me.

JJ soon had the junction box open, revealing hundreds of different-coloured wires running in all directions.

"Which house does he live in?" JJ asked.

I told him and eventually he spotted the right wire, took two metal clips and attached them.

Then he hooked the other end of the wires into a pair of headphones and handed them to me. I put them on and heard a dialling tone.

"That's his phone." JJ was wasting his time doing the occasional gig for villains. He should have been working for British intelligence. Unfortunately he got drummed out of the army for nicking rings off Argie corpses at Goose Green.

I clung unsteadily on to that BT pole 30 feet above the suburbs of south east London and tried not to look down. I'm not a great one for heights.

JJ leaned against the pole next to me and pulled out his *News of the Screws*. He pointed at the paper and mouthed the words: "To read," and began pouring over the tale of a transvestite politician who'd just run off with one of his wife's best friends. Sometimes you get a stupid answer twice.

We stayed up that telephone pole for about half an hour and fuck all happened, except a bunch of Kamikaze pigeons started dive-bombing us. They only gave up when JJ chucked half his cheese and pickle sandwich on the pavement.

Then someone started dialling from inside Marshall's house. Here we go, I thought, he's going to call his bookie and pick a few classic losers.

But it was Brenda Marshall. She was on the blower to some mate of hers and they yapped away for a few minutes.

Then she invited this other woman and her old man for dinner the following week. Bloody typical, I thought, she invites them over, but she has to come to our place. We'll see about that! They kept yapping.

JJ pointed to his watch. It was 75 minutes to kick-off time. Get off the fucking phone, I thought, get off the fucking phone.

Eventually, she did, but before they'd finished I picked up a tasty-sounding recipe for ginger spice pudding.

Nothing happened for another ten or 15 minutes.

JJ had been through the sports pages and was re-reading the dirty bits of a two-page massage parlour expose when the phone rang.

Maybe it was a bookie calling him to give a stack of tight odds.

No, it was a wrong number and I was starting to freeze my bollocks off. The earphones were making my ears sore so I took them off.

I turned to JJ.

"D'you think they've got two phones?"

He leaned back into the junction box. I was convinced we had the wrong phone. While Marshall was busy gambling his life away, I was getting a recipe for ginger fucking spice pudding.

Then JJ turned around.

"Only the one phone."

He went back to a story headlined: MY THREE IN A BED ROMP WITH HOLLYWOOD STAR.

As time went slowly by I got more and more despondent. The man doesn't bet on the gee-gees so he must be gambling on the football or nothing at all. That's it. And Marshall hadn't bet a fucking penny. It was half-an-hour to the Sunday afternoon kick-offs.

Fifteen minutes later someone picked up the phone. I recognised Marshall's voice immediately.

He starts putting money on the football and I mean really betting. He makes all three Premiership games that day, at £10,000 a game. Then he hangs up and calls another bookie and goes through the same routine again, this time at £5,000 a game.

At last I'd found out where all his dosh went. This stupid bastard was burying himself even deeper than before. That afternoon he was on the boards for £45,000 and who knew how long it'd been going on?

The bookies let him carry on because they knew he was a good earner, and when you're taking home decent wedge they don't give a monkey's how deeply you go into the hole.

As long as he kept handing in two grand a week or so I'd have let him keep betting, too. The odds were stacked against him ever getting even again. The bookies' attitude is, I own you, don't I? And as long as I know you're capable of earning I'll let you go on for fucking ever. Punters making consistent payments are rarely shut down even when they have little or no hope of ever getting even.

The real problems begin when they miss payments. The bookies call them desperadoes and Marshall was on his way to becoming one big fucking desperado.

Listening to that phone call clinched it for me. I knew he'd be back on at half time, trying to win both halves of a game or at least break even, but he'd fall even deeper into that hole.

I tapped JJ on the shoulder and gave him the thumbs up.

"We got him," I said. "Let's go."

He carefully folded up his News of the Screws, took the clips off the wires, wrapped up his equipment and we slid gently back down to earth.

I drove n back to Donny's place, pulled out my wallet and handed him four 50-pound notes.

"Good work, doctor," I told him.

I knew JJ would keep his trap shut simply out of friendship, but combining friendship and some decent wedge meant that little extra guarantee. Neither me nor JJ got home in time for the kick-off of the Sky game. But I got back in time to lay a few bets on some Far East races.

I'm not really into football these days, although no doubt my old mate Kenny Marshall would be avidly watching Sky at that very moment.

I ended up breaking about even with the Far East syndicates but Marshall was taken to the cleaners. He lost all three games – 45 big ones down the tube.

I took the missus up west to Chinatown for a meal that night but, truth is, my mind wasn't really on the chop suey and spring rolls.

She got the right hump when I wouldn't order spare ribs after overdosing on them at Cat's house. All I could think about was Kenny fucking Marshall. I should have been happy because now I knew for certain he was in the shit over his gambling, just as Twiggy had told me.

But something told me not to stop checking my rear-view.

One thing I do remember about that evening with the old lady in Chinatown was the message in the fortune cookie at the end of the meal. I put it in my wallet because it got me thinking.

"Don't make any decisions until you are sure."

Now I was sure. And it was time to make the most important decision of all.

The following day – Monday – I decided to check out Marshall's whole morning routine one last time to make sure he hadn't changed anything. He hadn't. Yet again I wasted half an hour waiting outside his favourite caff while he warmed up inside.

Sitting there got me thinking about how pissed off his bookies would be when they read about his untimely death in the *Evening Standard*.

I made a list of the places he might head for while I waited for his next move. Then he went and fucking tricked me again by driving across the river and into Victoria. He parked up on a meter and walked into a tanning salon on Erskine Street.

In my time I've seen blokes go into all sorts of places; brothels, football games, barges on the Thames, bus depots, even abattoirs. One target I was following went in a trannie bar once, which worried me a bit, especially when my target walked out a few minutes later with a six-foot brunette on his arm.

But I never had a geezer go in a tanning salon before.

Then I started wondering if Kenny Marshall was topping up on his tan before hitting the sun-drenched beaches of Copacabana. I was getting paranoid again. I presumed the salon was one of those unisex jobs when two blokes in shellsuits walked in a few minutes after Marshall.

But I knew something was up when Marshall came out more than an hour later exactly the same colour as when he went in.

Then something started happening that is quite a rarity in this game.

I wasn't just picking up Marshall's movements, I was picking up his rhythm. I was getting in tune with his movements, his vibes I suppose you'd call them. I knew his physical movements but now I could see what was going on in his head as well.

Majority of hits are just trace, track and shoot. But this wasn't the case with Marshall. We were on the same wavelength, but going in opposite fucking directions. Hopefully, only the one of us knew where we were heading.

From the tanning salon Marshall went back over the river towards Eltham. We ended up heading south to the A2 sliproad.

I hadn't looked once to see if I was being tailed, as I'd promised myself I would. Now, with nothing much else to do except listen to a bunch of phone-in wallies on Talk Radio I started paying attention to my rear-view.

A big silver Merc with two blokes in it was about four car lengths behind me. Something about it got on my nerves. So I put my foot down and noticed they sped up immediately. But they always stayed the exact same distance behind me. Now they were really getting on my nerves. When I moved from a left handlane into the middle, they moved too.

Finally, I put my indicator on, as if I was getting off at the next exit, and moved over to the left lane. Their ticker went on.

I watched them closely. When the exit came I sailed right past it. They did too! That's when I knew I definitely had some new enemies.

I dropped back from Marshall at the next exit off the A2 and took the slip road. The Merc followed. I drove half a mile before making a series of turns. My new enemies followed me for the first four turns, then dropped out of sight.

They knew I'd picked them up. Shame because I wanted to get close enough to take a proper look at them. They might have been familiar faces. I reckoned Kenny Marshall wasn't bothering to look over his shoulder because he had people looking out for him. There was also the possibility Twiggy was involved with that mob in the silver Merc and planned to have me burned the moment I took out Marshall.

Neither option was very appealing and the job itself was in serious jeopardy if they were Marshall's cronies and they knew I was on his tail. He'd either have to come at me with all guns blazing or do a runner, and do it quick.

On the other hand, if the tail came from Twiggy it wasn't so bad. He wouldn't think I knew he'd set it up. But he'd be a bit more careful in the future.

I couldn't do fuck all about any of it, so I closed my notepad for the day and headed home.

It was past seven by the time I finally found a parking space nearly half a mile from my house. Not having a car port like Kenny Marshall was getting on my nerves more than ever. I intended calling my number one bookie to see how my fillies were performing, then stay home and read up on my notes.

Some serious decisions about Marshall's future, or lack of it, had to be made.

But there was a barrel-load of noise and laughter when I walked in the hallway. Then I remembered the old lady was hosting a girls' night at our place. Every Monday night my missus meets with five of her mates at one of their homes and they play a bit of bridge, slag all their old men off and rabbit on about their favourite biceps in *The Full Monty*.

I've got to sit down and plan a murder and these girls are squeaking like a bunch of demented guinea pigs. They know I'm in the business but they don't know exactly what I do. If I'm handling some panty hose or a load of cutlery I give them first option.

When there's a lorryload of ciggies on the go I tell them what's on offer – and encourage them to spread the word amongst their friends. I often palm off between 300 and 500 cartons to the five of them. Same with the booze when they're in the mood. A lot of them flogged on their produce and copped a few bob profit themselves. Good luck to them.

The only party pooper is Dot, whose old man is a customs and excise officer and she believes she'd be helping finance organised crime.

"Anyone after some cheap fags?" I asked as I sat down and grabbed a cold leg of chicken.

The others started screaming and shouting as if they'd just spotted Engelbert Humperdinck and Tom Jones down at the local KwikFit. I told them all to call my old lady before Friday to stick their orders in.

I was deep into my chicken leg when Patsy, who's quite a tasty-looking brunette but has a high-pitched, squeaky voice that drives me up the fucking wall, demanded, "Haven't you got anything else?"

"Do I look like a fucking cash and carry?"

They all laughed and lapped it up, but I knew the old lady didn't like me swearing in front of them.

Patsy's old man ran a chain of chippies in Eltham and Erith. Sue's fella was an estate agent and I haven't a clue what Bab's or Vicky's husbands did.

But for the moment these ladies only had eyes for me.

"Yeah. I got some other gear on offer," I told them in my hardest villain's accent.

They were all ears.

"'Alf a dozen smutty videos starring some stud with a twenty-inch piece of tackle. Yours for a tenner each, ladies. Any offers?"

They laughed even more. Patsy put up a hand but then put it straight down again when she realised no one else was bidding. She could be a bit of a stroppy cow but those nipples of hers stuck out like bullets through her skimpy cotton T-shirt.

Just then I caught a glimpse of the old lady and knew she didn't like me spreading porno videos through the neighbourhood. So I finished my chicken and got up to retire to the bedroom.

"Where you off to?" my missus asked.

"I gotta go and plan a hit," I said in a loud, nasty voice.

The girls collapsed in giggles. Then I noticed Patsy looking at me a bit strangely. She raised her hand and shaped it like a gun, thumb up, forefinger pointing forward.

"Bang. Bang," she said, running her tongue along her lips. "You're dead."

Somehow she knew what I was up to. I didn't want to know how so I scarpered upstairs and left them to their bridge and chicken legs.

I checked in with my main man, Scotch Johnny, because there'd been a few upsets on the Far East geegee circuit and I hoped I'd still come out in the black. He confirmed that I was well up for the week. I wrote down all the winners and losers and made a note to set aside some time the following Tuesday to sort out my books.

Then I got out my Marshall notes. Concentrating wasn't easy with all those birds downstairs laughing their heads off comparing the size of their old men's dicks. I decided to firm up the next ciggie shipment there and then. I got on the phone and tracked down my middle man, a sweaty Russian fellow called Ludwig.

Ludwig had taken over a health club called The Aquarium just off Shooter's Hill a few years back. He got it on a contra deal after the previous owners got into serious hock with the Moscow mafia. Ludwig had turned it into a very unhealthy drinking den. Usually it was wall-to-wall with dodgy villains and a bunch of quiffy-looking tarts. Most of them ended up skinny dipping in the pool once the booze and drugs kicked in.

On Fridays and Saturdays some of London's oldest panto villains from the days of the Richardsons and the Krays would drop a tab of E and then start stroking old sploshers in the steamrooms. Ludwig was usually pumped up on speed and grating a hole in his cheek. He's always telling me to come over and grab a pint.

I didn't need much persuading that night.

Chapter Fifteen

I took the long route to Ludwig's place, stayed off the main roads and kept checking my rear-view. I had to know who was watching me before I dropped Marshall because people who tail other people have a nasty habit of turning up at just the wrong moment. The Aquarium was fairly quiet when I strolled in.

"Where's all the strumpet?" I asked Ludwig. The smell of chlorine from the indoor pool misted up my eyes within seconds.

Ludwig hadn't changed the water in years and told me he kept pouring in chemicals hoping to kill off all the piss and spunk. You'd never catch me doing a few laps in there. Ludwig shrugged his shoulders and grated through his teeth when he finally responded to my question about the lack of females on display.

"Is Monday night and is early. It get busy later, no problem."

Ludwig's cheeks had a dent the size of a fifty-pence piece and his Russian/American accent could really do your brain in, especially when he was munching on some of Colombia's finest.

"You wanna do some business now? I got lotsa orders for fags and booze," said Ludwig.

Ludwig represented a couple of very wealthy Russian faces from Pinner – a lot of them like it there because it's near Heathrow Airport. We'd teamed up on a number of business enterprises over the previous 18 months. I only dealt in booze and fags with Ludwig because Russians can get very fucking evil when it comes to anything heavier.

It was usually a straight cash deal. Ludwig would sub me £50,000 and expect that back plus £15,000 profit.

If we were nicked, which was highly unlikely, it was a straight washout – I didn't owe him a penny.

My profits, for sending lorries across the Channel and bringing back around 20,000 cartons of ciggies and 100 crates of spirits plus distribution, came to about £10,000.

Ludwig and his backers made the bigger slice, but then he was gambling their dirty money up front; all I was risking was my liberty.

That brings up the obvious question of, if I'm clearing £10,000 on booze and fags and not taking any big risks, why bother copping 20 big ones to knock someone off? There are a few reasons.

First of all, my fearsome reputation comes from plugging villains, everything else takes second place. The day I stop pulling the trigger my name goes down the swanny along with my earning potential.

Second, there's the thrill of the chase.

I kill for the same reason people who've made tens of millions off drugs continue to risk being banged up by chopping out a few lines of Charlie for their mates. It gets in your blood and then there's no turning back. I'd fucking die of boredom if all I did was organise booze and fags runs every month.

Third, there's a lot more security in pulling the trigger than hauling cancer sticks and giving people liver damage. Every now and again those VAT men at the customs and excise at Dover and Folkestone get a bit twitchy and I have to knock it all on the head for a while.

There's never a bad time for a killing.

I told Ludwig I needed his finance by Thursday night. He gave me the nod and told me to come back to the club when he had the shopping bag ready. It was past 11.30 by then and I reckoned the old lady's cronies would be getting sick of each other by now so I could head home.

I spotted one cracking-looking bird as I left Ludwig's but I had other things on my mind, so I didn't even stop for a chinwag.

As it turned out, I should've stayed because I had to hide in the bedroom while the wife's mates finished a last round of cherry brandies.

I hit the phone to "Disco" Dave Dixon. I don't know why

he's called "Disco", either. Disco Dave's my regular booze and fags manager but he can be a right ducker and diver at times.

He's a reasonable organiser and moves produce on quickly, which is the key to this game. Disco's more than a fence because he goes out and hustles for business. Like ciggies. Like booze. Even burglar alarms.

"Burglar alarms!" I screamed into the phone, laughing. "Didn't you see *Crimewatch* the other night?"

Disco wasn't listening to me. He just carried on the sales patter.

"Straight up," he said. "They're DIY burglar alarm kits anyone can install. Chucked a pony at the driver and he dumped the lot off at my cousin's lock-up."

I didn't have the heart to tell him about *Crimewatch* a second time, so I acted surprised when he told me what I already knew.

"Only problem is they don't have no instructions with them," says Disco, as if it's nothing important.

"So I've heard."

"What?"

"Don't worry about it."

Disco rapped on.

"Got two thousand units. Each one's fifteen quid and up in the shops. Yours for eight."

Disco's problem in life is he can only focus on one subject at a time. I told him not to go into business for himself. It'll end in tears.

"Why don't you give 'em away for a pound each? Then tip off a few local burglars and take a backhander from them?"

Disco Dave stopped and thought about my idea for a moment. He was still scratching his head when I started barking orders about the 20,000 cartons of fags and another 100 crates of spirits plus the cash to pay for them.

After a few more moments he finally got the message.

"What's my role, then?" he asked.

"Organise it. The lot. I got some other business on the go and I haven't got time to knock it all out. I'll give you the cash.

You get the lorry, the drivers, pick up the shipment, bring it back and deliver the lot. It's worth three grand in your pocket."

"You're on," he said.

I knew Disco Dave could handle it because the whole operation virtually ran itself. All it needed was an investment of time and effort.

Disco Dave was perfect: he had a lack of brain and a lot of time. I arranged a meet with him Thursday night with the cash. I wanted the lorry to leave that night so it could be back by the weekend, in time for Monday deliveries.

The house finally cleared of yapping housewives after I'd finished my call to Disco Dave.

"Win a few bob?" I asked the missus.

She frowned.

"No, I didn't," she said.

It was only a few quid but she got well grumpy about it.

"Gambling's going to be the death of us," I laughed.

All she wanted was a kip so I waved goodnight as she stumbled up the stairs.

I needed some peace and quiet to study all my notes on Kenny Marshall.

His daily routine was simple enough but then he went a bit off the rails in the afternoon and totally unpredictable after nightfall. Best option seemed to hit him as he made his rounds in the morning, or near his bird's house or at the drinking den in Eltham in the afternoon.

I started making a new, revised list of the potential hit locations. Next to each place I noted all the possible problems. Then I began eliminating each suggestion.

I had to get him alone and out in the open. That meant knowing the traffic situation and the nearest public transport. It was all on my manor so I knew the traffic situation well enough. I'd even taken careful notes about lights, stop signs, one-ways and schools in the area. (You try mixing it with a lollipop lady. You'll get more aggro than if you got nicked pulling the trigger on your target.)

It had to be a location that ensured quick, easy and dependable movement. I've heard of pros in the past who blew jobs because they didn't do their prep properly, from beginning to end.

I use side streets all the time because I know I can get through quickly. But there are certain things you just cannot cater for. When I knocked off number six in Lambeth a few years back, I dumped the bike I was driving, walked a couple of hundred yards to The Oval tube station and got on the Northern Line to Stockwell.

Only problem was, the train got stuck in a tunnel. It was the middle of summer but I was wearing a heavy sports jacket with a piece tucked in my belt.

So I'm sitting opposite a bunch of Swedish tourists stewing like a warthog holding a just-fired cannon which I need to dispose of – and it's burning my bollocks off. But there's no way I can take off that jacket. I start thinking someone has seen me plugging my target and tailed me to the station before calling the filth. I'm convinced I'm in a Northern Line log jam created just to nick me.

For ten minutes I sat there crunched up and hardly daring to move, sweat raining down in front of my eyes. Everyone in that fucking carriage seemed to be watching me.

I felt like jumping up and spraying the lot of them for being such nosey bastards.

Then the train began moving. Turned out they'd only stopped it because some miserable bastard had jumped in front of the train ahead of us. My point is, that that was an unforeseen problem.

My premier location choice had always been Eltham Green, but I was going off it rapidly. When Marshall went through the area on his rounds the traffic had been heavy which meant I couldn't scarper as fast as was possible. But it remained an outsider.

The mini-cab office on Peckham Rye was a non-starter because the traffic was even worse over there.

Marshall's girlfriend's house had potential but posed some different problems.

She lived on a one-way street which led to a stop-sign, a mini-roundabout and then on to a dual carriageway. Every 50 feet was a fucking fat concrete sleeping PC Plod.

Not only would every car halt at the stop-sign but half of Sydenham's housewives would be delicately mounting the humps at 15 mph. The nearby A2 was also a fucking nightmare for trafffic in the mornings. There were also a lot of kids living around the place. All it needed was one to pop out of nowhere and see something bad for their eyes.

Getting him outside his own house was an easier option, but I don't like violating a man's home. It goes back to what happened with my first missus. That includes the area around his house as well. Hitting a man in his front room or on his front lawn is asking for trouble. Then there was Mrs Curran ...

That left the drinking club underneath the pie and eel shop. Trafffic flow wasn't bad. After dark it was fairly quiet on the streets and the lighting wasn't up to much.

Even better, Twiggy's file said he often left the place after dark and there were lots of dark doorways I could loiter in.

Problem was, I couldn't know for certain when he'd be at the club or when he'd leave. He never seemed to stay for the same amount of time – there was no telling who he might come out with. Hitting someone walking along the street with a mate was not a good idea. A caff, pub or restaurant is a different matter altogether where people shit hot bricks and give 15 different descriptions of you to the cozzers.

One even bigger element knocked the club off my favourite location list. It was owned by Mustafa "Mad Turk" Arrit. Neither him nor his large family of psycho smack dealers would be too happy if someone was gunned down outside the place. Arrit was inside at this particular time but, out of a combination of common sense and respect for the Mad Turk and his family, I crossed that drinking den off my list.

Marshall needed to be out on his own at night. I reckon I can work anywhere at any time but dark is better. Unfortunately, I still didn't know what he got up to at night.

Then I thought about somehow getting him to come to me.

Usually, if you force a target to change his schedule to fit in with you it alerts him to what's up. Not a good move, is it?

Then it dawned on me that his bosses could get him to meet me without ever raising his eyebrows. It would involve other people, which is risky. Particularly when those other people include my old mate Twiggy.

But I'd just thought of a plan.

Of course, I'd only really know if the plan had worked long after the job had been forgotten. That was the key to it. If the job was forgotten I'd done it right. If not, I'd end up in a cold, damp cell with a ruined reputation – or a cold, damp grave.

I knew then that getting Marshall to me was the answer. I didn't know where, but south east London is full of perfect spots. I'd soon find one.

Meanwhile, I'd keep on the lookout for Twiggy while I was busy setting up Marshall for his final flutter.

I arranged a meet with Twiggy on Tuesday to see if his fish would swallow my bait.

Chapter Sixteen

Tuesday almost became a very rare day. Very rare indeed. First thing that morning I debated about whether to change motors so I had an edge over whoever was tailing me. But I already had an edge: I knew they were there. I stuck to the Beemer.

As I walked out of my house I checked out all the cars parked up and down the road to see if that big silver Merc was about. Not a sign.

I stepped out between two parked cars to cross the road, just as a black cab came round the corner moving up the street.

He had his yellow light on, meaning the driver had no passengers. Then I noticed the driver was staring right at me. I stepped back and waited for him to pass.

But the cab drifted over to the side of the road where I was waiting. He was getting closer and closer. His diesel engine was clattering away like a biscuit tin full of spanners.

By now his face was locked on me and he looked totally manic. He couldn't have been more than 70 feet from me, doing at least 50 mph and getting faster and faster.

For a second I was frozen to the spot then my reactions kicked in.

I threw myself on to the bonnet of a parked car behind me, bruising my thigh as I landed. Luckily, the momentum of the leap got me rolling across the bonnet until I dropped off the car on to the pavement on the other side.

I hit the ground with a thump and grabbed the loaded .38 I was carrying.

The cab screeched to a halt, leaving a trail of burning rubber on the street surface. The driver jumped out and ran towards me.

I crouched down behind the car front wing, put my finger on the trigger and aimed.

"You all right, mate?" the driver yelled.

Then he saw the barrel on the bonnet of the car. He stopped dead in his tracks.

"Don't fuckin' move or I'll blow you away," I said, as calmly as I could.

He stuck his hands up in the air, like someone had just rammed a lamp post up his arse.

"Sorry, mate. I just ..."

"Shut the fuck up!" I ordered. "Now lie face down on the motor and stretch your hands above your head."

He did what I told him and then I walked round and checked him for weapons. Nothing. I moved towards his cab, still watching him, and went through the motions of a search. Nothing.

"What the fuck's your game?" I demanded. "You nearly copped it."

He was in his late fifties, I'd guess, clean shaven with a boozer's complexion. Thick coke-bottle glasses with black rims. And a ski-hat.

He began turning round to face me. "I didn't see you ..."

"Don't move a fuckin' inch," I said. "Now talk."

"I'm sorry, mate. I been on all night. I was half asleep. Lucky I didn't kill you," he said.

"You're lucky I didn't kill *you*," I said.

I didn't know whether to believe a fucking word.

"What you doin' out this way?"

"Just dropped a punter in the high street."

"Where?"

"I told you, the high street." He was getting a bit nervy again.

"Where in the fuckin' high street?"

He named a block of flats I knew existed but the fact remained that he'd come too fucking close to knocking me off.

There's this pencil-thin line between paranoia and reality. I was bouncing back and forwards over it like a grasshopper on sulphate. And each time the line became more blurred.

I returned to the cab again, reached in and pulled out the cabbie's licence. The face in the photo was lean, had a beard and a full head of hair. I looked over at him. Then back at the photo. He might have shaved off his beard. It could be him.

Then I reached over and pulled off his woolly ski-hat.

He was as bald as a coot.

I shoved the barrel deep into his left ear. He winced to one side, his head bent over.

"What the fuck is your game?"

"I told you," he said, "I'm sorry I just ..."

I pushed the gun further into his ear drum, twisting it just a touch so the sight cut into his inner lobe.

Then I said quietly, "If you're the cabbie then who the fuck is this?"

I pushed the licence into his face and then held it a couple of inches in front of him.

He was shaking.

"That's my cousin," he pleaded, "this is his cab. I take it out some nights."

"Really?" I said coldly.

"I swear that's the truth ..."

I stood there for a moment, not knowing what to believe.

"If I'd been trying to run you over why did I stop?"

"Maybe you got a shooter?"

"What? I never fired a gun in my life. Don't even own a gun. You can ask my cousin. He'll tell you."

I released my finger from the trigger. There was no way to prove it one way or the other so I decided to pass it off as a dangerous accident. That incident should have been a lesson to me. I was spending so much fucking time thinking about what Marshall was up to and what Twiggy might be doing that I was in danger of losing the plot.

"Get outta here," I said coldly. "If I see you again, you'll get some of this."

I pointed the piece in his direction and held it there for a few more seconds. Then I put it away. The so-called cabbie ran to his vehicle and took off at high speed. I looked both ways before crossing the road to my motor.

I might yet regret our little encounter.

Later that morning I lined up a few punters to take delivery of my booze and fags shipment the following Monday but I couldn't get that cabbie incident out of my mind.

I switched my attention to Marty from the rag trade, whose shop was just off Peckham Rye. Marty owed me two grand for a previous delivery of booze and fags and had been ducking me for weeks.

When I finally got him on the phone he'd promised to pay up by the following Tuesday. Now it was Tuesday and I'd tried to bell him but I was told he was out. He was giving me the runaround again, so I went visiting.

Marty's shop was down an alleyway just near the main market on the High Road. When I walked in he was standing in his showroom, showing some old dear a roll of satin. When he spotted me he looked well pissed off. He excused himself from the old dear and beckoned me into his office.

Marty was about five foot five, straggly thin and had a silver Kevin-Keegan-at-FC-Hamburg bouffant job tied back in a rat's tail. He was probably in his mid-fifties, but he could easily have been older than Peter Stringfellow.

"Well, Marty," I said. "Hope you've got what I'm after ..."

He interrupted me.

"It's fine, my friend. But listen, I have a problem. I can't help you today ..." He seemed more concerned with not losing his customer waiting patiently outside. "One of my lorries was nicked last week and people just aren't paying their bills on time."

"Fuck them," I said.

Then I took a deep, long, noisy irritated breath.

"Don't fuck me about any more, Marty."

I was starting to lose it.

He shrugged his bony shoulders. "I'm sorry, my friend, but that's the score."

"I ain't your friend," I replied, "and you're the one who's gonna be sorry. D'you understand?"

"Just one more week, please?"

I didn't want to hear this. The strain of what had happened outside my house with that cabbie had put my head on a knife edge. I really hate myself when I get like this.

"Time's up. I want the money. Now."

"I told you, I don't have it …"

Marty was sounding irritated with me and that was making my headache even worse.

And then he started on like the pratt he is.

"What you going to do? Kill me for a couple of grand?"

He had a point. It was well below the going rate.

And by saying the magic word "kill" Marty seemed to slow down my runaway train of fury. I took another deep breath. Now wasn't the time for this sort of aggro.

"You're right, Marty," I said. "I'm not goin' to do you …" I paused and looked straight at him. "But I'll be back Thursday afternoon when we'll go and visit a friend who'll sub you the money. And then …"

Then Marty went and fucking interrupted me again.

"I'm not dealin' with shylocks."

"Stop fuckin' interrupting me," I said. "I'm tellin' you. Not askin'. Tellin'. You're going to get on with this geezer and then you're going to settle up and we'll never do business again."

I began to turn towards the door. His prized customer had long gone and he looked like he was heading to the lavatory for a very painless crap.

"Don't stain the fuckin' pan," I muttered.

Marty stood there like the bone-shaking pussycat he was. I just hoped he now realised I was being deadly serious.

Next I went straight over to Twiggy's used car emporium but he wasn't there. I left word with one of his valets that a friend of Careful Craig's had been in to see him. I said it was about a certain business arrangement and I would meet him at the Barley Mow at 10.30pm.

Then I drove off towards Marshall's place to see if he'd got home safely. I continually checked my rearview and there didn't seem to be anyone on my tail. But then again, I couldn't be certain. One old black Saab stayed close for quite a while and then disappeared. It didn't seem to be on the case. But I couldn't be sure, could I?

At Marshall's place I parked under a big oak tree in the hope its shadow would stop Mrs Curran from seeing me.

And I sat and watched.

After about five minutes the front door opened and someone walked out. With the sun directly in my eyes it was difficult to see who it was, but the style of walk looked familiar.

I watched as the figure got closer, feeling safe because my car was well hidden. He got closer and closer but didn't once look in my direction. He didn't have to.

He was about 30 yards away when I knew for certain.

Twiggy had just walked out of Kenny Marshall's front door!

Chapter Seventeen

Now you'd think Twiggy would suspect I'd spot him leaving Marshall's house but everything's got to be right in your face with Twiggy. Remember, he didn't even see that train coming when it chopped his arms off, so he might not have given much thought to my research work.

So why was Twiggy round at my target's house? It implied he was in league with Marshall which spelt curtains for me. I had to find out what was really going on.

If Twiggy was planning to have me taken out, I didn't want him to get wind of me knowing. My only advantage was that I knew what he was up to – and that he'd tie it in to the Marshall job. That left me still in control.

If Twiggy thought I knew he'd have me done in asap.

All this tension was getting to me so I decided to burn off some stress by trying out my weapons in the process. There is a well-known basement in Erith which belongs to a Spanish lady called Polita who's not in bad nick considering she's about the same age as Barbara Windsor.

Her old man was a familiar face called Tony who padded up the basement walls with soundproofing material from a recording studio in Maidstone which was knocked down to make way for a supermarket.

Unfortunately, Tony died a couple of years back but his missus kept the business going. Polita lets people use her basement for a small remuneration. For a few bob more she'll lay on grub and booze and she's got a mate called Denise who has a few friends who'll also pop round for a fee.

Also, people who've run into a spot of bother with other people have been taken down to Tony's basement for a chat. Personally, I only ever use the place to try out my latest tool. I needed to test out the .38 I'd got from Old Bill Wink to make sure it was up to scratch.

I go to Tony's basement four or five times a year, even when I don't have a specific job, to fire off a few rounds from my collection to keep them all in working order.

That day I stopped back at my place to pick up the new shooter and three different types of ammo. It was getting more and more difficult to get a solid supplier in south east London. Many guns were nicked without any ammo in them. I used to go way out near Brands Hatch to a little ammo man who worked out of a barn on his farm.

This same fellow also made up the special cartridges for my little gem of a hand shotgun. Since I'd hardly used any ammo over the previous few months I had plenty knocking around the house.

Whenever I carry a piece around I have this habit of putting it in a plastic bag and dropping the bullets in a jacket pocket. It's a sort of good luck thing with me. It also covers me with the filth because a loaded gun can mean three years longer than if it's empty. I know the law and I try to tread the line.

But the Marshall job had proved such a headache I loaded up the new gun as well as the one I always had with me when on duty.

At home I always kept the loaded piece in my wardrobe and another hidden by the front door at all times, despite what my missus thinks.

On the way to Tony's basement I stopped at a builders' yard and picked up four pieces of wood: one 2'×4', one 3'×6', one 1' board and a solid piece of ply. These would serve as my lab equipment.

Polita and I had a brief natter before I went downstairs and I promised to stop by for a proper chat on my way out. Then I got down to work.

First, I did what's known as a dry firing run – without ammo – to make sure the trigger mechanism was fully operational. This involves aiming the shooter and clicking away with the trigger a few times at one of Polita's paper targets up on the wall. It feels the same way whether you've got bullets in or not.

It helps give me a proper feel of the weapon. I stand there with my feet pointing forward about a shoulder distance apart. Arms extended but not locked.

I grip the shooter with my right hand primarily and use the grooves of my right hand for my left hand to grip. Always remember the left hand has more to do with the grip than the right hand.

Then I line the sights up. There are two on most handguns; the rear sight used to line up the white strip on the front sight. You need that white strip to go straight across the top of your target.

I always use the right eye. It's definitely better than my left. Just shut each of your eyes for a couple of seconds one day and you'll soon work it out.

Once I've got the target perfectly lined up, I flick off the safety and squeeze slowly.

That way you never know exactly when the gun will go off which means your body doesn't tense up in expectation. When that flame jumps out of the barrel and a snort of cordite hits the air you know you're in business. But, of course, all that comes later when I'm using actual bullets.

Next, I set up each of the boards against a cement wall and stepped back about eight feet. Eight feet was the furthest I could be from Marshall when I plugged him.

I usually like to be more up close and personal, then there's no chance of me fucking up and missing. You've got to be near enough to guarantee the job gets done.

In Northern Ireland the Provos call it giving someone an O.B.E. – One Behind the Ear.

Chilling fucking phrase, ain't it?

I had to test all three different makes of ammo I had with me.

The first was a hollow-point bullet which slashes around like a razor blade once it enters the body.

The second type was the flat-nosed bullet.

The third was a bog standard ball bullet.

I began by emptying out the shells I had put in the new .38 and replacing them with four hollow-points.

Then I fired one bullet into each board.

I repeated this with the two other types of ammo.

Twelve bullets later the smell of cordite was wafting through the basement and I felt a definite high. My hands were slightly trembling. I felt sharp and alert – almost like I'd snorted a line of Charlie.

Then I moved about three feet from the target and did the same thing all over again.

Now I had to calculate what it all meant.

I knew the piece was excellent the moment the first shot was fired but once I'd dug the remains of the bullets out of the wood I could work out the damage they'd inflict on Kenny Marshall.

Bog standard ball ammo comes out whole. Flat ammo comes out flat and wide, like a squashed bread roll. The hollow-point ammo will splatter because it spreads as it pierces the wood.

The big test comes with the ply because that's tougher and most resembles a human head.

The ply had been smashed to pieces.

I now knew the piece was superb and my natural choice of ammo had to be the hollow-point.

I went upstairs for a bevy with Polita and cleaned up my piece while we chatted. Weapons were her and her husband's hobby, so we talked guns and the wild men still using them on blaggings and whatever.

Polita told me the old south east London firms were fingering a lot of the younger cowboys holding up building societies and stuff like that because they were giving the old pros a bad name!

Apparently these young wallies often used pieces like the Glock 9mm semi-automatics. They spit out bullet casings which, as I've already mentioned, provide Old Bill with useful evidence. And the cozzers use the exact same weapon so they know them inside out.

Like I said before, it's the Wild West out there. The cozzers know it and the villains know it and there's no way it'll ever change.

The fee for the use of Tony's basement was £50. The latest word on the streets came free. Both were worth every penny.

As I headed over to the Barley Mow for my meet with Twiggy, a serious plan began taking shape in my mind. Letting Twiggy in on the details of the actual hit would give me more control.

If he thought I was in one location I could be somewhere else, nearby, keeping an eye on him.

That way I could still do away with Marshall, but if Twiggy made a move, I'd plug him as well. Maybe this contract wasn't so bad after all.

On the way to the boozer I backtracked a few streets a couple of times, just to be sure no one was on my tail.

I still got there by 10.15pm. Twiggy showed at 10.45 when I was deep into a plate of cheese and biscuits. We sat and talked rubbish while I finished my food. Then we left the boozer for a discreet chat.

As he got in my motor he really niggled me by slamming the door so hard it nearly came off its hinges. But I didn't say anything.

We drove up towards Kennington. It's nice and quiet in a motor and if you drive within the law, not many people spot you.

"So what's up?" he asked after we settled in for the drive. His tongue stayed in his mouth and I didn't hear one HISSS! from his pneumatic arms.

I hesitated because I didn't want him to suss anything.

"Nothin's up," I said carefully. "Just a few details need ironing out."

"Like what?" he snapped back, staring straight ahead.

"So far Marshall's routine has gone right off the map. There's half a dozen reasonable locations where I can take him out, but none of them are perfect. And he hardly ever seems to go out at night ..."

"What's that gotta do with me?" interrupted Twiggy.

"Give us a fuckin' chance," I told him, "I'm just gettin' to that."

He turned towards me.

"Well, I haven't got all bloody night."

I backed off a bit, something I don't usually do, because I didn't want a barney in the front seat of my motor. But his attitude was pissing me off bigtime.

Fuck it, I thought, I'll go straight for the jugular.

"Does Marshall know anything about all this?"

"What d'you mean?" He squinted at me as he spoke.

"Does Marshall know he's in the frame. Yes or no?"

"No fuckin' way."

"What about those two cowboys working for him? Would they 'ave tipped him off?"

Twiggy chuckled at that last remark.

"They haven't got the bottle."

"How can you be so sure?"

"'Cause they told us they met with Marshall yesterday to talk about the next blag."

Ding. Ding. Ding.

A bell was ringing loudly in my head. My built-in alarm system had just gone off.

So I asked Twiggy, "Where did they have this meet?"

"Marshall's got a few bob invested in some tanning salon over in Victoria."

"Well, well, well," I said to myself, as much as to Twiggy. "I saw a couple of likely lads walk in there a few minutes after him."

"Now you know."

"Now I know," I agreed.

He sighed and for the first time in that entire meet I heard his plastic arms hiss. Then he started speaking.

"There has been some other aggro, though. I was goin' to bell you about it."

"What?"

He paused for what seemed like an eternity, so when he spoke it sounded pretty fucking dramatic.

"Marshall's planning to do a runner."

"What kind of runner?"

"We're not sure. But he's told his boys this is going to be the last blag …"

"Maybe he's just closin' down the operation?" I interrupted.

He glared at me.

"Let me finish, please."

I let him carry on but no way was I going to say sorry. Twiggy shook his head with irritation. If he was having me on, he was going over the top.

But if this was legit then he was more of a fucking tosser than I thought.

"Marshall's cleaned out all his bank accounts and leant on his private punters to pay up on Friday."

"I was with him Friday," I said. "Didn't see him pick up any cash."

Twiggy snapped back double quick. "His missus did it. She's got more than £50,000 in her handbag …" Just then Twiggy's horrible sandpaper tongue came shooting out of his mouth. "He's about to do a Lord Lucan."

"When?"

"He told his toyboys the last blag's to be next Monday. It's gotta be just after that."

"But why's he taken all the cash out so early?" I was struggling to get my head round this one.

Twiggy shook his head from side to side and ignored my point.

"The MD wants to know how you're goin' to handle this."

I noted that he said the MD wanted to know, not Twiggy.

"I'll have to bring it forward, then."

They were putting me in a time box.

"When?"

I'd already decided deliberately to let them know everything so I wasn't too bothered. They could line Marshall up for me. That way if they made a move, I'd know when it was going to happen. And they'd be sure of getting me into an isolated spot on my own.

"Gotta be this weekend."

I paused and glanced at Twiggy's face. Not a flicker of emotion. I continued. "Will Marshall take orders?"

Twiggy nodded. "Of course he will. If we tell him to get on all fours and bark like a fuckin' dog, the only question he'd ask is 'how loud'."

I checked the rear-view as we moved towards London Bridge, but there was no one around.

"Good," I said. "Now if I tell you that, on Saturday night for argument's sake, I want him to meet someone somewhere, can you deliver him there?"

Twiggy answered very slowly and deliberately. "Woof. Woof," he said.

"You sure?"

He nodded and that tongue came shooting out yet again.

"I'll be in touch once it's firmed up."

I then swung the motor around and headed back south towards my favourite suburbs. I was thinking through the plan.

"All right," I finally said. "I want you to tell Marshall a big job's come up and he's the man for it. Tell him it's nothin' too heavy, but he's gotta identify someone."

I told Twiggy that Marshall was to meet a bloke at a specific location, and then they'd go to another location where he was to finger somebody for his new friend.

Twiggy suggested offering Marshall two grand for the job, to make sure Marshall wouldn't turn it down. No doubt he'd be suspicious, but he'd have no choice in the matter, unless he wanted a long heart-to-heart with the MD.

After outlining the plan, I wanted to ask Twiggy about my tail and his visit to Marshall's house. But he didn't give me any real excuse to turn the conversation round in that direction. Then I had a try.

"What's he been like in the office?"

"What, Marshall?" Twiggy took a few moments to think out the rest of his reply. "He's been a bit quieter than usual."

"And outside the office?"

He looked right at me. His tongue came shooting out of his mouth.

"How the fuck should I know?"

I shrugged my shoulders.

"Just thought you might have heard somethin'."

I was concerned he hadn't put me in the picture about his little visit to Kenny Marshall's house. He also hadn't mentioned why his two white rasta mates were tailing me.

Those alarm bells were still ringing.

If Twiggy was backing this caper those two muppets would know I'd picked up on them. But he didn't breathe a word about it. As he got out of the motor in the car park of the Barley Mow, Twiggy said he'd have to get the final thumbs up from the MD about my plan. But he didn't expect any problems. I thanked him, for what I'm not quite sure.

Then he slammed my car door again and I wished I'd had a go at him earlier. Clumsy bastard.

Tuesday had been a long day and thrown up more questions than answers. I had to move quickly on Marshall in case he did a runner. But had Twiggy just fed me the info to set me up?

Whatever the truth, all I had to do now was decide on the right location, which would take up the following day, Wednesday.

I took a small detour via Marshall's house that evening just to make sure he was tucked up in bed for the night. As I sailed past his place the lights were on in the front room and his motor was parked up for the night. Feeling reasonably content, I headed home myself.

I spent much of Tuesday night lying awake trying to work out where to get Marshall to meet me. Every time I thought I had the right place somewhere else popped into my head and the whole process started over again. I was looking for problems that often didn't even exist.

The location had to be isolated. Why do a man on a busy street when you can hit him on a piece of wasteground or under a bridge, in a cemetery or even a scrap yard?

But that spot had to be feasible. If Twiggy told Marshall to go to a meet on a rubbish tip, Marshall's nostrils would've

153

flared up more than Kenneth Williams' in *Carry On Camping*.

So what I'm after is the not-so-perfect perfect spot.

This kept me tossing and turning in bed for a few hours. Every time I closed my eyes I'd think of another location and start running through its potential. I managed more work just lying there than I had in my motor. But all this movement disturbed the missus.

"Whatever's on your mind," she whispered from the other side of the bed, "let it wait 'til tomorrow."

Then she went out like a light. She's got this way of throwing out the one-liners and then conking out pronto. I reckon it's because she's not really bothered by any of the more intense things in life.

Lucky her.

Pity I'm not the same.

Wednesday should have been a nice, lazy day. First thing I called my bookie and found out how my fillies were lining up. I had a few bob on me so there was no reason not to lay a few certs. Before I left the house that morning, I asked the missus about Sunday.

"Marshall's still comin' for lunch?"

"Haven't spoken to Brenda since I told you," she said, "but she sounded pretty definite about it."

Then I chipped in.

"Do us a favour? Call her today and let me know what the score is."

Naturally, she wanted to know why.

"Because …" I said to her. "Just give her a call, all right."

"What sort of answer is that?" she said.

That's when I stupidly lost it.

"Just call her up and find out, please."

She agreed but she wasn't happy. The not-having-kids issue was eating away at her again.

I don't blame her in a way. She needed something else to

think about besides her next shopping trip to Harrods but I'd laid my cards on the table right from the start. While we were courting she'd mentioned she had an ovary problem and couldn't get pregnant.

That helped me decide she was the girl for me. It might sound callous but after what happened to my first missus I felt I had a right to choose.

I didn't even think about adoption. It wasn't an issue.

When I get chippy with the old lady she either walks away from me or hits the fucking roof. It's always one extreme or the other with her. I never wanted a doormat who did what she was told without question, but on the other hand there were times when I could do without the grief. Suppose I want the best of both worlds. But don't we all?

This old debt collector I used to know told me once there were two basic types of wives.

"They either leave the handbrake on or they don't," he said.

I didn't know what the hell he was on about at first. But then he explained:

"The wife who leaves the handbrake on when she drives is the type who's well turned out and would never cause you any aggro.

"But she can't have much goin' on up top 'cos she can't even remember to release the fuckin' handbrake. Think about it.

"The ones who never leave it on are always in charge. They don't miss a trick which means they're on your back day and night. But they're much more of a challenge."

Which left my missus sitting right in the middle, I reckon.

I don't know what I really expected to find out by getting the old lady to call up Brenda Marshall. Suppose I thought it might help skim a bit of background info on my target's movements.

If Marshall's old lady blew out the invite that meant Twiggy probably wasn't telling porkies and Marshall really was about to do a runner.

On the other hand, if she said they were coming, that would tell me precisely fuck all.

Of course, it was possible they weren't planning a runner until later in the week. Then again, Marshall's missus might not even know her old man was about to get on his toes.

That morning I picked up on Marshall just as he was walking out of the caff as usual. I'd been with him about half an hour when I checked my rear-view. That fucking silver Merc was back again.

I immediately pulled away from Marshall. The Merc did not follow which was even more bloody confusing.

I pulled up for a breather and tried to work out what the fuck was going on.

The Merc had picked me up twice, both times when I was tailing Marshall. That connected the Merc with Marshall. They were either keeping an eye on him ... or me. I wished I knew which.

If the geezers in that motor were on his side, my cover was truly blown. But then why hadn't he done a runner yet? If they reported back to him that he was being tailed by me, he'd have been off like a shot.

That meant they must have been shadowing Marshall – and Twiggy must have put them up to it. But why? Again, were they after him or me?

I thought about whether I'd ever done anything to get in the MD's bad books.

Two specific incidents troubled me. I'd done a freelance puff run to Marbella for the MD's firm a few years back and pocketed a bit of his prized Moroccan Black on the sly. Maybe he got wind of it.

The other time was when I got pulled by the law about another contract killing. The filth turned the thumb screws on me and threw the MD's name into the ring. Naturally, I denied all knowledge of him or his firm.

But another shootist was collared after me and he put half a finger on the MD, who then got dragged in and nearly nicked.

A lot of people tried to make out I'd done the singing, which was bollocks. I thought I'd cleared the air with the MD a few months later.

But maybe he hadn't believed me, after all.

Twiggy had a reason to have me taken out at the same time as Marshall. Maybe the MD had sanctioned the double hit.

Call me an old worrier, but now I was sure I had good reason to be on edge.

Chapter Eighteen

This job was getting very time consuming and complicated. I was in real danger of letting my other businesses suffer so I called Disco Dave for an update on how my fags and booze customers were doing.

"It's comin' together fine," he told me.

"Remember to save a couple of dozen cartons for my missus and her mates," I reminded him.

"How many exactly? I'll make sure I keep them aside."

I thought for a minute. "Make it thirty cartons."

"Thirty?" said Disco. "You tryin' to give 'em all cancer?"

First Twiggy now Disco: why was half the fucking world trying to crack jokes all of a sudden? Me and Disco agreed to meet at the usual lock-up Thursday night so I could give him the cash and send our lorry crew on their merry way.

By now you'll have realised that I'm what you'd call a lone ranger in many ways. But there are times when I need to bounce all this shit off someone. Closest I ever came to talking openly about *everything* was with Cat. But that's only 'cause she's a good listener. She can't give me the right answers because killing is nothing more than a wanking fantasy to her but that day I felt a definite need to see her. So I gambled that she might be doing a spot of housework and gave her a call on the mobile.

"I'm only just getting out of bed," she said drowsily. Sounded like she'd been puffing on some wackybacky. I could smell it down the phone.

"Don't bother," I said.

By the time I got to Notting Hill she'd put on a pair of chunky, black strappy platforms.

"Too much sleep's bad for you," I told Cat as she swung the front door open from behind it so no one could see her starkers from the street.

I know it sounds fucking predictable, but Cat purrs away when she's on heat. I'll swear I heard it rising out of her throat as she stood there in her platforms. She didn't say a word but turned on one of her most evil smiles, cupped my balls in her hands and squeezed them just hard enough.

"You smell hot," she said.

Cat had this thing about smell, so do I. She even reckoned she could whiff when a bloke had just had a wank.

"It's a sweet, dank smell, Malcolm. And it's so horny," Cat told me during one bunk-up.

Back in her marbelled hallway that afternoon she informed me, "I know what you've been up to."

I enjoyed her little games.

"And what's that, then?" I asked.

She tightened her grip on my balls.

"You've been firing a gun," she said.

I tried not to hesitate and immediately came back with a chuckle and a response.

"Bang. Bang."

Cat had obviously got a sniff of cordite after my test run down at Polita's the previous day. I don't reckon she'd have smelt a thing if I'd just completed a contract but down in that pokey basement all the cordite seeped into your clothes and hair because there was no proper ventilation.

I looked into Cat's eyes. They were swimming in black treacle as usual. It made her seem more dangerous than she really was.

I like them a bit fucked-up just so long as they're not more fucked-up than me. Over the years I've worked out that the so-called normal people out there in the so-called normal world just don't gel with the likes of me. They want everything to work smoothly and safely for them and they're happy with their two-point-four kids and their nine-to-five jobs.

My manor's full of them.

After all, we're talking classic surburbia, ain't we? Makes me feel like a fucking alien from another planet. On the other hand, life must be so fucking simple compared with what I get up to. Truth is, you can't pin people like me down and we'd never be accepted back in civvie street, so we may as well cause some havoc.

And, there are a few hidden benefits to being a bit of a fuck-up. You cut through all life's crap and, if you don't go too far over the top, you're not a liability to others. Although some people might disagree.

So while Cat tightened her lock on my balls, she slipped her other arm under my jacket and pressed her fingers on my backbone. She ran her hand down the inside of the back of my trousers and at the same time pushed her passion fruit soft tongue in my mouth.

Then Cat gave my balls a rougher tug. I winced.

She led me like a weak little lamb towards her kids' playroom for a few hours of escape from the real world. I wouldn't dream of revealing all the tasty details of what happened between Cat and me that afternoon. But I will concede that her creativity knew no bounds.

One of her favourites was dressing me up in her panty hose. I didn't mind because it was a right laugh and a definite turn-on. She also liked me squeezing into her size 7 stilettos. Then she'd use the spikey heel to pleasure herself. That afternoon she put on her sternest black leather, calf-length riding boots and got me to lick the mud and dirt off them. Cheeky bird even pretended she'd stepped in a pile of dogshit that afternoon. But I didn't care.

We doubled our pleasure when she produced some stainless steel loveballs from her panty drawer. She proudly informed me they'd been left behind by that black girl she said she'd pulled the other day.

Cat could have been having me on but, knowing her, it was most likely true.

After a few hours of playing games, we lay back on the floor of her kids' playroom and Cat began telling me one of her saucy stories.

"Did I ever tell you about one of my most famous conquests," she asked, knowing full well she hadn't.

"Male or female?"

She laughed.

"*He* was captain of the England rugby team. God, he was a bore."

"So why d'you do him?"

"I liked his girlfriend."

"Naturally."

I paused and stared right into those two seas of black treacle.

"Bet you had him licking your toilet bowl."

"Much better than that ..." Cat was proud of what was coming next. "I made him jerk himself off while he drove his Aston Martin through Epping Forest ..."

"Sounds like a right wanker."

She ignored my not so subtle joke.

"It was hilarious. He wanted to stop the car and screw me but I wouldn't let him. We nearly hit about twenty other cars."

God, I fucking loved that posh voice of hers.

"Bet you stopped and gave him one in the end?" I asked, trying to sound like I didn't really care, although she could see my hard-on revving up.

"Of course I didn't ..." She sounded indignant again. "Stupid bastard lost control of the car, mounted a pavement and ended up knocking down a gate."

"Oh, dear."

But she wasn't finished yet.

"Then I made him lick his sticky mess off the steering wheel."

"Sounds a bit predictable," I said, just to wind her up.

"Bet you don't know what happened next?" she purred, rising to the bait.

"Bet I do." I paused.

"Go on, then, *Mister Master Criminal*. You tell me," she ordered before taking one long mouthful of air.

Naturally, I took up the challenge.

"You made him get out of the motor and left him standing there like a tosser."

For a moment she looked furious. Then a smile came across her face and she licked her top lip with the tip of her tongue.

"You're the most evil *shit* I've ever met," she whispered into my ear. A tiny globule of spit landed on my lobe as she said the word "shit".

"Takes one to know one," I said.

Just then I caught Cat looking at me in a really intense way. Her head was slightly tilted and those eyes were drilling holes into my brain.

"So who're you knocking off this week?" she said very casually.

That's when I broke my golden rule.

"Just some fuckin' toerag I went to school with."

"Sounds a bit close to home."

She had a point but my prick was stirring again so I kept playing.

"He deserves it."

"Don't they all," came the plummy response.

She was spot on, of course, so I leaned across and kissed her full on the mouth. It was more homy than all the sick and twisted stunts we'd been performing all afternoon.

And it stopped me telling her any more about job number 13.

On the way home from Cat's place I flobbed into my handkerchief and used it to give my face and neck a good scrub down. Then I threw the hanky away. Costs me £3 a time, but it's well worth it in the long run. Avoids all aggro from her indoors.

I had a busy night's work ahead of me, so I could only stop home for a short time that evening. The old lady had only just walked in a few minutes before me. She'd been over at her brother's house all afternoon.

My nephew, it turned out, was hooked on smack and they

were trying to decide how to deal with it. I advised the missus to keep out of it but that went down about as well as a crocodile in a knocking shop.

She started mouthing off at me.

"If you had a brother and he asked you to help, what would you tell him?"

Her lips snarled at me as she emphasised the "you".

"I'd get him locked up," I yelled back, "and then I'd knock some fuckin' sense into him. That's what I'd do."

I emphasised the "I".

She didn't like that one bit.

You see, the old lady was (and still is) definitely what I'd call a true civilian. She sees everything in black and white terms. Good and bad – there's no halfway house.

I suppose that's how she gets through life with a cunt like me. If she started thinking too much about the grey areas in between we'd soon be heading for splitsville. You might well be wondering why I married her if she wasn't one of those fucked-up type of birds I mentioned earlier. Well, the Cats of this world may be good when I'm in escape mode but they can't provide the long-term stability that stops me from going completely over the top.

I'd be nothing without the missus and I don't deserve her. That night she should have given me a good slapping and sent me packing after the way I'd spoken to her.

Instead I barked at her, "Did you speak to Brenda Marshall?"

She nodded. "They're definitely coming. I told them to get here about half twelve."

Then she added with a hint of sarcasm, "That all right with you?"

It was all right with me, I told her. And then I left. The old lady didn't even give me any grief for walking straight out of the front door. Maybe she was past caring. I wondered if perhaps I'd turned the woman I married into one of those divvy birds who's always leaving the handbrake on.

Hopefully not.

My mission for that evening was to find *the* perfect location for the big day. I waited until dark because I wanted the job to happen at night. Places that look fine in the daylight have a way of becoming useless in the dark.

There could be a streetlight reflecting right over the chosen spot. Or traffic might be re-routed down the road because of roadworks. Or the place might be swamped with dog owners walking their pets.

The bottom line is you have to recce the spot at night.

The first of my two favourite locations was in Eltham Green, right next to a sprawling estate of rundown 60s and 70s houses.

I drove there, parked across the street from the dog shit-infested green and sat and waited. It didn't take long to spot the dog owners patrolling the area. The late-night corner shop nearby catered to a steady stream of boy racers in knackered-looking Escorts and Fiestas.

And Eltham Green had obviously been rated as a "high crime area" by the local plod because pandas were sliding by about every 15 minutes.

On the positive side, there were some good places, like a bus shelter, to duck out of sight when my man appeared on the scene and, most importantly, Marshall wouldn't suspect anything when he was told to meet someone there. It was that *kind* of place.

Next I moved to my alternative choice at the far end of Bexley Village. This is a much quieter area with narrower roads that twist and turn through the village centre. People in the suburbs call it the countryside but there's not a lot of green around it.

Bexley Village is badly lit at night and contains a boozer that's been popular with some of the biggest names in south east London and Kent over the years.

Many of those bigtime names lived in gated mansions dotted around the place.

I knew the manor well from back in the days when I was a young runner for an old-timer called Jack Venables. Bexley

Village also happened to be pretty fucking dead at night which meant the filth didn't bother with panda patrols. I knew all the side streets and all the entrances to the nearby A2, M2 and M20.

Marshall wouldn't suspect a thing when he was told to meet someone in Bexley Village.

I soon found a specific street that was so poorly lit no one would spot anything, even though there was a block of flats right opposite.

I parked up nearby and began walking the area.

It was only about nine, but it was so quiet you could hear the hum of traffic on the A2 more than a mile away. I walked into the block of flats and up to the roof. It was empty and dirty. I looked over the side and homed in on my intended spot. It seemed perfect.

The shadow of the building almost completely blacked out the area below and there wasn't a streetlight within 100 feet.

I went back down, got in my motor and waited.

I waited for people walking their dogs.

I waited for other vehicles to pass by and light the area up with their headlights.

I waited for a panda car.

I waited for any kids larking around.

Two cars cruised by. Not one panda showed up. No dogs. No kids.

That's when I made my decision.

This is the spot where Kenny Marshall dies.

The only decision left was when? It had to be before Monday night and Twiggy would need a couple of days to arrange the meet. I also had to get hold of a decent motor.

Thursday night was definitely out because there was too much to organise.

Friday night was when I'd nick a motor.

That got me to Saturday, with Sunday to fall back on in case it all went belly up. Saturday night would be perfect. It was all coming together nicely.

On Saturday night I'd blow Kenny Marshall away with a .38, using hollow-point bullets, just past the A2 turn-off on the south-east end of Bexley Village.

As I slowly drove home I went over the plan in my mind. Twice. Three times. It seemed perfect. Marshall would be ordered to turn up for a meet at that spot on Saturday night at 10pm.

He'd be told he was meeting a familiar face who'd take him somewhere to identify another individual. That familiar face would be me. I'd tell Twiggy I was going to wait in my motor for Marshall.

Actually, I'd get there early and hang back in that block of flats. That way I could see everything happening in front of me. After Marshall turned up I'd let him sit and stew for a bit, then I'd just walk up to his motor and blow his brains out.

Then I'd get the fuck out of there as quickly as possible.

The missus didn't even mention my smackhead nephew when I got home late that night. We talked about a few other things, though.

"You gonna do the Sunday lunch, then?" she asked.

"What?" I said. In my mind, Marshall was already dead. Worrying about what food to give him for a lunch that he wouldn't attend just didn't matter.

"Shoulder of lamb," I told her in a flat tone of voice. "I'll do it Moroccan style with the tandoori paste marinade."

Just saying it made me feel hungry. If everything went according to plan we'd end up having the whole shoulder to ourselves.

"Brenda told me two of the kids are vegetarians," said the missus.

"What?" I'd already switched off the subject since it wasn't going to happen anyway.

"They don't eat meat ..." she said slowly in a slightly

impatient voice. "That's what happens when you send your kids to some nobby boarding school ..."

I looked at her blankly.

"They'll just have to eat a lot of fuckin' cous-cous," I said, not giving a toss.

"But you gotta give them some sort of alternative," said the old lady.

I let out a big sigh and took a long suck through my teeth.

"Tell you what," I said, "why don't you pop down to Iceland and get them some tofu fuckin' rissoles, all right?"

No wonder Marshall had a gambling problem. Boarding school must have been costing him a fortune. A lot of villains these days send their kids to these upmarket schools. I reckon most of them really wish they lived in the normal world so they're doing the next best thing by producing kids that might grow up to have normal lives, or so they think.

Anyway, it was time to stop talking about the menu for a Sunday lunch that was never going to happen.

"Do whatever you think, my darlin'."

I caught the missus looking at me a bit strangely then because usually I'm a right fussy git about food when we've got guests. But she didn't follow through on it, thank God.

Once she'd gone to bed I took out my notes and checked them over carefully one last time. Then I got a match and burned them to a cinder in the fireplace. I never like to leave any written evidence around the place. Then, as I looked into the flames, something a bit weird happened.

My eyes went blurry and I thought I saw Marshall's wife and kids' faces in the flames. I shut my eyes tight and shook my head. They'd gone when I opened them up again.

That's it. That's all that happened.

I didn't start worrying about what it all meant, but I did block it out of my mind at that moment. I'm not even sure why I've mentioned it here. It was probably brought on by a dose of the kind of guilt my old mum suffered from.

I don't want to go down that road again.

The burning of those notes marked the end of the planning stage of my job. Up until that point you never think of the end result. It's more like a game than murder. Usually, you never really consider that the man you watch, the man you tail, is going to cease to exist at a time and place you have chosen for his execution. On every hit, up until this point, there had always been something a bit vague about it all.

But now the real action phase would begin.

It's like a big jigsaw puzzle, really. You're trying so hard to finish off one small section you never get round to working out what the complete picture should be. The only way is to work one section, then another, and another, until the whole thing comes together.

Once the planning's over the so-called deadly business can begin. It's a bit of a reality check. Suddenly you've got all this fucking power. You're about to become the most important person in your target's life, although he'll have less than a second to realise it.

You're going to be the last thing he sees before the curtains drop.

It's a hell of a buzz. Good and bad vibes firing off in all directions. More of a high than any drugs I've ever come across.

I wondered if Marshall would even have time to consider the fates that brought us together.

Two lads grow up in the same neighbourhood, follow similar paths, know a lot of the same faces. I'd probably be the last person he'd guess would be there at the end. Fascinating to see how he'd react when he saw me, if he had time to recognise me, of course.

Then I remembered that slimy look he gave my missus when we said our goodbyes at Harrods, and I wanted him to know it was me before he died.

Chapter Nineteen

So, the scene was set. All I had to do now was put the whole thing in motion. I did this by driving over to see Twiggy on Thursday morning, at about 11am. It was the earliest I could get my head properly round the whole operation.

We walked up Sultan Avenue together, and then round the corner. It was all a precaution in case anyone was earwigging our little chat.

Only problem was that Twiggy has this annoying habit of bumping into you while you're walking along. The pavement just wasn't big enough for the two of us. Must be something to do with his balance on account of those plastic limbs.

"The MD says it's on," he told me, as his left claw clattered into my elbow. "He left it down to me to get Marshall there."

"Reckon you can?"

"You tell me where and he'll turn up. Simple as that."

"It ain't goin' to be that fuckin' easy," I said. "If I was him, I'd be watchin' my back."

At that precise moment Twiggy crashed into me again, even though the pavement was wide enough for at least five people.

"Gimma a bit of space, Twigs," I said. "For Christ's sake."

"What?" He stopped right up against me. Three inches from my face. Dog's breath everywhere, as usual.

"You ever been mugged, Twigs?"

"What the fuck're you on about?"

"You spend your time bumping into people. Must be somethin' to do with *those* things?" I said, looking at his pink plastic limbs. "They throw you off balance or what?"

His blank expression told me he still didn't have a clue what I was on about.

Instead, Twiggy pushed his face even closer to mine and spewed mutt's breath right up my nostrils.

"You've always got some fuckin' problem, ain't you? You

171

told me to get Marshall and he'll be there, all right? Bloke's got no fuckin' choice. I tell him the MD wants him to do somethin', he just does it. You worry about your own end and leave me to do the important stuff, all right?"

"All right," I answered, choosing to ignore the fact he was an ignorant cunt, "but he'd better be there. It's fuckin' cold that time of night."

Just then I caught Twiggy looking at me with a really nasty expression but he didn't say a word. So I kept the whole thing on track.

"Here's what I need. The designated spot is in Bexley Village where Pepys Road ends at a block of flats called Guildford Court. If he hasn't got his A–Z on him tell him it's just past Heath Road. There's a little area with trees in front of the block of flats. It's almost pitch dark ..."

I reckoned Twiggy would have problems taking it all in so I slowed down my delivery a bit.

"He's got to come in his own motor and be there by eleven at the very latest. Tell him it doesn't matter what time he leaves his house but he'd better show up by eleven ..."

Twiggy was nodding but I still wasn't sure he was taking it all on board. And I was about to start on the really important stuff.

"When he gets there he's got to make sure the door on the passenger side of his motor is open and sit there and wait. Tell him a familiar face, nothing more than that, is going to be there to meet him. Tell him they'll then drive to another location and then he's got to point someone out to this friend."

I let it all sink in for quite a few seconds.

My next sentence was for Twiggy's ears only.

I wanted him to know exactly where I'd be, even though I wouldn't really be there at all. I'd be close by, watching to see if their white rastas turned up to try to plug me.

"Now listen really carefully," I said.

He didn't respond.

"Fuckin' concentrate, Twigs," I barked.

This time he blinked his eyes and nodded.

"I'll be sittin' about fifteen yards away from that spot in my own motor. I'll sit low and he won't see me."

I paused yet again.

"You understand?"

"'Course I fuckin' do," he said.

"Then I'll pop out, walk over to Marshall and bang, bang." I turned to Twiggy. "Reckon he'll go for it?"

"He'll be on for a bunk-up in a monastry when the MD waves two grand under his nose."

What sort of joke was that, I wondered. But I didn't bother saying anything.

We walked on for a couple more minutes in silence. He collided with me three more times but I'd given up complaining. Clumsy bastard would walk straight under a bus one day. Good riddance. Then Twiggy surprised me by appearing to be concentrating on the job in hand.

"I don't fuckin' understand Marshall," he said all of a sudden. "Geezer makes fuckin' good money, his job's a doddle, and then he goes and lands himself right in the shit ..."

He paused and looked for a response in me. I didn't blink an eyelid. "He's not such a bad bloke, either. And he's a good worker. It'll be a shame to see him go."

I wasn't sure if this touching speech was for my benefit or not. Perhaps he was trying to make me think that he, Twiggy, was an arsehole with a heart of gold. Seemed unlikely since Twiggy would rather have seen me six feet under than Kenny Marshall.

But I gave him a standard response.

"We all got to go sometime, old fruit."

Twiggy looked at me very strangely then, like he hadn't heard a word I'd just said.

"You need a driver or a motor for this op?" he asked.

Twiggy's unique brand of help I required like the hole in the head I intended to put in Kenny Marshall.

"Na, I'm well covered," I said.

Twiggy did an awkward shrug and let out his first real pneumatic hiss of the evening.

HISSSS!

"Don't say I didn't offer."

Back at his second-hand car lot we moved off our separate ways. As he walked off I told him I'd check in with him Saturday morning.

We nodded to each other.

"Saturday," Twiggy said. "He'll be on a fuckin' plate."

"Woof, woof?"

"Woof, fuckin' woof," he agreed.

Thursday promised to be another crazy day. Part One of my other work involved taking a ride to see Marty, my tight-fisted little rag trade friend. Marty knew full well what sort of loan I would organise for him so, naturally, I presumed he'd have my £2,000 ready and waiting.

Naturally, I was totally wrong.

"What can I say?" he said like the wanker he was. "I couldn't get it. But I'll manage it in the next few days."

"Get your fuckin' Afghan on, sunshine," I interrupted. "You're gonna meet a mate of mine."

He sat there at his desk with a silly grin on his face. Stupid bastard just didn't get it. The nearest Marty the Mug had got to this sort of caper was watching *Starsky and Hutch*. He didn't have a clue that I meant business.

"What happens if I don't go with you?"

Simple question. Simple answer.

"You get hurt ..." I stopped to let that sink in. "Then we still go and see my mate."

He jumped up and grabbed his coat.

We hopped in a minicab – his treat – and headed over to an Afro-Caribbean restaurant I know on Camberwell New Road.

The bloke who runs the place just calls himself "Easy". He comes from somewhere out in darkest Africa, I think. He's got another name but I haven't a clue what it is.

Easy speaks in a soft accent that sounds like a cross between

Trevor McDonald and Idi Amin. He lends out cash at what the local building society would call "exorbitant interest rates". I don't know Easy that well, but he's handled a few financial matters for me over the years.

He always has a decent stash of readies lying around and there's nothing more liable to scare the shit out of a little rag trade greaseball like Marty than a loan shark the colour of pure Guinness. I ordered a couple of beers, one for me and one for Marty – my treat – and told Easy we had some business for him. He directed us towards a darkened booth near the back.

A few minutes later Easy wandered up and I did the introductions.

"Easy, this is Marty and he needs an advance."

A lovely smile came to Easy's face at that moment. His luminous yellow teeth lit up the room like a Christmas tree.

"How much you want?"

I said, "Two big ones, please."

Often I'd accept less than what is owed to me in exchange for the actual readies so I can simply pay the money broker for his services but I was so fucked off with Marty for dicking me around I decided to take my whole cut.

Easy looked at Marty. That smile of his seemed to have grown even bigger.

"How we goin' to work diss?"

Marty the Mug didn't have a fucking clue what he was talking about.

"What d'you mean?"

"I mean, how you goin' to pay me, man? How long you take? How much you pay every week?"

They eventually agreed to a two-year loan, which seemed much too long to me.

If Marty kept up the payments it would work out to about six grand, just to pay off £2,000!

Easy laid out the cash on the spot. Marty the Mug picked it up nervously and handed it to me without counting it.

175

"Aren't you gonna count it?" I asked.

I always say that to them 'cos it's good to see them suffer.

Marty and I took a cab back up to his place – his treat. He gave me some right rabbit on the way. I didn't give a toss because I had my readies.

"What if I can't pay him back? If I miss a payment?" he muttered nervously.

"He's called Easy 'cos he'll always work somethin' out."

"But what if I can't afford it?"

"Then he and his brothers'll pay you a visit."

He gave me a half-hearted nod.

"I've just done you the biggest favour of your life, Marty. I helped you avoid the ultimate interest payment. You owe me a big thank you."

He laughed miserably.

"Thank you," he said.

But I don't think he really meant it.

Half the cash I'd got off Marty belonged to one of my backers, but I didn't see the point in running over to deliver it. I'd just top up the money I owed that particular chap when the next shipment of booze and fags came in.

It was late afternoon and I had a bit of time to spare before the next meet with my Russian backer, Ludwig.

Some ways it's easier to kill a man than waste an hour.

So I dropped into a second-hand music shop just off Camberwell Green next to a boozer where I used to do some smalltime puff deals. I'd been looking for the *Motown Chartbusters Volume IV* album since I'd lost it during a house move years back.

When I first turned pro I was so fucking hyper I couldn't relax enough to listen to all the sounds I'd liked when I was a kid. Then, in my mid-30s I went on this cruise with the missus and she got friendly with a bloody awful couple from some place like Beaconsfield.

So I bought myself a walkman to avoid talking to them and my interest in music returned with a vengeance. Well, my luck was in that day because I found the *Motown Chartbusters* cassette in that shop. It was spotless and only cost me a tenner.

I started to think that maybe the Marshall job wasn't going to end in tears after all.

On that Thursday I took one more float past Marshall's house to be sure everything was still hunky dorey. I pulled up by my favourite lamp post and sat and waited and watched.

Marshall's motor was parked up in his car port and there was a light on in the front room.

So I waited a while.

I leaned behind the seat and grabbed my *Two Fat Ladies* cookbook off the back window shelf. Perhaps I'd ditch the Moroccan lamb and go for something more acceptable to the Marshalls and their veggie burger loving kids. I started flicking through the pages then suddenly slammed it shut.

Hang on a minute. They weren't going to get anywhere near my dining table. What the fuck was I doing?

Now, that's what I call bad karma.

I glued my eyes back on to the front door immediately. I was so knackered I started going into a bit of trance. So I opened the window to stop myself nodding off. Still my eyelids kept dropping. I snapped them open and tried to shake the tiredness out of my head.

Seconds later the lids completely shut down.

Suddenly I found myself in a penthouse flat with Princess Di's corpse laid out on a slab besides me. Then there's this almighty rumbling and the whole apartment block starts falling apart like an earthquake's just hit. My favourite dreamscape hero then appears like magic. As usual, he has exactly the same face and name as me. But it isn't me.

And he points his favourite 9mm Glock up my arse again.

Just then I feel this wet patch on the back of my neck. Was this fucker kissing me before he killed me? I was so freaked I snapped myself awake, which you can do if you put your mind to it.

I swung my head and turned. Jesus Christ!

This fucking huge hairy Alsatian was sticking its damp black nose through the window. I thought it was a canine division plod hound come to get me. Then I heard a familiar voice.

"Look who we've found for you," said Mrs Curran in a sing-song granny voice.

"What's that?" I said pointing at this huge hairy German Shepherd with pinhead black eyes.

Mrs Curran looked confused.

"This is Twiggy."

She was staring right in at me.

What the fuck was she on about? Twiggy?

Then I finally twigged it (sorry!).

I shook my head from side to side.

"That's not him. He's much too dark."

I leaned out of the window and went through the motions of looking at the dog more closely. Suddenly he jumped up with his hind legs against my immaculately clean car door and a huge sandpaper tongue came slopping out.

He nearly took my head off with one lick.

"He's so happy to see you," said Mrs Curran cheerily. "Are you sure he's not your dog?"

I patted his hairy flea-infested head with about as much enthusiasm as a mouse in a snakepit.

"Wish he was," I said, trying to keep my distance but at the same time forcing a friendly smile. "I really appreciate all this but this just isn't my dog."

"How can you be so sure?" snapped Mrs Curran.

"I know my own dog. He's the wrong colour for starters. This fellow's too dark."

Mrs Curran was thankfully lost for words for a few seconds. Then she tilted her head at me.

"I've kept this dog in my house for three days." She stopped, opened her mouth and asked hesitatingly, "If he isn't yours, then, whose can he be?"

I shrugged my shoulders.

"Where d'you find him?"

"This charming young boy brought him to me after he saw my reward notice and …"

"Reward notice?"

"Oh, yes. Didn't I tell you? I put up a £50 reward to find your dog."

Inside, I was splitting my sides.

"Mrs Curran, I don't know how to break this to you, but I think you've got yourself a hot dog."

I tried to say it very carefully, making certain the "hot" and "dog" came out entirely separately.

Naturally, she didn't quite get it.

"A hot dog?"

I corrected myself.

"A stolen dog. This kid must have read the notice and nicked the dog to order …"

I could see she was very confused.

"Dog-napping's all the rage these days."

"Am I going to be arrested?"

"You could be, unless you get that dog back to its rightful owner."

"But I don't even know where he comes from."

Mrs Curran started getting all shaky and I felt really bad about it. I told her to call the RSPCA or the old bill and they'd probably have a missing dog report.

Then I reached into my pocket and took out a nice, new crisp £50 note.

"You're a lovely lady, Mrs Curran," I said. "I really appreciate what you've done, trying to find that dog for me and my kids …" I handed her the bill. "Now you go on inside and call the police."

"You're absolutely right, Mr Randall. And don't you

179

worry because I'll keep looking for your dog until we find him. Poor thing."

She began walking away and turned back towards me.

"I promise you, Mr Randall, we'll find him."

I nodded politely and forced a smile.

At that moment the dog must have seen something of interest because it suddenly took off at a gallop, with little old Mrs Curran hanging on to the lead for dear life.

As they disappeared down her pathway I laughed my fucking head off so bad that I nearly hit another car as I pulled out and headed home for supper. A few minutes later I smashed the palms of my hands down on the steering wheel when it dawned on me what a pratt I was.

I'd just encouraged the one person who could ID me and place me outside Marshall's house to get in touch with the filth.

What a fucking stupid thing to do.

Chapter Twenty

The missus wasn't in when I got home, but she'd got in some fresh tuna from a mate of hers whose old man worked at Billingsgate. I was just preparing a Dijon sauce when the phone rang.

"Yeah?"

"Malcolm?"

"Yeah."

"Kenny Marshall here, mate."

I stumbled for a response.

"How you doin'?"

"Fine, my old son. How 'bout you?"

"Can't complain. Didn't recognise your voice when I picked up the phone."

"Right."

"I was expectin' the missus. She ain't here so I thought it was her checking in."

As I spoke to Marshall, one part of my brain was trying to sound normal while the other worked overtime sussing out what the fuck was going on.

"Sorry, mate, but we can't make it for lunch on Sunday."

I didn't respond for a couple of seconds while his words sunk in. Then:

"That's a real shame," I said, as disappointedly as I could, "the old lady was really looking forward to seein' Brenda."

Then, purely as an afterthought, I asked him, "What's up?"

His response was cold and calm.

"Nothin' really. It's just my old mum's gone and had a bit of a heart attack ..."

"Sorry to hear about that, mate."

Then he went and laughed for some strange reason.

"It's nothin' too serious. She gets one every time I take the wife somewhere without her ..."

We both laughed.

"Anyhow, we gotta be up at the hospital most of Sunday so we thought it best to duck out of your lunch."

"That's a real pity, mate. I was goin' to cook up one of my specials. Moroccan lamb roasted on a spit."

I knew I was going well over the top but I couldn't resist it.

"Sounds fuckin' wonderful. All I get round here are vegetarian hotpots and rissoles that taste like fuckin' cardboard."

"So I heard."

I was starting to feel sorry for him so I thought I'd better bring the conversation to a rapid conclusion.

"Let's try and make it another day."

Fucking liar.

"We could do the followin' Sunday?" he asked hopefully.

This was getting silly but I had to play along.

"Sounds good to me. I'll double check with the missus and get back to you," I said chirpily as I began grating some cheese.

The next bit I couldn't resist.

"Hope your old mum gets better."

"She will. Soon as she finds out she's fucked up our weekend. See ya, Malcolm."

"Goodbye, Kenny."

I carried on grating some cheddar but I couldn't get Marshall out of my mind. Using your own old mum as an excuse to do a runner seemed a bit strong.

But then again, Twiggy might have been telling me porkies about Marshall's plans to scarper. I wanted to believe Marshall. Which made me disbelieve Twiggy. Which made Saturday night a little bit more fucking dangerous. Which meant I'd better keep on my toes.

But then again, if Marshall was about to go walkies why was he talking about coming to lunch the following Sunday?

This was doing my brain in. I got so wrapped up in my thoughts I nearly grated the top off my thumb.

By the time I got to Ludwig's place – The Aquarium – it was swimming with women of all shapes, colours and sizes and a lot of leery fellows trying to pull them.

"You givin' away free Viagra, or what?" I asked Ludwig when I got to his table.

You'd be amazed by the number of old-time villains – some in their 70s – who love popping pills and snorting Charlie when they're in the party mood.

Ludwig was grinning and grinding his teeth as usual.

"Free pussy," he said. "They smell it coming."

I wasn't sure if he meant that as a joke. Thursday night, Ludwig explained, was always a lively night because it's near the end of the week and a lot of old lags are out looking to pull for the weekend.

I recognised one bankrobbing legend stroking a nastylooking blonde's leg as his tab of ecstasy kicked in. Ludwig and I talked about the rapidly declining number of decent, law-abiding citizens in the world for a few moments, and then decided it was a fucking good thing.

Then we walked over to his office. Ludwig moved like a bodybuilder pumped full of steroids with arms that seemed too short for his torso. As we sauntered along the edge of the indoor swimming pool a bunch of silicon tarts and some flabby-looking old boys with droopy tits were about to take a plunge into the musty green chlorine water which contained more jism than a sperm bank.

Once we got to Ludwig's office, he locked the door behind me and threw me a package, wrapped in brown paper. I knew the routine: inside were two smaller packages, each with about three inches thick of £50 notes.

"£50,000, my friend. You look after it, yes?" he said.

I didn't bother to count it. If Ludwig says a package contains a pound and a half of dogshit, you can be sure it is exactly one and a half pounds, not an ounce more, not an ounce less. Lot of faces reckon Russians aren't trustworthy but they're all right as long as you don't turn your back on them.

"See you next week," I said cheerily to Ludwig.

That's when I'd pay Ludwig his money plus profit. It wouldn't be wrapped in neat little brown parcels because my team gets paid with any denomination that's around at any given moment. Often that means fivers and even one and two pound coins. The old lady and I sit up all bloody night counting it. The kitchen table is covered in notes and brass and the two of us are packing them into hundreds and thousands.

Then I usually grab a few Tesco's bags and divide up shares – this is Ludwig's, this is mine, this is expenses. Ludwig obviously gets the biggest chunk. The next night I grab the Tesco's bags filled with loot and covered with a newspaper and pop over to wherever we've got a meet.

First time I did that, Ludwig went fucking mental. He couldn't believe how anyone would treat cash so casually. He wanted his money delivered in some posh leather briefcase until I pointed out it's much safer to carry it round in plastic bags.

Who'd expect them to be filled with readies?

Ludwig could be a right stroppy bastard at times but then he did come from Moscow where they'd plug you for 500 quid. My share of the profits from these operations can be anywhere from £5,000 to £20,000, depending on the size of the shipment. It usually works out around the £10,000 mark.

As I got up to leave Ludwig's unhealthy health club that night, he said, "You get Marlboro Lights?"

"Hard or soft?" I asked. When you're in business you have to know the produce.

"Hard."

Ludwig walked me out back past the pool which was even more lively than earlier. I was tempted to stop awhile but I was out of Charlie and the last time I scored off one of Ludwig's dickhead dealers I ended up with a gram of talcum powder.

Mind you, I've pulled a few birds in The Aquarium in my time. One of the weirdest I ever came across was this half-Italian, half-Indian woman called Peera, who turned out to be a copper's wife from Dagenham. First time we met I only got her phone number, but a couple of days later I was researching a job which involved popping over the Dartford Bridge into deepest Essex so I gave her a bell and asked her out for lunch.

It turned out Peera didn't drink or take any gear so at first I thought maybe I'd got her a bit wrong.

Then, as I'm driving her home after a very quiet lunch so she can collect her car and pick up her kids from school, my hand brushes her knee and her eyes lock right on to me.

Next thing I know we're having a massive snog-up on the stairs of her police-issue, red-brick, two-up two-down within spitting distance of Ford's.

Then I noticed she kept popping up for air to check the windows to see if anyone was watching.

"Thought you said your hubby was out on patrol all day?" I asked her.

"He is but he likes coming round for a cuppa about this time of the day."

Then, calm as an oyster, she gets back to business. No doubt Peera would have loved it if her old man had walked in on us. That first afternoon we didn't really get going on account of her having to pick up her kids but over the following few weeks I found out she was on a completely different agenda.

One afternoon she locked her thighs round my head like a nut cracker as I lay on my back on her beige shagpile and proceeded to try and empty her entire bladder down my throat.

Now I'm pretty much up for anything (as long as it doesn't involve kids or animals) but being drowned in piss on a tatty carpet in the lounge of some PC Plod's gaff in Dagenham didn't do much for my hard-on. The other reason I ditched her was far more important – she was a lousy kisser. Here was a girl with all these creative thoughts juicing through her mind and she couldn't snog properly. All she did was poke her tongue between my lips and leave it hanging there like a slice of slimy, uncooked liver.

Sometimes I think about giving Peera a call but the truth is that reviving bits on the side never works. Stick the good times in the memory bank and move on. That's what I say.

Back at the Aquarium that night, Ludwig wished me a good trip on the fags and booze run. Sometimes I drove the lorry myself and he thought it was one of those occasions. I didn't bother putting him right. Far as I was concerned, the more people who thought I was off the manor at the weekend the better it would be.

Me and Ludwig's bundle of readies then headed over to meet Disco Dave at the lock-up, a modest double garage off the Bermondsey Road. Certain chaps who were known to certain other chaps could rent these sort of spaces out and be sure no one would come sniffing around.

All sorts of merchandise ends up there, much of it from hijacked lorries. When I rolled up our 10tonner was already backed up against the double doors. Disco was inside the cab with two blokes trying to keep warm. I didn't hang about.

The garage was empty and every sound echoed. The lighting was so bad I couldn't even make out the other end of the lock-up.

"You all set?" I asked Disco and his two drivers.

They nodded.

I noticed that Disco looked a bit narked.

"What's your problem?" I asked him.

"It's flamin' school half-term this weekend," he said.

"So what?"

"Half of Kent is going across the water to do the same as us," said Disco.

His two noddies shook their heads at the same time.

"Then you'd better get a move on. When you back?"

Disco looked to the older of his two drivers.

"Should be Saturday night. But don't get shirty if we don't make it 'til Sunday dinnertime," came the reply.

"There's an extra drink in it for you if you get back here in the morning," I said in a serious tone.

Then I handed Disco the package.

"There's fifty big ones. It's not mine, so don't fuckin' lose it."

I knew he wouldn't, because he knew what would happen if he did. He handed it to the older of the two drivers. My parting words: "Be good. The lungs and livers of south east London are depending on you."

As the lorry slowly pulled off, Disco and I walked towards my motor. I asked if he'd shifted all of his useless burglar alarms. He immediately changed the subject.

"You here Sunday?" he asked.

"Maybe. I got some other commitments over the weekend. But I'll bell you whatever happens."

I left. All my other interests were now wrapped up for the week. I had nothing more to do. I was completely clear to deal with Kenny Marshall. All I had to do was get a motor and be at the spot early. I planned to be very, very early.

Although it was well past midnight when I got home, the old lady was still up.

"Where you been?" she asked me, which is a bit unusual for her.

"Getting my booze and fags boys on the road ..."

This was one operation I kept her well informed about.

"Tell your girlfriends they'll get their cancer sticks on Monday. Whose house are you at that night?"

She thought about it for a moment. "Jenny's. I'll write down her address."

"Good idea. Might as well bring the van over there. Make sure they're all drivin' and I'll help load their motors up."

We chatted for a few moments, husband-and-wife small talk, and then she announced we'd been invited to her brother's house for supper.

"When's that, then?"

"Saturday night."

Typical.

"No can do ..."

Her face was already clouding over.

"I told you never to make plans for me without askin' first.

187

You did it with the Marshalls and now you're at it again. What's the matter with you?"

Then she really got the hump. "Why can't we go?"

I started to lose my rag.

"Don't you understand fuckin' English? I can't do it. I got business."

"I can't just call my brother and say you can't make it."

"I got a better idea. Call your brother and tell him we both can't make it."

"Don't bloody tell me what to do. I might go without you."

I looked her straight in the eyes and lowered my voice.

"You ain't going ..." I said quietly. "It's not often I tell you what to do, but you're here on your todd all Saturday night."

She stopped yelling. She knew I was serious.

"Why?"

"Because I said so, all right? You gotta be here Saturday night because ..." I thought quickly, "... because I'm expectin' a fuckin' important phone call and I won't be here."

"What am I?" she screamed. "Your fucking secretary?"

Why did she always say that when she got narked with me? If only she realised I was the one taking orders, not her. Being the wimp I am I totally ignored that last remark.

"If anyone calls Saturday night you're goin' to tell them I'm having a kip upstairs."

I needed her there to establish an alibi in case of emergencies. A missus is the perfect alibi. She can't be forced to testify against her old man unless she volunteers and my old lady was not about to wave goodbye to all those Harrods shopping trips.

She went very quiet for a few seconds. She knew something big was up but she knew she couldn't ask me about it. That was our unwritten rule. The old lady never asked about the heavier side of my work. In return she got everything her heart and wallet desired.

Then I broke the silence when I suddenly remembered to tell her, "Kenny Marshall called. They can't come on Sunday. His mum's had a heart attack or somethin'."

She didn't respond, so I chipped in, "Why don't you call your bruv and tell him we can come Sunday night?"

"Sometimes," she said quietly, "sometimes ..." When she's angry she often doesn't finish her sentences.

I didn't want her having a go at me because we were having too many barnies at that time. We got especially tense just before a job. And that's bad karma. Then I thought I'd come up with the perfect answer.

"Come here," I said and tried to to give her a cuddle.

But she was far from happy and I was finding it hard to even put my arms around her. Then she looked up at me and I could see from the expression on her face she'd been stewing about a few things for quite a while. The missus wasn't good at hiding her feelings. What you see is what you get with her. She's a bit of a kid in some ways. But then so am I.

I tried to pull her closer. She looked up at me again. Tears were welling in the corner of her eyes.

"Malcolm, I know you hurt people when you're out working."

"What you on about, darlin'?"

"You hurt people, don't you?"

"Why you suddenly askin' me all this?"

Then she deliberately untangled herself from my arms. I knew that meant trouble.

"I was reading *Good Housekeeping* in the dentist, and there was this housewife who was married to a hitman ..." She paused to look at me for a reaction. I didn't look up.

"And he treated her just the same way you treat me."

I tried to compose myself for a few seconds. Defence or attack. Defence or attack. I didn't know which way to turn, thanks to *Good fucking Housekeeping*. At that moment I looked at her and I knew she knew. Yet she was still waiting for me to answer.

"If you think I knock people off then why aren't you scared I might do the same to you?" I asked in a jokey sort of way.

I was pushing it but I didn't give a fuck at that moment in time. I might regret it later but I couldn't let it drop for some weird reason.

" 'Cos I think you love me and I know you'd never hurt me."

"I thought hitmen were cold bastards who feel no emotion?"

"Yeah, but you're not like the rest of them."

"Then what's the problem?"

I pulled her back in my arms and suddenly felt a rush of affection for her. We kissed full on the mouth for the first time in weeks. As our tongues lapped hungrily at each other this strange sense of relief came over me.

Why was it always women who sussed me out? Maybe they were the only ones I allowed to get inside my head. Men couldn't be trusted. My dad was a classic example. Then there were those fuckers who killed my first wife. Oh, and don't forget the bastards I've plugged over the years. None of them would have understood.

Me and the wife stayed up another couple of hours watching some crappy porno video about three birds who go out shagging men and then killing them.

I broke open a bottle of bubbly and dug out some old Charlie I had stashed in the freezer. We both snorted a couple of lines and had some fun copying what one girl was doing to some stud on the video.

It's funny how every now and again the missus drops her I'm-a-normal-practical-housewife-in-the suburbs-routine. She's not really into the porn, but at least she's a good enough sport to go through the motions. It would have been the perfect moment to ask her if she and Kenny Marshall had enjoyed a bunk-up together.

But you know what?

I didn't really want to bloody know.

Chapter Twenty-One

The old lady was long gone by the time I got up Friday morning. I didn't have a clue where she was, out at the shops, having it off with a toyboy. None of it mattered just so long as she wasn't anywhere near Kenny fucking Marshall. I just hoped I knew enough to be thankful for small blessings.

So I lay there in bed going through my plan for the day. The only thing left to get sorted was a motor, but that had to wait until after dark.

I got up and made myself some brekkie; fried eggs, bacon, slice of toast and coffee. Then I opened up the *Telegraph* and went straight to my horoscope.

It said Friday would be a good day to meet new people "who have your best interests at heart", which proves what a load of old tosh the horoscopes are. But I'm still a sucker for them.

About 11.30 there was a knock on the door.

From the front window it looked like two of London's finest Plods, in anoraks. What the fuck was going on? I considered staying quiet and hoping they'd piss off. But I needed to know what was happening so I opened my front door.

"Yeah?"

"Are you Malcolm Deakin?"

"If I'm not he's gonna be well upset when he gets home and finds out I've been shagging his missus."

I don't know why but I was in a really good mood. But that didn't make them any happier.

"Get dressed, please. We need you to come down to the station and answer a few questions."

"Gotta warrant?" I always ask this one first because it really winds them up. They admitted they didn't but I wasn't going to make a fuss.

"I don't give a toss either way," I said.

They looked a bit confused.

"Gissa minute and I'll get me shirt on."

What the hell. I didn't have any other plans until much later anyway. It was obvious they wanted to talk to me about something. It had to be about job number 13. If I didn't play ball with them they'd just come back at me with a warrant. And that might prove a bigger problem because I didn't know when they'd serve it. Last thing I wanted was them finding a loaded .38 in my pocket as I was walking down my garden path.

So I made them feel important. Why not? The army taught me the art of respecting your fellow man. It can come in quite handy at times. In any case, small things have a habit of causing big problems. So far luck had been very much on my side but I've definitely sailed a bit close to the wind over the years.

One night I was on the piss up west and since I don't believe in drinking and driving I hailed a cab and asked the driver, "All right for a ride to Bromley?"

Cabbies don't like going out to the suburbs unless they're about to clock off and they live on the same manor. They can make a lot more dosh sailing round the West End. But this cabbie – he was in his early 50s I would guess – said he'd do it. As he drove me home we had a good chinwag along the way. When we got there I chucked him a pony and told him to keep the change. He was well chuffed.

Two weeks later I was shadowing a contract up a busy street in Knightsbridge when I looked across the road and spotted the law in the shape of two plain clothes plod who knew me well.

Unfortunately, I was carrying a piece on me at the time. I kept walking until I reached one of those wide streets in the middle of Knightsbridge when I stopped because the lights changed.

By some fucking miracle, the first vehicle to roll up by the lights was my pony express cabbie. I took it as a sign from heaven.

"Watcha," I said, "hold on to this for me ..." and in one swift motion I dropped the shooter on the floor next to him. "Get lost for a few minutes. If you come back and see me walkin' down the road, return it. If you don't, gimme a call (I gave him my mobile number) later."

He nodded and drove off. I walked another block and sure enough the law apprehended me.

"What're you up to?" old bill number one asked me.

"Doin' some exercise. What's the problem?"

"Mind if I search you?" old bill number two requested.

"'Course I mind," I said, "but go ahead and give yourself a hard-on."

He patted me down and didn't find a thing.

"Why don't you stay over the river where you fuckin' belong?"

"Whatever you say, constable."

Number one butted in. "We been watchin' you for more than half an hour. You're tailing someone up ahead."

"What you on about? I had a big dinner and I'm just walkin' it off."

"If he cops it ..."

I interrupted.

"Now, if you're finished, I got things to do ..."

And I walked away.

I must have gone another half a mile up that big road which takes you all the way to Heathrow – think it's called Cromwell Road – when my new best mate the cabbie pulls up.

"You all right?"

I nodded and jumped in the back and told him to take me across the river to Peckham Rye.

"Take your time. Want to see if we've got any company."

We didn't. I chucked him two fifties and wished him a happy and prosperous future.

That particular target took three months to hit. But once a job's accepted and the money's been handed over there's no going back. I finally got the bastard when he was back on my side of the river, naturally. Meanwhile, I was sure those two plodders wouldn't bother filing a report about our meeting in Knightsbridge.

The filth hate filling out forms almost as much as robbers hate the filth. They just wanted to make sure I didn't get up to anything on their patch. Then they wouldn't have to fill in any forms, would they?

Anyway, back to the two detectives who'd showed up at my house. As they drove me to the nick I had to ask the all-important question: "What's all this about?"

We were heading to the local copshop which probably meant it had nothing to do with job number 13. Just in case, I conjured up an alibi while I sat in the back of their motor. I'd tell them I'd been on my todd at home the previous evening reading the racing charts and watching the telly.

I should never have taken on this job so soon after the last one. Here I was on my way to the local copshop when I should have been thinking about pinching a motor. Eventually, we got to Bromley nick. Last time I'd been here was when I was a teenager and got pulled for flogging stolen Vespas. I was a bit of a Mod in those days.

First thing the two Muppets did when we arrived was take me into a little room and read me my rights. Then some detective I'd never seen before walked in.

"How you keepin', Malcolm?" he said.

I shrugged my shoulders.

"Doin' all right."

"Bet you are ..." He began looking over my sheet. "You've been in a few nicks in your time, haven't you?"

As it happened, I'd been given a tug for more than half a dozen murders, booked on one at this point, but never convicted.

"Not really. I like to keep out of trouble," I answered.

I wondered if he was going to mention job number 13.

"What you been up to lately?"

Old bill continued looking at my sheet as he spoke.

"Bit of this, bit of that. Nothin' to worry your head about."

"Of course you haven't."

Then he took a deep breath.

Here we go, I thought, and braced myself for a mention of number 13.

"Malcolm, you ever heard of a man called Terry Lattigan?"

I gave him an empty look and jerked my head back quizzically.

"Perhaps you know him as Billy White?"

"I dunno what you're on about."

Truth is, I'd never heard of him. I reckoned some villain had turned up dead and they were rounding up the usual bunch of suspects in the hope of getting a lead. Since I genuinely wasn't in the frame I could answer as truthfully as I could manage. I even threw in the odd joke to keep them amused.

But I drew the line at calling them "Sir" because then they'd know I was taking the piss.

An hour later they'd got nowhere. Then this smart-arsed detective tried to pull a fast one.

"Don't you need to call your brief?"

Now if I'd said yes, he'd have known I'd got something to hide.

"Don't reckon so," I said, "unless you know something I don't.

He looked well cheesed off at my response so I went in for the kill, naturally.

"Is that it, then?"

He gave out a half-hearted smile.

"On yer bike. But don't go disappearing into a cloud of smoke."

He didn't have anything on me and I *loved* that wound-up expression on his ugly face.

Just as I was strolling down the steps of Bromley nick, my Nokia started singing.

"Hey, Mister criminal," said a familiar voice, "you knocked anyone off today?"

Cat was on heat as usual. I pushed my mouth right up against the phone as some tasty-looking Indian WPC strolled past me with a flirty grin on her face.

"No, but I'd like to knock you off," I whispered.

There was a pause during which I could hear Cat's heavy breathing.

"What do I say if the police come round and see me, Malcolm?" she sighed. "What do I tell them about you?"

"Tell them everything you know and then give them a good time," I replied.

"What if there's only one of them?"

"Then you'd better get your handcuffs out, girl."

I thought I heard another female voice in the background then, but I might have been mistaken.

"Actually, I've got an officer lying here beside me, Malcolm. D'you want to speak to her," the Cat purred.

Phone sex on the steps of Bromley nick. There's a first time for everything.

But now was not the time.

"I gotta go, my darlin'," I whispered.

"Meanie."

"I'll call you early next week ..."

Before I'd finished saying it she'd put the phone down. Typical Cat.

I had to get moving to grab myself some transport for tomorrow's activities. There used to be a saying in Bexleyheath when I was a kid, "no wheels, no deals" meaning that without a motor it was almost impossible to make a decent wedge.

I had a car and a scooter by the time I was 15, even though I didn't have a licence. The motor was an Anglia low rider with twenty-inch alloys and a souped-up V6 engine. It went like a fucking rocket.

The scooter was mainly for trips down to the south coast on Sundays when the Mods were looking for a bit of aggro with those greasy Rocker pratts on their BSAs.

Obviously, next to buying a motor the easiest way to get one is to nick it. In fact, buying one is a fuck of a lot harder. You gotta fill out all those stupid forms and invent addresses and stuff.

I know blokes who can get you a nicked motor, any colour, any day of the fucking week. I've probably personally stolen near to 100 cars in my time. Some I've sold. A few years back I used to take them to Cyprus for a couple of Lebanese carpet dealers who had them resprayed, re-registered and flogged back into Europe. But most of the motors I've nicked were essential tools for my various business interests including everything from smuggling drugs to knocking off scumbags.

There's no question of ever using your own motor for a job. There is only one chap I know who does, but he doesn't do hits, just robberies. This geezer's an expert mechanic and has his car so souped-up that Plod can't keep up with him on the open road. In order to keep that same motor he has to constantly paint it and switch number plates. That vehicle's been at least 15 different colours so far and he's got more plates than the NAAFI.

And, just to be on the safe side, when he first got it, he registered it to a scrap yard.

Seems a lot of effort when all he has to do is go out and nick a car each time he does a job. All I need is a motor to get me from A to fucking B and then get away from there even faster. I'm not interested in phoney plates and all that bollocks because I won't have the motor long enough for it to matter.

It takes at least two days for stolen vehicles to get on to the police computer and I was going to nick mine on the Friday night, use it Saturday night when I plugged Marshall and then dump it. I wasn't even going to drive it during daylight hours so there was no way I'd get a tug.

Mind you, on one occasion I did nick a black cab to use on a job.

My plan was to sit near the target's girlfriend's house and then cruise by when he came out. I'd watched this bastard long enough to know he never, ever used his own motor. So I picked up my man in the cab, drove half a mile and plugged him.

Great thing about a cab is you can lock the back doors just by pressing on the brake pedal. Very handy if they try and do a runner. Which he didn't.

The other unusual thing about that job was that I made an

197

extra £4.50. Just after I'd nicked the cab I was driving to Camberwell with it when some geezer hailed me.

So, just for a laugh I picked him up. I think he said he was a film director or producer, on his way to see a bit of crumpet, I reckon. He told me some great gossip about Tom Cruise. The fare was £4.00 and he bunged me a 50p tip. Don't knock it.

By the time Bromley's finest detectives had finished their shift, I'd had supper, managed a barny with the wife and got ready to leave the house, it was dark outside.

I took a pair of disposable transparent latex gloves, like a doctor wears. They weren't in the same league as the black, elbow-length ones Cat liked putting on, but stretching them over my fingers certainly gave me a bit of a tingle. I also had a few lengths of wire which would help me break in and get the motor started.

I already knew what model I was after.

I wanted a dark-coloured, newish model BMW Three Series with nothing unusual like a black rubber aerial or some bird's name sprayed across the windscreen. I headed for the neighbourhoods with law-abiding residents living in blocks of flats with limited parking facilities which meant there were lots of cars out on the streets.

Very few people in these areas ever find parking spaces close enough to their buildings to keep an eye on their car. Even if someone did see me fiddling about with a door lock, you can lay odds they'd probably think I was just another mug who'd left his keys in the ignition. Most of them wouldn't even think about calling the cozzers. They don't want to get involved, for which myself and many others are eternally grateful.

I began my hunt for a suitable vehicle across the water in Pimlico but from the moment I left my place I kept an eye out for a tail. I was looking for either that big silver Merc or the filth. No doubt plod hadn't finished with me. No way would I nick a motor on their patch or anywhere near my usual manor.

Or anywhere near where I was going to do away with a target, for that matter.

All I needed was to be driving to a hit and have the owner finger me in his motor.

I scouted Pimlico and Victoria for about 45 minutes without finding what I wanted. Next I tried Chelsea and soon spotted the perfect vehicle in a street just off the Embankment near Cheyne Walk. It was a dark blue, four-door '92 Three Series Beemer. A nippy motor with a reputation for reliability but they didn't come with factory-fitted alarms back in those days.

My next problem was finding a place to park my own car. I didn't want a ticket placing me in Chelsea which connected me to the motor I was about to pinch. Eventually I found a legal spot just across Battersea Bridge.

Then I walked briskly back across the river and hung about for a few minutes checking out the area near my new motor. It was surprisingly quiet.

I whipped on my gloves on for a bit of surgery and got down to work. I poked the wire about inside the rubber window lining until I hit the central locking system. Ping. I was inside.

Then I opened the bonnet and ran a wire from the battery to the solenoid and the car roared to life. The whole job took a couple of minutes. Once the Beemer was fired up, I checked the fuel gauge. If a jalopy doesn't have the petrol to get me out of that area I'll turn off the engine, lock the door and abandon ship.

I'd never take a nicked motor into a garage to buy fuel. Garage forecourts are covered by security cameras.

There was a time I wouldn't have cared. That was when I made a decent wedge nicking cars so I'd always bring a short hose and siphon enough petrol to get out of the area pronto.

That evening my luck was in because my unknown benefactor had a half-full tank which would more than easily get me over the river and to a locksmith I do a bit of business with. Locksmiths are still, even in this day and age, God's gift to absent-minded housewives, S and M merchants, and villains.

A good one can rustle up a key for anything from a pair of handcuffs to a Chieftain tank. And I knew the perfect man for my newly acquired Beemer. This particular bloke, who will remain unidentified because he is still very much in business and unknown to the filth, has been working for some of the major south east London firms for at least 20 years. He's efficient, dependable and keeps his trap shut. All of which makes him pretty fucking expensive to employ.

This geezer's got his own house and motor repair shop over in Dulwich and, because of the unusual hours kept by many of his clients, he didn't mind being woken up at half past two in the morning.

I pulled my motor into his garage and watched him get down to work. He was a real craftsman. First he pulled the ignition out and checked the serial number. Then he asked me if I wanted a key made for the existing ignition in the car or a totally new ignition switch. It didn't really matter either way so I went for the easiest route – just a new key.

Then he opened his toolbox. This box was about three feet long by about a foot and a half high and contained some of the fucking strangest instruments I've ever seen. He checked some BMW manual he had against the make of car and ignition serial number, turned on one of his cutters, and made a key for me right there on the spot. Then he did the same for the door. At this point I didn't know if it was the same key or not, but I ended up with two keys, one for the door, the other for the ignition.

The price of the job was £200. It took 45 minutes. Fucking magic is what I call it.

While the locksmith was working on the key I checked the battery, the electrical system, even the tyres. The only thing that didn't work was the clock on the dash and the light inside the glove compartment. They never work on Beemers. I'd checked the brakes while I was driving over and they were in good shape.

All in all I had a fair old motor.

It's not always that way. I've stolen knackered jalopies and had to dump them half a mile down the road. Now, armed with my new set of keys, I needed to find a good place to keep the Beemer out of the limelight until Saturday night. I chose a 24-hour car park on some wasteland just off Camberwell High Road. Another tenner down the swanny.

It was 3.30am and I had to find a cab.

Eventually, I flagged down some headcase in a battered old Sierra with a half-bitten black aerial – an obvious fucking minicab if I'd ever seen one.

"Where you goin'?" he asked as I opened the back door.

A waft of puff hit me straight in the face. I didn't reply until I was in the back seat. I knew he'd be well pissed off when I told him to go to Battersea at that hour.

"Battersea," I said.

"No way, man," he replied flatly. "Can't go to Battersea now, man. Is wrong way for me."

"There's a score in it for you," I said hopefully.

I'd swear there were cobwebs in his dreadlocks.

"What yo' wanna score, man?"

Then I looked at him – hard.

"What?" I said even more confused than him for a moment. He was so shitfaced he thought I was after some puff.

I pulled out a £20 note and waved it at him.

"Twenty quid says you'll take me to Battersea."

"Right on."

He dropped me a few blocks from where I'd parked my motor and I flung him the twenty.

"See you about," I said as I got out of his smoke-drenched Sierra.

Just then he began pulling something out of his jacket. For a split second my own hand dived in next to my piece. What the fuck was he doing?

Then he pulled out a business card.

"Yo' need a ride. Just call. Any time."

I looked at his bloodshot eyes and reckoned he'd had so much whacky-backy he wouldn't remember where he'd picked me up, let alone my beaming face.

"Thanks," I said, slamming the door shut.

I was so wound up I knew I'd never get any kip for hours so I drove around for a bit trying to sort my head out.

And I thought about tomorrow.

At 11.00pm, Marshall would show up. Hopefully (remember, I still wasn't totally sure at this stage) I'd walk over to his motor and blow his brains out. In theory that would be the end of it. But I expected more.

Then I put myself in Twiggy's head.

I knew that once I started walking towards Marshall's car I'd be out in the open – a sitting duck. That's when Twiggy might try and cut me down. And remember, Marshall, or whoever was sitting in his motor, would be tooled up. Somebody could move in behind me and I'd be caught in the middle of the crossfire.

All I could do about that was run like hell and keep my head down.

Then again, I could wait in the playground next to the block of flats, and make my approach from the front of the motor. That would only work if Marshall turned up on time. If he was late I'd get so fucking cold my reflexes would be shot to shit.

But there was a simpler alternative.

I took it for granted Marshall or some ringer (I'm assuming there'd only be one person in the motor) would be tooled up and the second I approached the car they'd start blasting away. I could avoid this by staying close to the back of the car and the wall beside it. That would cut down on the shooting angle from inside the motor.

But then, if this was a set-up, there wasn't much I could do about it, except hope my luck held out.

I reckoned I still had the upper hand because I wouldn't be where I told Twiggy I'd be. I also planned to get there early, and wait until after 11. These were all small factors when it came down to the wider picture, but they gave me a chance to cover my back.

It was gone four in the morning and I was still driving around aimlessly, so I decided to check out my killing ground.

I got to Bexley Village and circled the block three times. It was pitch dark and there was nothing happening. I was about the only vehicle on the road. I parked up. Still no sign of life. No dog walkers, no joggers, no motors driving through. The shadows played nicely across the area and filled my chosen spot with darkness.

I got out and walked around for a bit. There was a slight breeze from the high buildings which would help muffle the pop of my shooter. I walked over to the back door of the block of flats that overlooked the location and strolled in.

The hallway was lit by a single, flickering lightbulb. I grabbed a dustbin from just outside the door and put it under the bulb. Then I climbed on to it and unscrewed the bulb with a handkerchief. I didn't need any more light than nature would provide.

I also realised this was a much better place to hide before the others showed up.

Then I sailed over to Marshall's place. There were no lights on. I don't know what I expected to find but I felt like a soldier on the eve of battle, covering and re-covering my plan over and over again. It was like that in the Falklands, just standing and looking over Goose Green at all those Argies. You feel like you're floating. Everything around you doesn't seem to be part of you. It's well weird.

I only joined the army because I thought it would keep me out of trouble. It might sound stupid now, but I really didn't intend spending the whole of my life on the wrong side of the law. Trouble was, I'd always been a bit of a loner even back in those days. I didn't fit in with army life and in the end they were glad to see the back of me.

I don't talk much about the Falklands and all that stuff

which is why I've not mentioned it much here. It's better off forgotten. It pisses me off the way everyone these days is supposed to come out and share all their experiences. There are some things in life you keep to yourself.

My dad never talked about what happened to him when he served in Burma during World War II. After what I saw in the Falklands I understood why.

On the way home that evening I stopped at an all-night caff I know and demolished some bacon and eggs. Then I went home and slept like a baby for the remainder of the night and into the middle of Saturday morning.

A clock inside my head was counting down the minutes and hours now. I knew it wouldn't stop ticking until Kenny Marshall was dead.

Chapter Twenty-Two

Saturday turned out to be fucking freezing. When I woke up the sky was a dense, dark, grey colour and it looked like rain, even sleet or perhaps the end of the world. Reckoned it would be rain for me, end of the world for Kenny Marshall.

The bad weather didn't bother me. It would keep people inside and cut down on other people's range of vision. Naturally, the first thing I did that morning was read the horoscope in that morning's *Telegraph*.

I tore it out of the paper and have kept it ever since. This is why:

"There are times when the faster you run the slower you appear to be moving, and with certain people trying to undermine your confidence you would do well to stop, look and listen before progressing any further.

"The Sun, currently in your birth sign, is enabling you to succeed – but only if you refuse to be intimidated by those whose greatest fear seems to be that you will run rings round them."

Problem with horoscopes is that they're like mirrors. You only see what you want to see. I carefully folded the scrap of newspaper, put it in my pocket and belled Twiggy.

"I'm comin' past your place in an about an hour," I said. "You gonna be there?"

"I'm glad you called," he answered, then paused. "There's something you need to know."

"What?"

"Not on the blower. Walls have ears and all that bollocks."

"See you in an hour."

"All right."

Then I sat down with the rest of the *Telegraph* and tried to catch up with what was happening in the world. The *Telegraph* is much better then those stupid little redtop comics. Can't believe a fucking word they say, can you? The missus won't even have them in the house. Says it's embarrassing if she's got company, especially if it's any of her snotty mates from the golf club.

Most of the time she's more bothered about matching the lounge curtains with a new three-piece suite than worrying about my chosen profession. I blame it on her father, of course. He was a snotty bastard and, naturally, he thought I wasn't good enough for his daughter.

The old boy had a stupid handlebar moustache and people thought he was some toffy-nosed ex-naval officer. Nearest he got to active service in World War II was floating off Ramsgate with the Royal Navy Reserve. Silly sod got his suits and shoes handmade and spent a fortune on poxy Fortnum and Mason food hampers every Christmas. They lived out in a fancy detached house near Maidstone.

Yet all he had was some crummy job in an insurance company.

When the old boy died it turned out everything was on the never never. He'd even borrowed cash to set up a lovenest with a toyboy in Catford. My missus's poor old mum was left with fuck all, except a £30,000 American Express bill and a big mortgage to pay off.

Even worse was the fact that the old man treated my missus like shit when she was a kid. She was the oldest of five and that bastard used to knock her about if she ever dared open her mouth. By the time I met her she'd shaken off most of her father's airs and graces because she hated him so much. They only ever rose to the surface when she kicked up a fuss about things like matching settee covers.

The only thing of interest in the paper that morning were the best runners for the weekend race meetings. At that precise moment in time, Kenny Marshall was probably doing the same thing I was, except he was checking the Premiership form.

I once plugged another fellow who had a similar problem to Marshall's. I got him on a Sunday night – poof – he was gone. Now here's the funny side of it: I was later told that Sunday had been his best gambling day in years.

This poor bastard had bet on eight or nine races and won

every one of them. It wasn't enough to pay everyone off but it would have helped him get a stay of execution.

The day of any hit you shouldn't get nervous. If you're confident it breezes by, but start bricking it about what's happening and you're asking for trouble.

I was thinking a lot about Marshall, but I was still confident. And curious. I wondered what Twiggy really had in mind for me this Saturday evening. I also did what I always seem to do on the day of an actual hit – think about the first few hits I carried out.

That very first one was a piece of cake. Bang. Bang. You're dead. Simple as that. Straight through the eye as he sat there snoring in his local boozer. I was 28 years old, not long out of the army and working as a runner for a well-known fence. This bloke made his name handling £15 million worth of gold bullion from the legendary Brink's-Mat blagging out at Heathrow Airport back in the early 80s.

This fence then offered me £5,000 to knock off some geezer he thought was about to grass him up to the cozzers.

I was already on a roll. People knew how I'd dealt with those bastards who'd kicked my first wife to death. From those early days I came to terms with a few important issues: If I live, I live; if I die, I die. Funny old world, ain't it? That's the way I am. I've done everything I've wanted in my life. I've seen what I wanted to see.

There's only one piece of unfinished business to take care of – that piece of dogshit who ordered the hit on me and whose Muppets killed my first missus will be getting out of prison soon. When he does I'll have him.

Death doesn't bother me.

Just like Kenny Marshall, I'm going to cop it eventually. If I die a few years sooner, what the hell, I've had a good run.

Dying can't be that bad – I've never heard any complaints.

My main concern is that I don't end up laid out on some greasy marble slab at the MD's undertakers in Millwall alongside a load of filthy used bank notes. I'd rather be reduced to ash at one of those quiet little crematoriums they have near most seaside towns on the south coast.

The only other thing that really bothers me is who turns up at my funeral. I can think of loads I don't want within a mile of the service. Most of them are hoods who think I'm some friend of theirs. Maybe I should put their names down on a list and leave it with my trusted brother-in-law.

As it happens the only hits that got to me were the three or four I did after those first two – before I'd made a name for myself as a fully-fledged pro.

I planned them carefully but I spent too much of my time turning my arsehole inside out worrying about them. I now realise the key is to stop planning, stop moving things around and just go for it. That's what being a pro is all about.

I tailed one target for eight days before deciding where to plug him. This bloke was a regular at a sex dungeon in Bayswater. Don't know how he got his rocks off being given a thrashing by some bird he's paying who doesn't give a shit. They've got to care, haven't they? My target used to stumble out of that dungeon in such a state he could hardly walk. Which meant he was not on the lookout for anyone on his tail.

The street outside this dungeon was a good location because my man had to get in his car and drive along a road with a bunch of sleeping policemen on it. Then he'd hit a mini roundabout that was always chockablock with traffic. That slowed him down nicely.

The moment I saw him come out of his vehicle I was going to move off to the end of the road in my motor and head him off. I'd be sitting there waiting for the traffic to clear so I could get across that roundabout. He'd pull up behind me and stop. And wait.

Then I'd get out of my motor like I had engine problems or a dose of roadrage or whatever and walk right up to the window of his car and plug him. Only problem was he never turned up again at that dungeon. And I couldn't exactly go ahead without him. So much for my great plan.

So I went over to his house, but it looked like he was away. I spoke to a postie and it turned out my target had gone on holiday for a couple of weeks.

I had to sit tight until he got back and start the whole tailing process all over again. It took another ten days, but I finally nailed him in a car wash.

I finished skimming the form in the *Telegraph* and drove over to Twiggy's crummy used-car lot for our long-awaited meet. He came scarpering out of his garden shed office like the overgrown, armless ape he is and hopped in my motor.

"Cold enough for you?" he asked after slamming the door. Before I could give him a pissed-off look, he let out one of his customary pneumatic hisses. His question about the weather being cold was the one I always had to answer first.

"No, it's not," I said. "Wish it was about ten degrees colder. My granddad was a fuckin' Eskimo."

He looked at me and didn't know how to react. Another hiss from his pneumatic arms broke the barrier of silence.

"Is he lined up, then?" I asked.

"Just about. He'll be there. When he came over yesterday I told him there was a job for him for tonight. He didn't seem bothered."

"He must have looked a bit curious."

"Nope."

"Doesn't make any fuckin' sense. He should be brickin' it about anything off the map."

I'll swear Twiggy backtracked a touch when he saw the puzzled look on my face.

"Well, he might 'ave hesitated for a second. But when I told him there was some extra wedge in it he seemed well chuffed."

I shook my head from side to side. Some people will do anything for money, I thought.

"What d'you tell him?"

"We had a good rabbit. He went for it, hook, line and fuckin' sinker. I told him to be at that spot in Bexley village at eleven."

Twiggy was getting so excited telling me all this he was delivering his lines in a breathless, rasping voice.

"I said someone who was known to him, a mate, would come to him, get in the motor and tell him where to drive."

"What d'you say about the fella he's supposed to finger?"

Twiggy shook his head.

"Nothin'. I said the contact would tell him while you were driving over."

"What? That's it?" I said dryly.

"Oh, he did ask how many bodies would be there. When I told him just.the one, he seemed happy."

There was only one detail missing.

"D'you tell him to keep the passenger door open like we agreed?"

Twiggy let off a long, ominous HISS! at that moment.

"Fuck it," he said, drawing it out. "I forgot. Bloody hell! I'm sorry, mate …"

He's sorry and I'm going to be standing on a street tooled up, trying to get into my target's locked motor. His fucking apologies wouldn't open that door. This is why I prefer operating on my own. When I do it myself it gets done and done right. I guarantee that no one cares about your own life as much as you do.

"You'd better see him, then," I spat out the words tersely. "I didn't plan to, but I s'ppose I'll have to. I'll go over to the office and meet him when he calls in. It's not a problem."

I looked him right in the eye.

"It is a problem," I said seriously.

"What do I tell him if he asks why?"

"How the hell do I know? Tell him I don't want to stand there in the freezing fuckin' cold. There's nothin' strange about a bloke wantin' to get in a car quickly. In fact, it'll make him think it's not a hit. If it was a hit I'd just pop him through the fuckin' window."

I made a mental note to be prepared in case the door was locked, as I fully expected it to be. Twiggy seemed a bit too relaxed for my liking. I wondered how fast that sandpaper tongue of his would come whipping out of his mouth if I fronted him up about seeing him leaving Marshall's place that day? But I decided not to.

I wondered how hard that tongue would have worked if I'd asked him who was trailing me? But I didn't bother with that one, either.

I'd simply be tooled up and prepared for all eventualities.

"Is he still planning a runner?" I asked Twiggy out of the blue.

Twiggy made a face.

"S'ppose so."

"Don't you know?"

"Why the fuck would I know?"

"Fuckin' marvellous," I said sarcastically.

His tongue came whipping out yet again.

"Don't start for fuck's sake," he snapped back at me.

He meant it as a threat and I took it on board. Now wasn't the right time to have it out with him. Another minute of awkward silence followed.

Then I asked him, "What was it you couldn't tell me on the blower?"

Twiggy got a bit dramatic then.

"Marshall's just got himself a piece."

Piss. Fuck. Shit. Bollocks. I said it as quietly and calmly as I could.

"Nice of you to share that with me. How d'you know?"

"His gunsmith belled us. Got a call last night."

"What kind of piece?"

It didn't really matter, a gun is a gun is a fucking gun.

"Automatic. Is that bad news?"

I looked across at him like he was the wanker I'd always thought he was.

"No, it's fuckin' great news. Can't wait to read my obituary in the fuckin' newspapers."

211

"Sorry, mate."

"Like fuck you are."

As it happened, I had fully expected Marshall to be packing, but I was more bothered by the way Twiggy told me about it. The info pack he'd provided said he didn't own or use a shooter. But how could someone in his line of business not need to carry a bit of protection?

More importantly, why did Twiggy lay it all on the table? One likely answer hit me like a ton of slate.

But then he broke the ice.

"If you need some help, the MD said to tell you he'd provide any back-up you need. Whatever you want."

This was why I thought he was letting me know about Marshall's piece. It was a perfect excuse for Twiggy to be live on the scene.

I prodded my finger into his chest.

"You just stay the fuck away from there. You understand? I don't want to see your fat, ugly face or your twiglet arms swinging anywhere in the vicinity. Is that clear?"

"Yeah."

I'd already decided that if Twiggy showed up that night I'd take him out.

"Now fuck off and tell Marshall what I told you ..." I paused. "If he gives you any earache about the door being unlocked tell him I don't want to get caught in the rain."

We drove back to his second-hand car dump just as the rain was starting up again. A few minutes later, as Twiggy got out of my motor, I grabbed one of his plastic claws. It felt horrible.

"And, Twigs?"

"Yeah?"

He was spitting through his teeth by now.

"Don't slam the fuckin' door this time."

I let go of his fake limb. He didn't answer but I'll swear he slammed my door even harder than before. At that moment in time I wanted to kill Twiggy a lot more than Kenny Marshall. He was such a useless tosspot.

On the way home I thought about Kenny Marshall and his gun and concluded there was no point in losing any sleep over it. If I was quick he'd never get a chance to use it. People not used to handling guns don't really want to actually fire them. You're going to take your time pulling that trigger if it's your first kill.

I knew that however shit-scared Marshall might be, when he saw me walking towards the motor, he'd hesitate for a moment.

He *thought* I was a hitman, but he didn't know. He couldn't be certain I was there to kill him. After all, we're mates. He'd take a moment or two to think about what the MD might do if he shot me and I was legit.

While he was considering all that, I'd kill him.

But I still didn't understand why Twiggy had bothered telling me about the gun. He either wanted an excuse to visit the location or he wanted to make sure all my attention was on Marshall and his automatic.

Another shooter would come at me from the rear, while I was all wound up with what lay ahead of me.

Then again Twiggy could have been telling the complete and utter truth. Maybe he was genuinely looking out for me. Remember, he'd have to face the MD if the whole operation turned into a bloodbath.

All this anxiety made me come up with something that might save my skin. It wouldn't take care of everything but it would certainly help.

I pulled over at a DIY store and went in.

It was bucketing down when I got home. I'd pissed away most of Saturday doing fuck all, really. I checked on the geegees and had yet another ruck with the old lady.

It wasn't a good day to be feuding. When I left the house on the Marshall job I wanted to be straight as a die not all over the shop, if you know what I mean. I needed to be calm, relaxed, so I tried to keep things as low key as possible.

I started the ball rolling about four o'clock.

"You talk to your brother?"

She was so late answering the bell for the first round that she didn't even fucking reply. I repeated myself.

"I said, did you talk …"

Then she came out defending like a real trooper.

"I heard you! I called them."

"And?"

She threw her first punch.

"What d'you care?" she jabbed. "You don't give a toss."

I hit back with a jab of my own.

"I told you. I got other things on my plate."

She then took a wild swipe that missed.

"What's more important than your family?"

I tried to duck that one.

"Give it a rest."

Then she tried a new tactic, something I'd never heard before.

"You want a rest? I'll give you a permanent fucking rest. You can bet on it. You might even win a few bob for a change."

I tried a probing left hook.

"What you on about?"

She really let loose with some nasty head shots then.

"Stop telling me what to do all the time. I've had it with you. I want out of this marriage. That clear enough for you?"

I reckoned the best offence was good defence.

"Don't be daft," I sneered stupidly.

But she was on a winning streak.

"Shall I spell it out for you?"

"Why not?"

"Tonight I'm going to stay here and if the phone rings I'll say you're asleep. That's tonight. But I might not be here tomorrow."

I got in one last body punch.

"Suit your fuckin' self."

End of round one.

Round two was short and sweet. She chucked a bit of lunch at me around 5pm and sniped, "I hope she's worth it."

I laughed and hit back.

"You're a right laugh, you are. I told you, this is business I'm going on. Business."

She laughed mockingly.

I looked her straight in the eyes. Maybe I'd ask her about her mate Kenny Marshall. A couple of seconds of silence followed as I began to take a run at it.

Then I completely bottled out.

"What d'you reckon buys all your fancy gear and that flashy little Fiat and all those theatre tickets and presents for everyone in your fuckin' family? Where's all that money come from?"

She didn't reply, just as I knew she wouldn't.

"Now fuckin' sit tight here like a good girl and do what I ask, all right?"

Just to seal my victory I walked over to her and kissed her on the forehead.

"You're my missus and there's no one else I give a flyin' fuck about."

It was the truth, even if I milked it for all it was worth. I didn't need this sort of aggro. It can be a right pain. I knew of a pro once who made a big song and dance over cheating on his old lady. She got her own back by hiring a detective to tail him. He followed this geezer right to his next hit. It ended their marriage, as well as the hitman's career.

That fight with my missus rated as a five on the ten-point Richter scale. There hadn't been that many punches, but the ones that landed did quite a bit of damage. I expected there'd be a few rematches yet.

She sat down with her knitting at about 6.30 and started watching *Blind Date*. I fucking hate that programme. I stretched out on the couch, asked her to wake me at 8pm and leaned my head back and grabbed forty winks. Cilla Black's whining Liverpudlian voice was grating through my nut so bad I could feel one of my headaches coming on.

At the end of the day there was only one thing on my mind – Kenny Marshall. I'd soaked up so much about him that my body was swelling with all that knowledge. From this moment on, until the job was completed, Kenny Marshall was going to fill my every thought. Everything I'd learned about him over the previous few weeks was doing a spaghetti junction through my brain. It was all coming at me from every direction.

This phase, the action phase, is undoubtedly the most important – and dangerous – part of any job.

It's the ultimate test and will magnify any cock-ups a hundred times. There were decisions to be made, some without much time to consider. They were decisions that were made simply by reaction.

Decisions that might cost me my life.

I splashed cold water on my face, more from habit than necessity, just to be sure I was firmly back in the land of the living. At about 8.30 I started getting ready. I don't have any special – or lucky – gear for a job. I just call it dressing to kill.

If you wear the same clobber too many times you end up being connected with a number of different hits, but I do like to dress down for a job. Grey, black and blue are the favoured colours.

For this job I picked out a pair of dark grey trousers with a plain, black shirt. I would have liked to wear a jumper, but it might get in the way if I needed to get my piece out double quick. I did allow myself the luxury of a dark blue scarf my sister-in-law knitted for me the previous Christmas.

Always dark socks and a pair of black trainers. White socks light up at night and the trainers grip the surface in all weather.

I topped that lot off with a loose-fitting black anorak. I had some warmer jackets but they all had labels that could make me easy to find.

I took off my wedding ring but left a cheap, fifty quid diver's watch on my wrist. I checked it up against the kitchen clock, which runs on Old Lady Time – ten minutes fast so my missus won't be late for her life.

I also packed two fresh pairs of transparent latex hospital

gloves. Overall I looked pretty normal, which is just what I wanted. The idea is not to stick out like a bottle of Scotch in a baptist church, but also not to look too ordinary, either.

In the real world, I wouldn't ever wear these trousers and shirt together because they don't look very inspiring. But I wasn't planning to pull any crumpet tonight.

The last thing I did before leaving the house was check on my weapons.

So as not to involve the missus, I picked up my shooters while she was out of the bedroom and locked myself in the bathroom.

I intended to carry three pieces: the new .38 which I'd got specifically to use on Marshall; the .38 I always carry in case I need extra firepower; and my dandy little mini shotgun, in case I have to shoot quickly and hit my target at 20 feet. That gun could also buy me enough time to aim my .38.

I loaded all the shooters up as I sat on the toilet. I used to wait until I'd got to the location, but then I heard one tale about a hitman who worked the same way as me, loading at the scene-of-the- crime-to-be.

Unfortunately, one night he began loading up and the ammo fell right through the chamber. He'd grabbed the wrong bullets, and the job never happened.

Now I always load before I leave.

I filled one jacket pocket with about a dozen extra shells and stuck the muffler in the other pocket, picked up the torch and checked its batteries.

Then I took a good long piss.

I left my house at about ten minutes before nine.

"What time you back?" my missus asked, sounding more curious than concerned.

"Late," I said.

"What does that mean?"

I shrugged my shoulders.

"It means when I'm finished."

She turned her back and walked away from me.

"Don't make a racket when you come in."

That was the least I could do for her.

My plan had been to grab a cab to the car park, and pick up my nicked motor, but it was still pissing down and the weather on the telly had said it was going on all night. I knew I'd never get a cab in this weather, so I took my own motor, which was risky in case it got ticketed or something while I was knocking off my target. But I didn't have much choice.

As I drove over to Camberwell I wondered exactly what Kenny Marshall was up to. He was probably finishing off his last supper at that moment.

The nicked Beemer started first time in the car park. It took me around 20 minutes to get over to Bexley Village. I deliberately went very slowly.

When I got there I drove through it as if I was on the way somewhere. I took a careful look around but there was nothing happening.

Then I drove through the other way. And a third time. You could have heard an ant running on the tarmac. It was that quiet.

I turned the motor around one last time and went through the village from the other direction. No sign of life. I parked it up and sat there in complete silence for a few minutes, just looking around. The rain made the streets glisten as if they'd been scrubbed clean for a special occasion. It was cold and there wasn't a soul out on the streets.

I was totally alone.

I gripped the steering wheel hard and felt those latex gloves tightening around my fingertips. The old chap stirred. What I wouldn't have given for naughty night nurse Cat complete with her own black rubber gloves and platform boots.

But now it was down to business.

Chapter Twenty-Three

On my manor we call Kenny Marshall's problems "A 3-Card Trick". That's the moment when all the cards come tumbling down; birds, booze and gambling. He'd only just scraped through to qualify for two out of three.

And that set me off thinking as I waited there in the dark.

About Marshall.

About him and my missus.

About Twiggy.

About the next two hours.

Like a boxer in the last few moments before entering the ring, or footballers huddled in the changing room before kick-off, I was psyching myself up to kill Kenny Marshall.

It had to be done.

I've learned one fucking important thing in this game. When you kill someone, you've really got to hate them, or at least hate what they represent. Every time I pull that trigger I'm killing the people who killed my first wife all over again. Killing those pieces of scum. That's why it doesn't really bother me.

And Marshall was one of them, no matter the cut of his suit or how good his manners were. He was vermin like the rest of them.

I know you've heard all this before but I want you to understand just how bitter I am about what happened to my first wife.

Bitter equals guilt and guilt equals obsession and obsession equals violence.

As I sat there, climbing some imaginary mountain of retribution, all this stuff raced through my head. But on the surface I was calm, collected, and totally prepared. You have to be in this game. I parked the motor, just as I'd told Twiggy I would do, about 20 yards from where I expected Marshall to pull up.

It was at a spot where I could watch him from the back door of the block of flats.

I checked my weapons one last time and then got out of the motor and walked the area. I looked in all directions, taking in everything. The excitement was so intense it felt like steel-winged butterflies were flying around in my stomach, getting faster by the second.

No matter how many jobs you do there is this surge of power that rushes through you during that final countdown. I could feel that familiar tingling from the tip of my dick to the tip of my toes as I waited and watched for Marshall to show up.

It felt fucking brilliant.

A controller like him is never late. They have to be on time because their schedule is usually so tight. I didn't know for sure where he'd be coming from but I presumed it had to be his house. That meant at about 10.15 he'd get in his motor to set off for our little appointment.

Meanwhile, I was on the lookout for any bodies that might look like they were Marshall's or Twiggy's pals. But it remained silent as stone, apart from the rain drops hitting the concrete.

Then I thought about Twiggy again. If he was going to hit me this evening he'd be turning up early as well.

I eventually strolled casually in to the block of flats. The back entrance was still open. The bulb hadn't been replaced and so the hallway was dark. I stepped inside and stood watch, out of the cold. It was 10.25.

I was approaching that magic point when thinking ceases and movements and reactions kick in.

I could hear myself taking short, sharp breaths. They felt very loud but, of course, I was the only one hearing them. The buzz was making me feel a little bit frisky.

First it was a feeling of disconnection from reality.

Then my thoughts came fast and furious.

Vivid images kept snapping past me.

My first wife arrived and stayed for a while.

Then an image of my .38, a beautiful piece of precision engineering.

I saw what happened when I pulled the trigger.

I watched as the bullet spun towards its final destination. Then it exploded in Marshall's skull. A poetic sight.

He's on the floor. No movement. No sound. Nothing.

Then those fast-changing images died and were replaced by my blanking-out process. If a human being can travel back through time and bring back all his animal instincts then this is the moment. Pressure of life, money, work, relationships. All of that didn't mean a fuck. Now it was down to basics – survival of the fittest. Me.

I was at my peak but I knew it would soon all start to fade. Emotion was trying to battle its way back into my head. Trying to drag me into middle-ground, half-thinking, half-caring, half-reacting. I fought back against the change. It was all a sign that the trigger should be pulled sooner rather than later.

At 19 minutes before 11 a black Audi drifted down the street. As it passed my motor it slowed to a snail's pace before picking up speed once again and heading off up the street.

Another 20 yards or so, just out of my vision beyond the back door of the block of flats, I heard it stop.

I opened the back door slightly so I could arch round and see what was happening.

Nothing. The driver was just sitting there. It wasn't Marshall.

But in the dark I couldn't be sure exactly who it was. I slipped out of the door and moved alongside the wall of the building towards my motor.

I reached under my jacket and pulled out that new .38 just as I saw the driver's door of that other car open. A shadowy figure struggled to get out and then turned towards my vehicle. I shoved my hand in my outside jacket pocket, pulled out the silencer, and screwed it on while still watching his every movement.

As he'd opened the door the interior light had flicked on for a split second and then I'd heard a familiar noise.

HISSSSS!

Twiggy had come to say farewell.

I watched as he lumbered towards my motor.

He must have expected to find my body slumped in the front seat.

Someone was supposed to have knocked me off before he arrived. I wanted to see his reaction when he realised I was very much alive and kicking. As he got nearer to the motor he brought his pink plastic limbs up in the air at an awkward angle, almost like he was surrendering, but he couldn't get them up very high. What the fuck was Twiggy up to?

Then he got to the motor and peered in. His head shot back up in a millisecond. He knew I was out there and he knew I had him in my sight.

Twiggy stepped back sharpish from the motor, but didn't try to run. Instead, he took a look around, slowly at first, but then faster and faster. I could see the steam of his breath backlit by a distant street light. That old familiar hissing sound came drifting across when he made a significant movement.

I slipped along the side of the building to get nearer to him, keeping my body flat against the wall. I didn't make a sound.

At the corner of the building I was about 25 feet from the motor. Twiggy was standing on the other side, in the street, with a mass of German steel between him and me. I'd never get him so I waited.

I still felt on an invincible high. I knew I had to keep hitting the spot.

Whatever Twiggy's game was, it had gone seriously wrong because I was about to wipe him out. Then he let his prosthetic arms drop back down, leaned his body slightly and began moving towards the back of the car.

His silhouette made him look like some sort of cumbersome, demented ape. I picked a target spot about six feet behind the motor. When he got there I'd squeeze the trigger.

Problem was Twiggy didn't seem in a hurry. His head was moving from side to side, then he'd rock on his heels to take a swift gander to see if I was moving in behind him.

Slowly, he got nearer and nearer to my designated spot.

I flicked the safety off the .38 and levelled it. Twiggy continued ambling towards his own execution. Then stopped, looked around and in a low, urgent voice rasped in the direction of where he thought I'd be hiding.

"Malcolm! Malcolm! Where the fuck are you?"

It saved his life.

Keeping completely back in the dark, I called back in a low voice.

"Keep the fuckin' claws up in the air and walk to the middle of the road."

In the silence our voices seemed incredibly loud.

As he moved away from the car, pink plastic arms up as high as he could get them, I darted in behind him and grabbed the collar of his coat. I threw him across the car bonnet and heard the prosthetic limbs clatter against the metal.

"What the fuck ..."

I poked the gun hard enough into his forehead to make a permanent dent.

"You've got ten seconds to tell me what the fuck you're doin' here."

He tried to stand up straight.

"Leave it out ..."

I kicked his legs away from under him and he keeled over like a shopwindow dummy. And I was still counting.

"Ten. Nine."

I looked behind me. No one.

Then I pressed the heel of my shoe hard into his cheek. So hard I could feel his dentures wobble as I continued counting.

"Come off it, Malcolm. I'm not here to take you out ..."

I knew then he was probably right. He couldn't talk very clearly with his mouth being pushed up against the tarmac so I pulled him to his feet, but kept his back to me.

"You got six seconds. Five."

I couldn't see his mouth but I'm sure his tongue was working overtime.

"I came to tell you Marshall's bringing help with him tonight."

I stopped counting.

"Go on."

"One of his two rastaboys called us today and said Marshall had hired them for a job tonight."

The dropping temperatures turned our breath into even whiter puffs of smoke as we spoke. I could hear the fear in Twiggy's voice. And his dog breath smelt like he was rotting from the inside.

"What you on about?" I snapped back at him.

"What am I on about? I'm fuckin' on about Marshall telling them he wants back-up for this meet."

It was a good move on Marshall's part. He had to have some sort of get-out plan.

"Why didn't you get hold of me earlier?" I asked.

"I tried," he said, still breathless. "Been calling Careful all fuckin' afternoon and evening. Couldn't raise him and I don't know how to get you direct. I had to come out myself. For fuck's sake."

He sounded genuine. But all these unanswered questions were still exploding inside my head.

"What about that cabbie?" I asked him.

"What fuckin' cabbie?"

"Don't gimme that crap!" I said. "Otherwise I'll fuckin' blow you away!"

It was the obvious solution and I was sorely tempted.

"That cabbie who tried to run me over, that's what I'm on about."

"You're fuckin' losin' it, mate. When I settle with someone, I do it myself. No hired gun ..." he looked at me at that moment, "... settles my personal scores."

For a geezer whose life was hanging by a thread, Twiggy was doing a superb job answering my questions.

I didn't know what the fuck to do, but I knew I had to do it fast.

Marshall was due any minute and I didn't want him dipping his headlights at me as I pointed a .38 at Twiggy. He'd take off on a runner that wouldn't end 'til he got to fucking Rio or wherever. So I decided to tow Twiggy along.

"Turn around and keep those fuckin' claws up in the air."

Then, as I quickly patted him down, it suddenly dawned on me that armless Twiggy couldn't have fired off a piece even if he'd wanted to.

"You're a wanker, Twigs. Not a cunt 'cos cunts have character." I had to get it off my chest. "D'you understand? You're a fuckin' wanker."

Then I held back for a second to see if he showed any signs of remorse. Nothing.

So I continued ...

"You been after me a long time, Twigs. It all makes sense."

He laughed half-heartedly.

"So you thought I ..."

"I still do," I said, interrupting.

At last we were talking the same language. A hundred thoughts flashed through my head. If Marshall didn't show up I'd know Twiggy was behind the entire scam. Then I'd definitely have to pop him.

"Take your belt off," I told him.

"Leave it out," he grizzled.

"Take the fuckin' belt off. NOW!"

Then I realised he'd take all night on account of those plastic crab's claws. So I grabbed the eye of the belt with one hand and yanked it until the belt came loose. Twiggy's strides hit the deck. Not a pleasant sight. He stood there in a pair of grey, baggy Y-fronts. Then he tried to hook the trousers back up and went down like a sack of potatoes.

"Don't move," I barked down at him.

He looked like a beached whale. I ordered him to put his plastic hooks behind his back and wrapped the belt around them as tightly as I could. Then I pulled up the back of his trousers so that he could hold on to them with one of the hooks behind his back.

He wouldn't be running off anywhere. Now I had some extra time.

Just then Twiggy let off an all-too-familiar HISSSS!

I ignored it at first but when it didn't stop I wondered what the fuck was going on.

HISSSSS!

"Knock it off, Twigs."

HISSSSS!

Suddenly Twigs' plastic arms started flailing around wildly, fighting against the belt that held them behind his back.

"Cut it out, Twigs," I shouted.

HISSSSS!

"I can't."

I pointed my shooter right at him.

"Bye-bye, Twigs ..."

"For fuck's sake! I'm not doin' it on purpose!"

My finger began squeezing on the trigger slowly so he could see I meant business.

"Pressure pump musta smashed when I fell over," he whispered hoarsely.

HISSSSS!

Twiggy's plastic limbs were clattering around like Pinocchio on speed. I put the gun away.

This had to be sorted before Marshall showed up.

HISSSSSS!

It sounded like one of those espresso coffee-making machines – only louder. I leaned down, pulled open his shirt, exposing the metal canister pressure pump. Twiggy arched his neck to take a look at what I was doing. Sheets of rain were driving across us both. His arms were still jerking all over the place and I was running out of patience.

"There's a switch under the canister," he wheezed breathlessly.

I found it and pushed my thumb down on it hard but nothing happened. I pulled my shooter out again.

Twiggy almost shat a basketful of bricks on the spot.

Then I turned the gun around and smashed the butt down on his pressure pump. After three mad swings it finally fell off with a clump. Twiggy's supernatural arms fell dead. He looked mortified. I'd just wrecked his ability to eat, drink, drive and fuck in three swipes of a gun butt.

Then I hauled him up with one hand, which wasn't easy, and prodded the .38 in his ribs.

"Over there."

I walked and he waddled like a penguin over to his motor where I turned off the ignition.

Then I dropped the keys in my pocket.

And Twiggy carried on moaning and groaning.

"When the MD finds out ..."

"Shut it!"

I pushed him in through the back door of the block of flats and brought him into the hallway with me.

"Sit down!"

"I'm fuckin' soaked," grizzled Twiggy.

"And stop fuckin' moanin'."

I made him sit on the floor. Then I leaned down and shoved the notch of the barrel half an inch up his left nostril. His tongue was wearing away his top lip. His eyes were huge balls of sickly grey in a bloodshot sea.

"I want some fuckin' answers," I said quietly. "Who's been on my tail while I've been watchin' Marshall?"

"His two blagger boys. They only told me tonight. Marshall got 'em to follow him for back-up. They picked you up, but they told Marshall it was all a coincidence."

"What the fuck did they go and tell him that for?"

Twiggy looked a bit diverted by something. I noticed a big wet patch appearing on his trousers.

Then I smelt his last pint of bitter.

"Malcolm," he snivelled, "those geezers are on our payroll now. They know that when Marshall dies they'll live. They ain't gonna help him, I swear."

It's got to be worth noting here that Twiggy was, after all, talking for his life. If his answers got on my nerves, I'd blow him away on the spot. We both knew that and the puddle on the floor proved it, too.

"You knew they were tailin' me?" I said.

"I told you, we only found out today. They hadn't told us earlier 'cos they didn't think it was important ..."

"Well, it fuckin' is now," I pointed out.

"They're a pair of right fuckin' idiots," continued Twiggy, "they only belled us about it when Marshall asked them to tool up for some protection."

"But they tailed me when I was in my own motor? They've got my number plate. They could tag me to the filth if they wanted. What's the score with that, then?"

"There's no way they'll tag you, Malcolm," he said. "It won't happen."

"What makes you so fuckin' sure?"

A lot of lives, the two rastaboys, Twiggy's, even Marshall's, depended on his reply. If I didn't like the sound of it, I'd have to put Marshall's hit on ice for a while.

"It's obvious ..." said Twiggy, who seemed to be gaining a bit of confidence now that his death sentence had been put on hold. "They'll end up six feet under if they grass you up. The MD would have 'em both put down instantly."

It all made sense. Those young blaggers might be a bit slow, but they definitely wanted to continue drinking Ribenas. My real problem was Twiggy. Shooting him was the easy solution. I'd tell the MD some load of rubbish, like he got in the way of some friendly fire. So what? Then I realised that if he wasn't telling porkies, Twiggy had come out here, at considerable risk to himself, to help me.

"Why d'you come here if you fuckin' hate me so much?"

"I got a job to do and that's to make sure Marshall is done. The MD asked for you so I got you. I have to see it through. But I promise you – none of this was for you."

I couldn't fault Twiggy for his honesty, which probably meant I'd have to give him the benefit of the doubt. I'd never have coughed to as much as he had, but then I'm a bit of a sneaky bastard when I want to be.

There was still one question bugging the life out of me,

though. It had to be sorted there and then. It was almost 11 and Marshall would be on the scene at any moment.

So I steamed in: "Here's the big one, Twigs. Get this right and you win the fuckin' jackpot. What were you doin' at Marshall's house the other night?"

Twiggy didn't even pause for breath.

"His old mum had a heart attack and he couldn't get over to the office and to the hospital in time for visiting hours. So I picked up the takings."

'Just like that?" I said.

"Yeah. Just like that."

"Who d'you think you are? Fuckin' Tommy Cooper?"

I didn't expect Twiggy to get it, but he smiled. I believed him. I wouldn't swear by him, but I believed him. He'd just prolonged his life expectancy. Now back to the main problem – Kenny Marshall.

I couldn't knock him off with witnesses around, even if those white rastaboys were in the MD's pocket. If they saw me killing Marshall they'd have to go as well, and two more bodies could cause me a lot of hassle. The filth don't give a toss about one villain getting knocked off, but when three go down, it turns into what the papers call a manhunt.

Remember those three E merchants over in Essex who got blasted as they sat in their Range Rover? Boys in blue went ballistic over that one. Then I decided to test the water.

"Maybe I don't think it's the right time to do it," I said.

"Then he's off on that big white bird on Monday. Fuckin' one-way ticket to Ronnie Biggs' back yard."

"What about his mum?"

What sort of stupid fucking question was that?

"She'll live."

I asked him one last time if he thought Marshall knew he was the target. He shrugged his shoulders.

"He might know now. But when I spoke to him this morning he didn't. His mind's on other things."

I knew the feeling. I'd go ahead and kill Marshall but plan A was already out of the window. I couldn't shoot him here. Twiggy was here. The two rastas were still here somewhere. Half of fucking Scotland Yard could be out there by now for all I knew.

Plan B needed to be something quick, clean and easy. Then I made a very dangerous decision. For the first time in my career I decided to just play it by ear. I'd wait and see how it all panned out.

The-man-with-the-plan now had nothing but gut instinct to go on.

All I had over Marshall was the fact I *knew* I had to kill him while he could only suspect what I was up to. Twiggy sat quietly slumped on the floor. The waft of piss reminded me of the bog at Bexleyheath Secondary Modern. I checked my watch. It was just after 11.

"I hope you're not tellin' me porkies," I said to Twiggy, without taking my eyes away from the window, " 'cos if Marshall doesn't show, I'll know you stitched me up." I looked down at him very quickly. "And then you'll get the bullet."

Twiggy looked pathetically at the floor when I glanced at him. One minute had passed. A second minute passed. Still nothing happening outside.

It was 11:06.

Twiggy started shaking. His skin looked a bit green and his eyes were closed. I checked his belt and leaned down behind him to loosen it a notch. Then I realised he could easily slip out of the belt if he disengaged his pink plastic limbs, which were pretty useless anyway. I pressed my shooter into his earhole and he stirred.

"Get over there," I said waving the weapon in the direction of a fat heating pipe that ran from the floor to ceiling.

"What?"

I didn't answer. I grabbed his collar and dragged him across the floor by his jacket, leaving a trail of piss behind him. Then I pushed his back up against the pipe and undid the belt behind his back.

"What's happenin'?"

"You'll find out soon enough."

I pulled off his soaked jacket and ripped the arms off his shirt, exposing his two prosthetic lifelines.

"What you doin'?"

Without uttering a word in reply, I undid the leather braces that held his left arm in place and pulled the plastic arm off his elbow socket.

Then I did the same with his right arm, leaving two red stumps of flesh.

I chucked the fake limbs into a huge refuse bin just outside the door. Then I span him around by his ankles and put his feet up against the central heating pipe. I weaved the belt around his feet and then behind the enormous pipe. Twiggy had even stopped whinging by this time, which made it all a lot easier.

Half a minute later I heard an engine running outside. The silver Merc, with those two bimbos in the front, sailed by slowly. Hopefully that meant Marshall would be just behind them. Two minutes later my target drew up in the space he'd been directed to.

Marshall left his engine running as he sat there. He was no doubt looking in all directions. Then he turned the car engine off, and switched out his lights. Long, thin shadows from the branches of an overhanging tree flickered across the inside of Marshall's vehicle.

Marshall leaned across the front seat and opened the latch on the passenger side. Then he clasped his hands behind his head and stretched back on the headrest. He was sitting comfortably.

I watched. I knew his automatic was sitting on the seat next to him. If he was really scared, the moment he spotted me he'd start shooting.

So I held back inside to give him time to cool down, let the tension ease up. Get him more used to his surroundings. The peace and quiet of a nice little Kent village. I remained just inside the doorway, hands at my side, watching him and panning the area. I'm certain his eyes moved more than once to the rear- view.

And so we waited. I don't really know what for. Perhaps it was for the perfect moment when the man on the diving board feels totally up for it.

But it had to be soon.

I watched for the lights of the Merc on the rear window of Marshall's car, because I couldn't see back down the road. But Marshall's two lapdogs didn't seem to have returned. Everything else attracted my constant attention. When the wind blew up a bit I wanted to know why. Were the filth hanging about waiting for me to make a move? Were there any punters out and about?

Down on the stone floor, Twiggy lay wet and quiet, except for an irritating wheeze. At least the hissing had stopped. It was still possible Twiggy had pulled me into a trap and when I was halfway to Marshall's motor his two cowboys would open fire on me.

At almost 11.30 I took a long, deep breath, checked my muffler was properly screwed on, and began to move towards opening the door. Then, just as I my hand turned the knob, Marshall moved around in his motor. I went motionless. Had he seen me?

What the hell was he up to?

His car door opened and he stepped out. I moved away from the door back into the shadows. Marshall looked around, carefully walked to the front of his car and stopped. What he did next turned out to be yet another surprise – the sort of thing that had been plaguing this frigging job since day one.

He did something I never thought I'd ever see a target do just before he met his maker.

He pulled down his trousers and took a crap.

Right there in the middle of a little Kent village, Kenny Marshall was taking his last crap. At least it proved he was worried. Inside, I was laughing.

In some ways Marshall was a lucky man because taking a crap is a luxury no hitman could afford out in the field. If I'm about to pull the trigger and I've got to take even a piss, I have to hold it back or piss in my pants, which ain't pleasant. Taking a shit is simply not allowed. That's why on the day of every job I'm super careful about what I eat.

No fruit, beans or orange juice because that's what makes you unload. All this seemed to indicate that Kenny fucking Marshall had only a vague idea he might be enjoying his last day on this planet. Cocky bastard even had a box of tissues next to him. Marshall sorted himself out, jumped up sprightly and walked back to the side of the motor.

He took another look in all directions and stretched before taking off his jacket and throwing it across the front seat. It was real brass monkey weather that night. Yet Marshall was sweating enough to have to take off his jacket, as he stood there, leaning against his motor, waiting.

I squinted hard and just made out the black grip, shoved into his belt, of a shooter.

That's when I began to get a bit shaky myself.

Under my breath I muttered something like, "Get back in the motor, you fuckin' pratt."

"What?" Twiggy whispered up at me.

"Button it," I whispered. It was an order.

I hung back because there was no way I could move out into the open with him standing outside. He could leg it in any fucking direction he chose. I wanted him in the front seat of that motor, trapped like a slug in a kid's jam jar.

Finally, he climbed back in the car. Now I could get down to business.

The .38 was still in my hand as I got to the door. Twiggy's eyes were focused right on the barrel as I turned towards him. I paused a moment. He shut his eyes really tight. He must have been saying a prayer. I pushed the tip of the barrel right up against his closed left eyelid.

"Keep 'em shut." I paused for effect. "There's a good boy ..."

His eyelids fluttered nervously but the shutters stayed down. I pressed the gun nozzle harder into his eyeball.

"If you're tellin' porkies I need to know now."

The eyelid without the gun barrel pressing against it opened. The iris was setting and closing like a flower blooming in slow-motion.

"Shut it!"

He immediately did as he was told.

I switched the barrel to that eyelid.

"No more chances, Twigs."

He didn't utter a sound. I left the nozzle there for a few seconds longer, then I pulled the gun away.

I checked to see I hadn't put the safety catch back on. I hadn't. Then I stuck it back in my trousers, keeping my latex mit on the handle. Twiggy's eyes remained firmly closed.

I reached into my pocket and pulled out the torch. Bending down close to the ground, so there'd be no reflection, I flicked it on and off quickly. It worked perfectly.

At that moment Twiggy opened his eyes again. I don't think he could quite believe he was still alive. I put my finger to my lips. He got the message.

I reached into my trouser pocket and silently dropped his car keys between a crack in the floor. After one more long, deep breath, I checked the .38 a final time and headed towards the door. Kenny and I were going for a drive.

I left Twiggy crumpled up there looking like that fresh lump of steaming, rancid turd Kenny Marshall had just deposited on the gleaming, rain-soaked tarmac.

Chapter Twenty-Four

It had stopped raining. The only noise was the squeaking of a swing as it moved gently backwards and forwards in the playground opposite.

Perhaps someone had been sitting on it a few moments earlier.

I started walking towards Marshall's car. Slowly at first, then I upped the pace a bit. It was about 30 yards between the building and his motor. Normally I'd cover it in less than 30 seconds. I don't know how long it took that night, but it seemed like a fucking eternity.

Twiggy, still lying in a puddle of his own piss, was long forgotten, a part of my distant past.

Everything was now. The moment.

I split that 30-yard walk into three different compartments in my brain. The first ten yards I looked to my sides and behind me, trying to see that silver Merc carrying the two white rastaboys, or spot anyone who might hit me from behind. I couldn't see the Merc, maybe they'd scarpered. There was fuck-all happening behind me.

As I walked I went right through a big puddle which I didn't even notice until my shoes and socks felt soaked. That helped make me angrier.

The middle ten yards I studied every inch of the area in front of me. I made visual arcs, something I'd learned in the army, each a bit wider and deeper than the one before it. If anyone was going to bounce out of the playground towards me I needed to pick him up super-fucking-fast.

The final ten yards belonged to the Kenny Marshall compartment of my brain. I upped my pace, but not too much. As I made my way towards him he must have been bricking it.

Bricking it to be there.

Bricking it about meeting somebody.

Bricking it because he was holding a loaded shooter in his hand.

If he did pull that trigger instantly, the odds of me walking away were not good. I needed to give him the sort of surprise that would stop him shooting on sight. I put my left hand into my belt and pulled the new .38 free. But I still kept it under my coat, completely concealed.

I took another look over my shoulder, just to be sure the silver Merc wasn't around.

Maybe I could still just bang him and walk away. No, I couldn't risk it. Unlike Twiggy I remained convinced they'd grass me up if plod did the asking.

I pulled my .38 out of my belt but kept it tucked inside my jacket.

Just then I sensed something else was wrong. Badly wrong. But I couldn't make out what it was. Don't you hate that feeling? You know there's a problem but you can't work out what it is.

It was only when I looked down at my hand gripping the handle of my gun inside my coat that I realised I still had on those latex gloves.

Marshall would go into a blind panic if he spotted them.

I put the gun back in my belt and stopped by the wall. I could only get one hot, sweaty glove off in time. So I shoved the other hand in my pocket and hoped he wouldn't notice. Five yards from Marshall's car I looked straight at the back of his head and I'll swear I caught his eyes in the rear-view mirror. He shifted his body so he was facing the passenger door. I knew that shooter was gripped in his hand.

I stayed as close as I could to the motor and got into the blind spot between the back window and the rear window on the left side of the motor. The only noise was the rain which had started falling lightly again and was splattering on the car. I stuck my left arm as far away from my body as I could, pointed the torch right where I guessed Marshall's head would be, and turned the beam on.

Nothing happened.

Normally I'd expect a bloke to blast away the moment the light went on. As long as my body wasn't behind it, I wouldn't get too badly hurt.

But he didn't fire and I ripped the door open so fast it almost bounced back on me.

As predicted, he was holding the piece in his right hand pointing it more or less in my direction. His eyes were beady and he did a swift Twiggy with his tongue.

"How you doin', Kenny?" I said as calmly as I could.

I slid into the passenger seat to find myself looking down the barrel of a gun for the first time in years. Marshall had a sort of blank, deer-caught-in-the-headlights look on his face. He was sweating buckets. He knew who I was, but he couldn't work out what I was doing there. He guessed I was a hitman, but he didn't know he was my target.

So he did nothing.

Kenny Marshall just sat there with his gun pointing right at me looked fucking terrified. Moving ever so slowly, I wiped the shooter away from my direction with the tip of my finger on the end of his barrel.

"My old man," I said quietly, "told me never to point weapons at people unless I planned to shoot them. Silly old sod didn't even like me using my water pistol."

I took my other hand off my own piece, but it was a great comfort to feel the bulk of it in my waistband, easily accessible. Just then Marshall snapped out of his trance.

"Hello, Malcolm," he said, almost brightly. "Didn't expect to see you here."

I smiled.

"Can't beat a surprise party, can you?"

Marshall didn't know how to handle it. Was he the target, or what? He should have just plugged me full of holes on the spot but he wasn't used to handling a gun so he hesitated, and hesitated.

"Depends who gets the surprise?" Marshall said finally.

It was a cool reply in the circumstances.

"Let's get goin'."

"Where to?"

"I'll tell you as we go."

He put his piece on the armrest between the front seats, turned forward and started the motor.

"What's that torch in aid of?" he asked as naturally as he could, but I knew he was very curious.

"It's dark out. Had to be certain it was you in the motor ..." I looked down. "What's the shooter for?"

He tried to act casual.

"I didn't know who I was meeting. Been havin' a few hassles recently with certain people."

"Hassles? What kinda hassles?" I asked, as if I didn't know.

"Hassles," he repeated.

But he didn't elaborate.

As Marshall started backing up the motor I took a long look in the vanity mirror of the sun visor. About 50 yards back a pair of headlights flashed on and off, then stayed on. The two muppets were back in their Merc. Then I picked up his gun and looked across for his reaction. It was a 9mm Glock. Kenny Marshall really was an amateur. He tried not to notice as I played with the gun in my hand.

"These Glocks are a liability, Kenny," I said.

I swung further towards him, gripping the gun tightly and looked straight at him.

"Fuckin' casings go everywhere ..." I paused. "And they have this dodgy safety catch on the trigger."

He couldn't take his eyes off my forefinger lightly stroking the trigger.

Then Marshall tried to prove he was a gunsmith.

"But all you have to do is squeeze the trigger lightly and it comes off automatically."

Marshall was trying to drive and watch that trigger all at the same time.

"That's right," I said, quietly. "Squeeze a bit harder and ..." I turned the gun right towards him then. "Pop pop. You're

238

dead." We looked right at each other that moment. "I told you, they're a fuckin' liability."

I turned away. I didn't want to freak him out yet. We had a journey to take first. I also had to lose that tail and decide where to take him.

"Head out towards Swanley," I told him. I knew I'd come up with something. Secluded country lanes would make it easier to lose a tail that didn't want to be attached in any case. Those blaggerboys knew the MD held the key to their future, so they weren't going to be too serious about following Marshall, especially once he made it clear he was trying to lose them.

"Yeah," I said calmly, trying to set something up. "I know what you mean about hassles. I got a few of them myself. That's why I brought the torch."

"What's up with you, then?" said Marshall, trying not to sound too interested.

"Just hassles," I said.

We both laughed. He seemed to be relaxing. We headed silently down the M2 as I tried to think of a location Marshall would find acceptable.

My first thought was a deserted layby under the triple flyover junction of the M2/M20/M25. But Marshall's supposed to be fingering someone, that's the cover story, so I knew he wouldn't fall for such an isolated spot.

Where would he expect to find a crowd? The answer was pretty obvious: at a boozer. That meant a nice big, dark boozer car park. I thought of boozers I knew out in the sticks with big car parks.

"When you get to the Swanley turn-off," I told him, "take the West Kingsdown road."

He nodded. It was only then I noticed his driving wasn't too hot. Maybe it was his nerves, but he kept cutting corners and not stopping at roundabouts. I really don't appreciate bad driving. I had Kenny Marshall's life in my hands that night, just so long as his driving didn't mean he had mine in his. I'd have said something about his driving but I didn't want to get the target upset at such a crucial stage of the job.

We sat there in silence for a while which also wasn't healthy because it gave him a chance to think up all sorts of plots. A bit of diversionary conversation was required.

"How's your old mum doin'?"

"Better," he said, a bit surprised at my question. "Doc called it a mild heart attack. Bit of a warning, really."

"Yeah, but you gotta take those sorta warnings seriously," I said.

Just then, Marshall swerved the car round a corner and nearly mounted the bank of the road. I don't think he even noticed the look of fear on my face caused by his fucking awful driving, although I did mutter something along the lines of "Take it easy, Kenny."

Another awkward silence followed for a minute or two.

"You know, Malcolm," Marshall eventually said, "we ain't been that close over the years, but I'm fuckin' glad it was you out there tonight. Thought I might be for the chop, if you know what I mean?"

I pursed my lips together and slowly nodded in agreement.

"Yeah, I know exactly what you mean."

If he'd been so happy to see me then why didn't he tell the two rastaboys to pull out. I still believed he was trying to lead me into a corner. Then I leaned forward and looked in the rear-view.

"Think we got company."

He made a big show of squinting into the mirror.

"You sure?"

"They've been with us since we left the village."

"They wouldn't be tailing us?"

"Not us," I said, "me. Told you I had a few hassles."

Marshall went quiet. I'd thrown him right off his guard. He couldn't tell me about his cowboys because he was supposed to be on a legit job with no need for personal muscle.

"You're gettin' too fuckin' paranoid," he said.

I chose to ignore that remark.

"Bang a right here."

It was pitch dark and we were just entering West Kingsdown, a well-known Kent village filled with huge fuck-off modern detached homes. Many of them have been built with the proceeds of some of the area's most legendary crimes. It's where numerous south-east London villains go once they've earned their first million. First right took us down a quiet residential street. We then did three more turns in slow succession.

Marshall was driving like an old dear out on a Sunday outing. The silver Merc stayed behind us.

Then I noticed him nervously checking it out in the rearview.

"Fuckin' told you," I said impatiently.

"Jesus," he said almost as believably, as he squinted in the mirror again.

"We gotta get shot of this lot," I said.

"How do we do that, then?"

Without warning I jammed my right foot down on top of his right foot, sending the pedal to the floor. The car reared up and took off at a gallop. I kept it slammed down until we were doing about 50 on a narrow road, passing a row of shops followed by some dull-looking grey-brick bungalows.

Then I let my foot off his.

"For fuck's sake, Malcolm. You'll get us killed."

"No chance," I said.

Then we made a few turns and shot out of a junction. The Merc had gone.

We headed towards a roundabout that would send us back on to the M2 in yet another one of those uncomfortable silences. Five minutes later, Marshall cut through the atmosphere like a runaway Chieftain.

"What's gonna happen to this bloke after I put the finger on him?"

A perfectly reasonable question under the circumstances. But I didn't want to answer it. I shrugged my shoulders.

"Not a lot. Just need to know he's the right man."

"Right man for what?" asked Marshall, who knew the answer to the question before he'd asked it.

I didn't respond. It would just make him more worried. But it didn't stop him blabbering.

"If you're gonna pop him, I don't want no part of it."

"Chill out, Kenny …" I paused and smiled. "Who d'you think I am, a fuckin' hitman or somethin'?"

His head rolled from side to side for a second then. It would have dropped off if the hinges had snapped.

"Well," he said slowly, "I've heard rumours. You got a reputation."

"Reputation for what?" I asked.

"You know …" he said.

I couldn't resist the next bit.

"If I was a hitman, Kenny, you shoulda blasted away when you saw it was me. I could've been sent by whoever you've got hassles with."

Just then, Marshall swerved across the centre lane of the motorway in front of a juggernaut. I crouched down with my hands over my head ready for impact. Somehow, we missed the artic and Kenny looped back into the centre lane. I noticed his eyeballs were flaring and watering all at the same time.

Instead of shouting and screaming at him I said, "Don't worry, Kenny. You're in safe hands."

As we went over the flyover junction between the M2 and M20, I focused my sight on his head and picked out a bullseye, just behind his bitten-up left ear.

I don't usually get this close to a punter, three feet is normally just fine, but here I was less than two feet away and if I stretched my arm out I'd have cut it to point blank range. But then bits of his head would splatter all over me. Not very pleasant.

Just then Marshall interrupted my train of thought, which was a bit irritating.

"Remember that tosser Bob Townley we was at school with?" asked Marshall.

I snapped straight back into present time.

"Yeah," I said. "I heard you was biffing his old lady …"

Before I'd even finished saying it I knew I'd just been a complete pratt. I only knew about it because it had been in that file Twiggy provided. An incredibly uncomfortable wall of silence followed.

"How d'you fuckin' know?" said Marshall.

"Everyone on the fuckin' manor knows."

"Bollocks. We haven't told a soul."

"Well, I heard it from two different people."

"Who?"

"I can't fuckin' tell you that, can I?"

But he wouldn't let it rest.

"I don't fuckin' believe you."

"Look, Kenny, it's not a big deal, mate. We all put it about a bit. You know what birds are like, they yap to all their mates."

"You sayin' she told someone?"

"If your missus was knobbin' some geezer d'you really think she wouldn't tell her best mates?"

A few more awkward seconds of silence followed. Then I decided the best line of defence was attack.

"Bet she's a right little goer," I said.

Marshall didn't know which way to turn.

"Best fuck I've ever had," he said proudly.

"That's what I said about your old lady when I had her in your four-poster," I said winking.

Marshall looked confused.

"How d'you know we got a four-poster?"

I didn't like the way he was staring at me. Then he slapped the steering wheel and chuckled. Silly wanker thought it was all a game. He was like that at school. Too anxious to please. Then I thought about him and my old lady.

"If my missus was cheatin' on me I'd have her and her boyfriend plugged."

I'll swear Kenny Marshall's face went a strange shade of green and his hands gripped the steering wheel extra tightly. Marshall couldn't make up his mind if we were about to become re-acquainted best friends or something much worse. Just then we narrowly missed hitting a newspaper van in the slow lane of the dual carriageway.

I didn't say a word.

Then Marshall tried a different tack.

"Got any birds on the go?" he asked.

"There's one on the boil," I answered.

"Bet she's some tasty young blonde," he said, trying hard to be matey.

"Nah. I prefer brassy older ones any day. Young birds give you nothin' but aggro," I told him.

Having a decent chinwag made the time go faster and seemed to help keep him calm.

So I carried on.

"Older women are more of a laugh and they're not so fuckin' demanding." Marshall nodded in agreement but I don't reckon he understood what I meant.

"Yeah," I said, "there's only two golden rules when it comes to totty."

Marshall nodded nervously.

"They've gotta be into sex. Might sound obvious but there's loadsa birds out there who wouldn't know a glass of spunk from a marguerita. All they're on the lookout for is some real luuuve ..."

Marshall chipped in.

"And we don't want any of that romantic stuff, do we?"

Maybe he'd finally got a handle on what I was on about. So I continued with my totty thesis.

"And, of course, they've got to have a good sense of humour ..."

"Goes without saying," agreed Marshall.

I don't know why, but at that moment I casually reached my hand into my waistband, transferred the .38 into my inside jacket pocket and checked to make sure the muffler was still tightly screwed on. It was. Marshall saw nothing. He kept his eyes on the road.

Perhaps I should have felt a bit of sympathy for Kenny Marshall. But no one appreciates you feeling sorry for them in life, do they? I certainly don't want anyone feeling that way about me. Marshall took my momentary lapse into silence as an excuse to start nervously rabbiting on about the old neighbourhood where we grew up. Another good reason to pop him.

But I let him ramble on.

I was back to being the-man-with-a-plan and nothing else mattered.

I picked up his words here and there as he went on about the cost of Beemers and some such shit. Like I said a long time back in this story, it's often best to let people rabbit. You soon hear the fear in their voice.

"I heard you like a flutter," he said, snapping me out of my own thoughts.

"What?" I asked.

"You ever been seriously in hock to the bookies?"

I didn't answer. He did me a favour and kept rambling.

"I've been there, mate. And it fuckin' hurts."

I didn't want to hear about something that might, just might, make me feel sorry for him.

"Bang a right here, mate," I said, telling him exactly where we were going. I then mentioned the name of the boozer.

"You ever been there?"

He said he hadn't. But more importantly, he stopped rabbiting about gambling.

"It's a good place," I told him. "Stays open 'til two and they do some superb grub. You should take the old lady there sometime."

"Definitely."

We were both lying. I knew he wasn't going to live long enough to go there. He thought he was off on a one-way ticket to coconut grove within 48 hours. I couldn't actually see Kenny Marshall soaking up the sun and pickling in booze. He just wasn't the type. When villains run they nearly always end up returning to their own manor. It's safer on home ground.

If anything happens to you abroad you can't just bung an old mate in blue a few bob and move on, but back on your own patch there's a network of cronies always on the lookout for you. Come to think of it, he probably wouldn't have survived long even if I hadn't got him. I had a chuckle to myself then. I was sitting next to a fellow who was breathing, who was alive, and already I was thinking of him in the past tense.

The last hour had been a fucking strain for a pro like me. All this rabbiting had watered down the killing buzz I needed to go through with a job. I'd started to relax and that was bad news.

As we got closer to Marshall's death scene, I tried to refocus my mind on the task at hand.

Mind you, every time I had to witness another bit of bad driving it made me feel better about popping him. Then Marshall pissed me off even more by rattling on again.

"You know, I was thinkin' that …" he began.

"Give it a rest, Kenny. I've got a fuckin' headache."

He looked at me a bit oddly, then. Our eyes caught each other and he immediately turned away from me and looked straight ahead. I have no doubt that at that moment, for one brief uncomfortable beat, just a whisp of time, he knew for certain. Then, hopefully, he must have denied it to himself. I didn't really mind him knowing because he couldn't do fuck all about it.

We finally got to the boozer just past midnight.

"Head for the back of the car park," I told him.

He then pulled up so close to another motor I'd have to be Kate Moss to get out the door.

"Not here," I ordered. "Over there's better. I don't want anyone knowin' we're here."

"But no one will recognise this car."

"Please, Kenny. I know this bloke. He's quite an operator."

Marshall reluctantly reversed out of the spot and nearly hit the car next to us. Pratt.

As we moved to the more deserted parking place, I reached into my jacket and got a good solid grip on my new .38. My eyes panned the car park fast. My instincts were up to speed once more, trying to spot any potential witnesses. A motor was leaving across the other side of the car park. No way could they see anything.

The car park itself was quite well lit, but the spot we moved into was overshadowed by an old barn which flooded the car with darkness. I saw what appeared to be the edge of a field behind the car. The shooter stayed inside my jacket until he'd stopped the car, put it in park, killed the engine, turned off the lights, and then turned to face me.

That's when I pulled the .38 out and pointed it right at him.

Marshall looked at the gun and froze. I mean froze fucking solid.

He knew. At that moment he knew.

Panic affects different people different ways. Some realise straight away what's happening, accept their fate and know their time's up. Others start screaming. Some even try to say something but nothing comes out.

From Kenny Marshall I got fear, sheer fucking fear.

In the one split second before I started pumping bullets into his head he crunched his body up, leaned hard against the door, and stuck both his hands out towards me to try and deflect the bullets.

"See you 'round, Kenny," I said in the brief beat of time as my finger squeezed hard on the trigger.

Don't know why I said anything. Can't remember ever saying anything on a job before, but I can definitely recall myself saying, "See you 'round, Kenny," to him.

It was the only sound before I fired. The words sort of echoed.

"See you 'round, Kenny."

"See you 'round, Kenny."

"See you 'round, Kenny."

That O.B.E. spot I'd earlier earmarked was turned away from me, so I just aimed a shitload of bullets into his skull.

The .38. made a muffled POP! POP! POP! as I fired. The silencer did a good job. No one even standing next to the motor

247

would have heard it. But even so, the shots sounded pretty fucking loud to me.

The force of the first shell drove his head to the right and against the window.

The second and third bullets made his body jerk about, but he was dead when that first bullet crashed into his brain.

All three hit the spot because, at that range, it would have been impossible to miss.

I had a stroke of luck when the first bullet exited from the back of his neck and bedded itself in the car door just below the level of the window, which would have made a hell of a racket if it'd shattered. Not much blood spurted about the place, but a thick, steady stream flowed down the front of his face, running down the side of his nose and then veering off to the left of his mouth.

After I stopped firing, the sheer momentum of the bullets made his body slump down, straight down, then against the door.

For a second I thought he was going to hit the hooter, which I definitely did not want, but he missed the steering wheel completely.

I sat in the motor and put my other Latex glove back on. I felt an overwhelming sense of relief as I snapped the air bubbles out of the fingertips to make sure they stretched smoothly over my hands.

Then I unscrewed the silencer, placed it in one pocket and the still warm .38 in the other. The sudden, overwhelming silence was deafening, if you know what I mean. But it wasn't uncomfortable. The job was done. I took a long breath and smelt the cordite wafting through the warmish car interior. That whiff reminded me of all my previous jobs. Then I made sure Marshall's body was lying low enough so no one close by would see it. I didn't like the way he was staring at me so I closed his eyelids and tilted his silly hat over his face.

From a distance he looked like some old drunk sleeping it off after a night on the piss. Then I glanced around the car park to see if anyone was about.

There was a group of four or five people walking out of the boozer. I sat there and watched them drive off. They didn't even look in my direction. I pulled out one of my brand new £3 hankies and rubbed my prints off every place I'd touched, including Marshall's 9mm piece of rubbish Glock. Then I dropped it back in his pocket to ensure the filth got the message that he was just another gangster who'd copped it.

I got out of the motor and carefully rubbed my dabs off the passenger handle. I stayed at the back of the car park, keeping to the shadows, hopped a fence and walked off into the field. When I was far enough away I switched on my torch. I moved swiftly and with purpose. I felt good. The high was still there and I knew it would provide the fuel for my safe departure.

I never once looked back and the most comfortable silence of the whole night was only broken by the sound of my latex gloves as I pulled them off my hands while I walked through the frosty grass in my black trainers.

Chapter Twenty-Five

Getting the job done was only half the fun. Even a perfect hit will end in tears if you get nabbed with the evidence: in this case, that new .38 and muffler. Some pros don't pay attention to such details. They sling a piece in the river or stick it in their sock drawer or even drop it behind a hedge.

In the trade we call them convicts because guns are in the habit of coming back to haunt you. Did you know the Met even has a special unit of divers who do nothing but look for weapons? They'll never find my dabs on one. I wasn't going to dump that .38-with-silencer in any old place and risk some kid finding it. I intended to wipe it off the face of this earth for good.

The moment Marshall slumped forward on that car seat he became just a big piece of nothing as far as I was concerned. My first priority was working out how I'd get back to the suburbs and pick up my own motor. That car I nicked back in Bexley Village didn't bother me. There was nothing to connect it with me. I would have dumped it anyway. Who cares if the cozzers stumble on it?

As I marched through the fields behind the pub car park I checked out my clothes in the darkness to be sure I hadn't ended up with any claret on me.

Not a speck. My mind was now firmly focused in on the next stage of the job. I'd head back on to the main road in a couple of minutes. But I couldn't afford to get a ride too near that boozer. I remembered a 24-hour service station near the M20 roundabout about two miles down the road. I decided to call a cab from the garage because it was far enough from the location not to matter.

Then I got to thinking what a fuck-up this entire job had been. Just to top it all off, it started pissing down with rain again.

More than half an hour later I called a local cab company

whose name was plastered on a payphone in the garage forecourt. I never use the mobile in case the cozzers check my phone bill. Soon I was on my way to Maidstone, the opposite direction to where I needed to go just in case the boys in blue did get wind of my involvement. There I grabbed a second cab back into the suburbs to that all-night car park.

Finally, more than two and a half hours after doing away with Kenny Marshall, I reached my own motor. By now I urgently needed to ditch that weapon. I'd already been holding it for too long.

After getting out of the car park I whacked on a War cassette and listened to a magic track called "The World is a Ghetto". That got me in a better mood. Music calms the savage beast – and good soul music certainly cools down a hyped-up hitman, if you know what I mean.

I headed back towards Bromley, through the Beckenham Woods area with very specific plans on how to get rid of that gun and silencer.

I kept to the quiet shortcuts even though there was no traffic around. That's when I tried a calmer review of the Kenny Marshall job. I wondered if Twiggy was trying to get his pink plastic limbs out of that dustbin. I doubted it. His trousers were probably round his ankles by now. My encounter with him wouldn't exactly improve our friendship, but I had no choice in the matter.

I knew the MD would give me a bit of aggro, but business, as they say, is business.

By the time I got to Langley Park, near Beckenham Woods, it was past three in the morning. The heavy rain had cleared the air and everything looked crystal clear in the moonlight. If luck was on my side, Marshall's body wouldn't be discovered until daylight. With bad luck someone leaving the boozer, taking a piss alongside the motor might spot his bullet-riddled corpse.

If I got rid of everything by noon on Sunday I'd be in the clear. The chances of being pulled by plod were dropping by the minute. I slowed down just as I reached the Royal Beckenham

Golf Club, slipped into the car park and waited for a few minutes. I felt calmer but, interestingly, I couldn't feel the cold at all, even though I could tell from my breath it was a lot nippier here than in Bexley Village.

I even felt one bead of sweat slowly rolling its way down my spine.

I got out of the car, slipped across the car park and stood by the low fencing that bordered the golf course itself. The missus took golf lessons here. I took a look across the green and then hopped the fence and headed confidently across the fairway.

Big detached houses loomed off to the right and seemed very near in the blue moonlight. I headed up a steep hill that led to the first tee. There were so many trees bordering this part of the course that it was virtually pitch black except for a few shadows playing games with my head. The grass smelled sweet. The view when I reached the top was so good that for a moment I forgot the purpose of my mission. The golf course spread out below me, little rolling black hills.

I crossed a little bridge that carried golfers from the tenth green to the eleventh tee. Shining my torch before me I eventually got to the eighteenth hole where a small lake bordered the tee. I reached into my pocket and pulled out the silencer. Plunk! I dropped it casually in the water. It sounded deep enough to do the trick.

The muffler on its own didn't really prove much, should anyone ever find it. A rusty silencer and no gun to connect to it. I loved the idea of dropping it in such a snotty place. I'd worked here as a Saturday caddie when I was a kid and I really loathed those old wankers who trotted round the green in their poxy plus fours treating me like shit.

Why did I bother throwing away the silencer after spending good money on it? I just call it another safety precaution for my own piece of mind. The gun was a lot heavier and much more important to the filth so I hung on to that. I had plans for it.

I got back in the motor and headed towards Catford, where I knew a small ironmongers on Garrett Lane to which I held my own key. It wasn't a big place but it was bloody handy at that time of the morning.

The only light I put on in the workshop was a fluorescent strip over the workbench. That meant no one could see me from the outside.

First off I got hold of my man's electric hacksaw and sliced the barrel right through at the base. Then I split it down the middle long ways, right down the seam.

Next, I took each of those sections and cut them in half, lengthwise again. The barrel was now just four lumps of metal.

Then I leaned the remains of the shooter up on the workbench, opened the hammer and smashed the fucking shit out of it. It was very therapeutic. I even smashed up the firing pin because, if the filth did get hold of my cartridges, without a firing pin there was no fucking way they could match it up to a specific gun.

I took all the bits, dropped them in three plastic bags and got back in my motor and headed towards home via a specific scrap yard I knew near the main Eltham roundabout by the old A2.

I slung the motor up round the corner from the locked entrance and carefully wiped all the dabs off each piece of the shooter just for safety's sake.

Then I slipped over the fence towards a bunch of scrapped vehicles and threw the cylinder in the open boot of a smashed-up Capri. The stock went through the sunroof of a wrecked Granada. Then each part of the barrel ended up in an Austin Princess, a Citroën and God knows what else.

No one in the world could find all those pieces and put them back together again. And they'd soon end up in a poxy box of crushed metal after those motors went through the mincer.

Seems like a fuck of a lot of trouble to go to, and it is, but after carrying out a job, especially one with all the headaches involved in the Marshall hit, you're so keyed up you need something to keep you busy for a while.

Some shootists I know go out and eat a slap-up meal. Others

are desperate for a bit of nookie. Me? I take my time getting shot of my weapon. Then, if it can be arranged, I go out for a meal followed by some slap and tickle.

Morning was edging its way on to the horizon. The whole disposal operation, from the moment Marshall copped it until I'd finished spreading the gun, had taken about four hours. Now I was heading home to try and get some kip. Sunday was another work day. My fags and booze were arriving and I was gonna be at the lock-up to welcome my team home.

The missus was dead to the world when I crept in and, as promised, I was careful not to wake her. I felt completely knackered, but I just couldn't switch off and get some shuteye. The old brain was still motoring. I got up and crept to the bathroom, knocked back a couple of paracetamol and then lay there in the dark so as not to wake the missus. But I remained as high as a kite.

At about 6am I made yet another run at trying to get some kip. I recall tossing and turning for a bit. I even tried a wank in the hope that when I came it might shut my brain down.

I focused my memory bank camera on Cat's latest performance but her face kept being superimposed by Kenny Marshall, which was really doing my head in.

Kenny Marshall wearing nothing but a pair of platforms and trying to make me give him a blowjob. My hard-on crumbled faster than a dynamite demolition job on a sixties tower-block.

Eventually I drifted off into semi-consciousness. Thank God I didn't dream about Marshall.

I did suffer that recurring nightmare about being shot up the arsehole – the cruellest way to kill a man. And to cap it all, the face of the person who shot me – was me.

I was waiting the 15 minutes it takes between entry of the bullet and certain death when the missus got out of bed, and woke me up in the process.

It was just after noon.

I opened one eye and turned to one side to make sure my arsehole was still intact.

"Anything happen last night?" I mumbled.

No reply. She still had the hump.

"Did anything happen?" I repeated.

"Nothin'," was all I got.

She didn't even look at me as she said it.

Couldn't even remember what she was pissed off about.

"Anybody call?"

"No."

Then she sighed heavily.

"I want you to call my brother today and say you're sorry."

"Good idea."

Mate of mine told me recently that's what they call being passive aggressive in a relationship.

He reckons it works more often than not.

"Just make sure she doesn't suss it out or else you're back to square one," my friend told me.

If the missus had just bought a Rembrandt at the Tate Gallery I'd have said, "That's a nice idea. Let's hang it above the horse brasses."

Meanwhile, based on her initial responses, I knew she wouldn't be thrilled if I asked her to rustle up a bit of breakfast. Cowardice overcame hunger and I bottled out of asking. I'd pick up something on the way to the warehouse.

"Did your *job* go all right last night?" she said sarcastically.

"Yeah. Smooth as ..."

I stopped mid-sentence because I couldn't think of anything that could have gone *so* unsmoothly.

I started again.

"It went all right."

"I'm *so* pleased," she said in a tone of voice that sounded about as genuine as Hilary when Bill told her Monica gave good head.

Then, for the first time since waking up, I thought about Kenny Marshall. In those few hours of sleep I'd shut him out completely and I wished I still could. The missus mumbled something else but I didn't take much notice. Slowly, and not without a bit of difficulty, I rolled over and sat up.

I was still fucking knackered and stiff as a board. I felt like I had a splitting hangover. I struggled to the bathroom and chucked some cold water on my face. One at a time, very unwillingly, my eyes fully opened and I squinted into the strong daylight pouring through the bathroom window.

Next I belled my brother-in-law. His phone was off the hook so I called Disco Dave.

"What's happenin', then?"

"Nothin' yet," said Disco in his most businesslike voice. "Lorry should be here by four. I'm gonna catch the Charlton game on the telly and then go over."

"You got some helpers comin' to break up the load?" I asked.

Taking the cartons of cigarettes out of the boxes and splitting the crates of booze to fill orders is the pain-in-the-arse part of bootlegging. It can take a full day just to split the produce into specific orders. I usually hire in a few lads and give them a fiver an hour, plus a good bung when the job is done.

I call it putting something back into the community because it helps keep the kids off the streets.

"You comin' over, then?" asked Disco.

"That's the idea," I said. "Got to check out a few dead certs, then I'll be there."

"Come early if you want," he offered. "I got one of those little hand-held tellies. We can put our feet up while the staff get to work."

I walked down the newsagents to check the papers out while my brother-in-law was engaged on the blower. I didn't make them, which was a relief. Obviously, no one had found Marshall too quick. At about 4.00pm, something came up on the local TV news, buried near the end of their bulletin. The newsreader just said a body had been found in the front seat of a Ford Scorpio by a chef as he was leaving the boozer at around 5am. The unidentified driver had been shot three times in the head in "what looked like a gangland killing".

The newsreader – a pretty brunette with a nice set of teeth – went on to say that plod were investigating. That meant they knew fuck all. The programme didn't even have any footage from the scene-of-the-crime.

The average London detective is underpaid and overworked. He's got more crime on his hands then he can handle, and he's going to pick up the same wage slip every week whether he solves them or not.

That means he's very selective about which cases he puts any real time in to. The murder of law- abiding citizens rightly gets the bulk of his time. The topping of one criminal by another is a long way down his list of priorities.

A lot of Plods reckon it's a result when one villain knocks off another. One down, ten thousand to go. There's little glory and a lot of going through the motions for detectives when a hit is carried out in south east London.

And some of those officers are so bent they don't like to upset local firms by pressing too hard on a well deserved "Gangland Rubout", as the papers like to call them.

So, without an informant, an eyewitness or a gun the chance of cracking such cases is almost nil.

That's why, once I'm away from the scene of a crime and have disposed of my tools, I know I'm 95 per cent in the clear.

Chapter Twenty-Six

I don't know how they found me, or why they bothered, but I got pulled on Monday afternoon as I was coming out of the races. That Sunday I'd fulfilled all my booze and ciggy commitments. The deliveries had begun and as I wasn't needed at the warehouse until Monday evening to pick up the cash, I celebrated by driving to Windsor for a flutter.

I'd just got back to my motor after the sixth and final race when these two twats approached.

"Are you Malcolm Deakin?"

It sounds predictable but the script never changes.

"If you know who I am," I said, "what's the point in asking?"

They both smiled. We all knew the routine.

What really bothered me was that they'd tracked me all the way to Windsor, and then stood and waited near my motor until the last race was over.

They could have saved themselves a lot of trouble by knocking on my front door. It seemed like a classic rounding-up-the-usual-suspects routine.

"Raise your hands, please," one of them said very politely.

Plain clothes plod don't often get nasty. I didn't mind them searching me because I had nothing to hide. As I've said before, I never carry a piece right after a job or even keep one in my motor, and if I read about a hit in the *Telegraph*, I stop carrying a piece altogether. Better safe than sorry.

I put my hands in the air and held them up rigid.

"This all right?"

One of them nodded.

"Lean against the car please."

I pushed my weight forward and did as requested. It reminded me of Twiggy on Saturday night. It felt like months ago. The plod patting me down knew full well he wouldn't find anything, so he didn't try very hard.

259

"Mind if we take a look at your car?"

They couldn't have it all their own way.

"You got a warrant, then?"

They looked at each other. They obviously hadn't. I shrugged my shoulders and surprised them.

"Go ahead. I got nothing to hide."

I handed the keys to the goon standing nearest the door. He opened it up and began poking around. My motor was cleaner inside and out than the Queen's roller on the home straight at Epsom on Derby Day. By this time we'd drawn a bit of a crowd in the car park and that's when I got a bit shirty.

"You nickin' me, or what?" I said to the one standing next to me.

"Just need to ask you a few questions."

"Fire away."

The second goon stuck his head out of my motor.

"Nothing," he said to his partner, who turned back to me.

"You're required back at the nick," said the brighter one.

Alarm bells started ringing.

"What?" I asked.

"My guv'nor wants a one-on-one, Malcolm."

Those bells were turning into sirens and they'd just called me by my first name. Familiarity can breed real contempt.

"Off we go, then." I shrugged and we headed for my motor.

One of them sat alongside me while his partner picked up his Cavalier.

I just hoped that all this bollocks would make the late, not-so-great Kenny Marshall happy.

Chapter Twenty-Seven

My passenger for the ride identified himself as Detective Sergeant Rodney Pearce, from C14, the Yard's organised crime unit. Rodney was in his late-30s, well over six feet tall and the proud owner of a beer gut, an occupational hazard of most plain clothes plod.

He was no more keen on being in my motor than I was in having him there.

"Where we off to, then?" I asked.

He didn't answer. Making me sweat a bit seemed a cheap shot.

As we drove out of Windsor, I spotted his partner's blue Cavalier in my rear-view. Made a change from a silver Merc. The other detective overtook us on the main road and my new mate DS Pearce instructed me to stay on his tail. Many villains, especially from my manor, waste half their lives slagging off the filth and trying to cause them maximum aggro but I take the attitude that they got a job to do just like the rest of us.

Mind you, if I had a daughter I wouldn't be too keen if she came home one day and said, "Dad, I'm going to marry a DC on the Flying Squad."

You've gotta draw the line somewhere, ain't you?

DS Pearce remained untalkative. Every time I asked what was happening, he said, "You'll find out soon enough."

We drove over the M25 in virtual silence. It made a pleasant change from that fucking chatterbox Kenny Marshall. Then Pearce surprised me.

"How d'you get on with the horses today?" he asked.

I had won a few bob, but I didn't feel like revealing that to him.

"Why?" I asked. "Wanna join my syndicate?"

He laughed, which was a turn-up for the books. Our only bit of excitement came when his mate charged so far ahead of us as we came off at the Coulsdon turn-off that I got caught at a red light.

"I'll have to drive if you can't keep up with him," Rodney said.

I shook my head and told him, "I just been out with a mate who's the worse driver in the fuckin' world. I'll stick behind the wheel if it's all the same to you."

I like those little injokes that no one else understands.

'Just keep up with Gary, please," said DS Rodney Pearce.

Gary turned out to be Detective Constable Gary Meadows, his other half.

After we got through Croydon I knew we had to be heading to the C14 regional offices. Now I understood why they picked me up at the races. They wanted a nice day out in the country. I still needed to know who'd told them I was there, so I plugged away at Rodney. He shrugged his shoulders.

"One of your mates gave us the nod."

"I don't have any mates," I said, still trying to work out who'd stitched me up.

He considered that response for about ten seconds.

"That's sad," he finally said.

Couple of minutes later we were walking into a small, empty conference room with the standard long table and a handful of chairs. There was nothing on the walls except a calendar. The room was illuminated by a long, dirty, orange fluorescent strip light. Rodney gave me a chair and suggested I sit down and wait.

Couple of minutes later this woman comes into the room.

She was black, which in any south London nick is a rare sight. She didn't ID herself but the other two goons stood to attention so I knew she had to be the DCI in charge of the district C14 unit. She marched across the highly polished cherry vinyl floor in an impressive pair of four-inch heels.

I wasn't too happy about seeing her, and it had nothing to do with her colour or sex.

You see, normally in roundups they just drag you in, give you a hard time for an hour and then push you out the door. DCIs don't get involved unless they're planning to really pin something on you. Also, if you're previously acquainted with the plod in charge, a word in the right ear can often get you out of that nick in minutes.

So here I was with a woman DCI I'd never seen or heard of in my life. It wasn't a good start.

What really got to me was that she reminded me a lot of my first missus, who was a similar shade. Back then, some of my so-called mates made some snidey remarks about me marrying a black girl. I haven't talked to any of them since. My old mum didn't give a toss and that was all that counted. As an outsider, I've always been on the same wavelength as a lot of black people. I know what it's like when you don't fit in.

My first missus told me that's what attracted her to me in the first place.

Anyway, the first thing this power-suited woman DCI did was read me my rights in a very educated accent, which was even more confusing. I'd heard my rights so many times I knew them better than the national anthem. But because she was saying them I listened more closely.

I had a right to a brief. I didn't have to answer any questions. Well, I told them, I'm not going to answer any questions and I want my brief down here pronto. (In the old days your rights consisted of a good slapping in the backroom of the station house but at least you could slip them a fifty and be on your way).

"If you've done nothing wrong," the lady DCI asked, "what d'you want a solicitor for?"

"None of your fuckin' business," I told her.

I wanted to see how she'd respond to a bit of lip.

"Mr Deakin, we don't know each other but I would appreciate a little respect."

"Sorry. That was out of order," I said, and I meant it. "You're in charge here, not me. And being so well educated, you're going to ask me some tough questions and me being so stupid, I'm liable to give you the wrong answers. My brief will tell me what I should and shouldn't answer."

Just then Rodney came forward and whispered something to the lady DCI, who then backed off.

263

He moved closer and smiled wearily in my direction like a door-to-door salesman on his 50th call of the day. I was about to get a dose of good cop, bad cop.

Well, well, well, what have we here, officer? Even my cousin's eight-year-old knows this routine. He sees it every night on *The Bill*. Rodney kicked off by offering me a cigarette. I declined but that didn't put him off.

"I'd cool down a bit, if I were you," he said, trying to perch casually on the edge of the table.

The sweat on his forehead glistened in a blue grey colour under the amber striplight.

"You look a fuckin' sight hotter than me, mate," I replied.

"Look, Malcolm, we just need to sort out a few things, then you can be on your way."

"Either I walk now or my brief comes down. You got something on me then go ahead and charge me."

Rodney looked back at the DCI for direction. The DCI nodded and I'd swear a slight, sexy smile came to her lips. Rodney got up and lumbered off.

Then she chipped in, "All right, call your brief."

I was thrown for a moment. I smiled on the outside but inside I was getting a bit shaky. I'd only nagged them about the brief because I wanted them to let me take a walk. The usual routine, when I pushed them like that, was they'd see me to the door.

So I got hold of my brief, sharpish.

I just prayed there was no way they knew what I'd been up to.

I judge briefs by only one rule: how quickly they can get me out the door. I don't care about the fees (as I've said, that's down to the faces who hire me and take care of my legal exes).

I don't want to know about problems and pleadings. I just want to know how soon I'll get out.

My brief at that time was, and still is, a wonderful gent called Cyril Roote. Mr Roote, as I've always called him and will continue to do so, would walk me straight out the door, I hoped. Mr Roote is a smallish bloke with wire-rimmed specs and a mop of thick, grey hair. His office is just off Hatton Garden and he loves a plate of chopped liver at the Nosherie most weekday lunchtimes.

Mr Roote began by defending petty villains on legal aid in north London. Then he invested in property in the late 70s and found that some of his speculating involved partners from the criminal underworld. They made him a member of their exclusive club and he defended them on a variety of charges and won. These days he's a very rich, powerful brief with some of the best "business" contacts in London.

Mr Roote had been recommended to me when my previous brief made the mistake of telling another pro to accept a manslaughter charge instead of pleading not guilty to murder. That's just not the way a good brief operates.

Anyway, Mr Roote got down to Croydon just as fast as his maroon Bentley Turbo could carry him round the M25. He doesn't make a packet off me but he gets excellent brownie points from the MD, who'd hired me for the Marshall job – and Mr Roote knows how to turn those points into crisp new notes.

While we were waiting for Mr Roote to arrive, plod tried to ask me a few questions, but I kept my trap shut. What they thought didn't matter. It was what they could prove that would cause the problems.

I went over the job step by step in my mind.

Maybe someone had seen me. That had happened before. Twice. Once the witness had to go on a surprise holiday just before my trial and the case got thrown out.

Another time the potential witness realised he'd made a mistake and told the court I was not the guilty man. That realisation saved all our lives.

Mr Roote eventually walked in the door dressed in a light brown checked tweed suit with a tacky-looking bright yellow waistcoat complete with watch and chain. Bit like Toad of Toad Hall. He immediately informed Plod that his client (that's me) had been illegally detained (I hadn't been) and demanded that I be immediately released.

Naturally, it didn't cut much ice. Eventually he calmed down and asked to be left alone with his client (me). Plod reluctantly withdrew. The two most important rules in life are take good care of your old lady and never lie to your brief. I could tell Mr Roote the lot because our conversation was privileged, meaning no part of it could ever be used against his client (me).

I knew the filth wouldn't bug the room because that would probably get every case in the station thrown out of court.

Mr Roote's eyes looked a bit puffy and red. He'd probably been on his third Vodka Martini when I called.

"All righty," he sighed, "let's hear it all. What do they think you've been up to?"

Up until this point it never dawned on me that Mr Roote didn't have a clue what I'd done. The filth hadn't mentioned a word about it, either.

"Murder."

He shook his head. This time he didn't even look at me. I think he knew the answer before he asked the question.

"Did you?"

I nodded.

He gave out a slight chuckle.

"Why can't you stick to something safe like drugs?"

Mr Roote took off his specs and wiped them.

"Well, what happened?"

I told him the whole story.

I told him about Marshall.

I told him why he went.

I told him about getting pulled by plod.

I told him about the job itself.

The only thing I left out was the names of the chaps who contacted me and hired me. Then Mr Roote asked me to go right through it all over again.

"Right," he said after hearing it a second time. "Is it possible they have anything at all?"

"Anything's possible."

"What about witnesses?"

"I didn't see any."

I paused and thought about Twiggy. Maybe he was getting his own back? A phone tip? Didn't seem his style, but it was possible. Twiggy couldn't land me in it, though, because he was in it himself. If I went, and I found out he'd stitched me up, he'd go down as well.

What about those two white rastaboys? The stick-up men. How about them?

I didn't think so. In the dark, at the distance they'd been sitting, they couldn't possibly ID me even if they knew who I was, which they didn't.

Hang on. They did have my number plate. But they wouldn't go to the filth, surely? I remembered Twiggy on the floor, squealing for his life: "Malcolm, those arseholes got nothin' to gain and their lives to lose if they turn you in."

"Where's the gun?" asked Mr Roote.

"Gone."

"Are you certain the victim died?"

"Saw it on the local TV news."

We both nodded slowly. Mr Roote reached into his briefcase and pulled out a legal pad of yellow lined paper.

"Now, this is what I want you to do," he said. "When they come back in and start asking questions, answer them to the best of your ability. I'll tell you when to stop if you're going too far. We have to find out if they know anything. And, Malcolm ..." he paused, "... when I tell you to shut up, you shut up."

"Whatever you say, doctor," I agreed.

"I have no doubt," he said, "it would have been easier than being your solicitor."

I mentioned to Mr Roote that so far plod hadn't even said why they'd brought me in. I didn't want him giving away anything, either.

We invited the Met's finest back into the room. I looked at my watch. I still hoped I might make it to the lock-up that night and deal things out to my customers. It was already almost six o'clock. The DCI walked back in with a cassette machine in her arms. She put it down and was about to plug it in when good old Mr Roote started strutting his stuff.

"My client and I agree he should co-operate in any way he can," he told them. "Naturally, I'll guide him over certain issues.

"Naturally," came the lady DCI's response.

She looked irritated as she tried to work out why the cassette recorder plug didn't seem to want to go in the socket.

"Naturally ..." she repeated through gritted teeth.

Then Mr Roote interrupted.

"I'm so sorry but I didn't catch your name."

The DCI looked up at him from the floor socket where she was still trying to jam the plug in. Her skirt had ridden halfway up her thigh and the moisturiser was glistening on her ebony legs. I could smell the scented skin cream.

"Julie Cater," she said, a bit impatiently. "Detective Chief Inspector Julie Cater."

Funny thing her name. It just didn't seem to belong to a black woman. In a strange sort of way it made me even more intrigued by her. Mr Roote stuck out his hand.

"Cyril Roote. Nice to meet you."

DCI Julie Cater nodded but made no effort to shake his hand. Eventually, she got the tape recorder going and stated the time, date and location of the interview. Mr Roote charged straight in once again.

"Let me begin by informing you that my client has no idea why he is here. He has advised me he has done nothing wrong."

"Right," DCI Cater nodded. Then she turned back to me. "Do you know Kenny Marshall?"

"Marshall?" I scratched my head naturally. "There's a lot of Marshalls round these parts."

"He lived on Eastbourne Road, Bromley."

I gave the matter a lot of thought.

"Doesn't ring a bell."

"He was brought up in the same neighbourhood as you," said Julie Cater.

I waited and went through a few motions.

"Yeah …" I paused for a few seconds thinking what to say next. "Yeah, I knew one Kenny Marshall …"

I put the emphasis on *one*.

"Yeah, we knew each other when we was kids. And, you're not going to believe this, my missus and me bumped into him and his old lady in Harrods couple of weeks back. Is that the fellow?"

Cater nodded.

"What's he been up to, then?" I asked.

"He was found dead yesterday. Shot in the head three times."

"Really?" I asked with as much surprise as I could manage, which wasn't much.

"Perhaps you saw it in the papers or on the television?"

There was something about the way she said television instead of TV or telly or the box. I paused for a deep breath.

"Nah. I stick to Channel Four racing. Gave up on the real world years ago. Nothin' but bad news."

I looked at Mr Roote for direction, but he was scribbling away on his legal pad. I needed to work out what the filth had in mind. I wasn't too worried, but I'd be a liar if I didn't admit I was a bit concerned. Once I got in a similar scenario which ended with me spending almost a year in custody at the Scrubs, waiting to be dealt with. (And waiting for witnesses to plan their holidays.)

So I asked for a glass of water.

Rodney, who'd been standing quietly in the background, went off to get the water. That was when they changed tactics.

"How much money do you have on you?" asked DCI Cater.

"On me?"

"On you."

"Don't know," I said, and I didn't, but they weren't going to let it drop that easily.

"Take a guess."

So I took a guess.

"Six, seven hundred quid perhaps."

"Where d'you get that money?"

I looked at them both for a moment and took a long sigh.

"None of your fuckin' business ..." I started to say in an angry voice.

"What my client means," Mr Roote interrupted, "is that he would prefer not to answer that particular question."

"Is that right?" Cater asked, turning to me, her full, swollen lips pouting like a goldfish.

"Spot on," I agreed with Mr Roote.

"All right," Cater said into the tape recorder, "suspect declines to answer."

Her teeth were big and white and she had a brilliantly straight, almost Roman nose. But it was that voice which really got me hot under the collar. Just then Rodney turned up with my water. As I slowly sipped it the questions grew more specific.

"What were you doing in the Swanley area Saturday night around midnight?" asked Cater.

Good question. The wrong response could concede I was in the borough.

"I wasn't," I told them. "I was tucked up in my bed."

"Prove it."

"Don't have to. Don't have to prove nothin'. You're the people who have to prove I did or I don't or I was or I wasn't."

Mr Roote laughed.

"What kind of car do you drive?" asked DCI Cater.

I told her.

"Must have cost a few bob?" she asked.

"Got a good deal off a mate."

"Thought you didn't have any mates?" interrupted Rodney. He'd remembered what I'd said to him in the car earlier. I nodded my head slightly and gave him a smile because it was a half-decent response.

Then there followed a lot of moving about, shuffling of

seats and bits of paper by everyone except Mr Roote and myself. I sat there, hands folded in front of me on the table. Occasionally I leaned back to take a stretch. Mr Roote was still scribbling away.

"You own a gun?" she asked.

"Me?"

I was a bit shaken by that one.

"Yes, you."

Mr Roote immediately held a cautious finger up in the air. "That would be against the law, wouldn't it?" I asked.

Mr Roote put his finger down and returned to his yellow legal pad. I started to believe they didn't really have anything on me, except a hunch. Maybe they were just rounding up the usual suspects. They were trying to make a hopefa case – which means they were hoping for any kind of clue that would smoke me out.

For the first time since we were at Windsor Race Course, the other detective, Gary Meadows, opened his mouth.

"You've been ID'd near Bexley Village on Saturday night."

I raised my eyebrows.

"You reckon?" I said calmly.

I didn't believe them. They had to try and nail me for doing something wrong – someone spotted you, you left a dab, the victim didn't snuff it instantly and ID'd you. Something, but it was up to me to ignore it all.

"Think you got me mixed up with someone else."

"I doubt it," said DCI Cater, "but we'll find out when we get you in a line-up."

I was so transfixed by those silky smooth legs that the words "line-up" didn't immediately sink in. Then I woke up to the fact this was very bad news. A line-up implied someone really did spot something and the filth were going to pin it on me.

And the cozzers have been known to pull a few strokes on line-ups.

Putting up five redheads and one blonde when the witness

knows it's a blonde who did the job is what I'll write here rather than the obvious racial version. At that moment I know my face looked ashen. Cater and Rodney looked at me. I raised my eyebrows and shrugged my shoulders.

"Will you take a paraffin test?" Cater asked.

This would show if I'd fired a gun recently. I didn't know whether or not I'd fail. It had been more than 36 hours since I knocked off Marshall, but I wasn't wearing gloves at the time.

"No," I said.

"Why not?"

"Don't feel like it. Don't have to. Don't want to. That's three reasons."

I was getting well pissed off with the whole saga by this stage. Kenny Marshall wasn't worth all this fucking aggro.

"How much longer you gonna be?" I asked.

DCI Julie Cater laughed.

"Depends on you."

Then she went through the entire fucking routine that plod always believes will trap a suspect.

Question: D'you know so-and-so from Bexleyheath?

Answer: Never heard of him.

Question: Where did Marshall come from?

Answer: Same road as me in Bexleyheath. You know that.

Question: Have you eaten at this particular boozer where the body was found?

Answer: No way, I heard the Guinness was cloudy and the food gives you the trots.

Question: Who were you with on Saturday night?

Answer: My missus. Ask her.

Question: Did Kenny Marshall ever place a bet with anyone you know?

Answer: I don't know anybody who places bets.

Question: How much were you paid?

Answer: Paid? For what? What you on about?

Question: Why don't you tell us all about it? We've got a witness, you know.

Answer: Fuck off and fuck your witness. I was home with my old lady Saturday night.

This went on for at least an hour, with the questions always going back to Marshall. The filth will batter away at you with questions down one side and the other if you let them. Then the increasingly delectable DCI Cater changed tactics.

Question: "Whoever killed Kenny Marshall must have *fucking* hated him."

She hadn't sworn once before. It was wonderful to hear. Then I realised for the first time she had the bluest eyes I'd ever seen in a black woman since my first missus. I looked straight into them without moving an inch.

"Why's that then?"

"Because the killer pumped a lot of bullets into him."

She stood up at that moment and moved closer to me.

"So?" I replied, trying to sound as if I didn't give a toss.

"So," she repeated, looking down at me. "He was already dead after the first bullet hit. There was no point in firing any more. Not very professional, was it?"

I took a long snort of her moisturiser. An awkward silence followed. Must have lasted all of half a minute. Then she walked around to the side of the table and looked across at me.

And you know what? Her hands were on her hips just the same way every woman in my life has done in the past. It freaked me out for a moment.

"Didn't your wife used to know Kenny Marshall?" she said, smirking at me.

I took a long, deep breath. I needed to compose myself.

"What sorta question is that?" I asked.

Mr Roote stood up.

"What is going on here?" he said.

"Didn't your wife used to know Kenny Marshall?" she repeated with lips glistening.

Mr Roote popped up again. But I waved him down.

"Who gives a fuck?" I said.

"Doesn't it bother you?"

"How can it bother me if I don't know about it?"

Cater clipped across the vinyl in her heels without saying another word. Then she stood in that familiar pose in the far corner of the room and turned back towards me.

"Do you sleep well at night, Malcolm?"

"Like a baby."

"That's not what I heard."

I took another deep breath to compose myself. Was it the missus? She was certainly pissed off enough to land me in the frame. Maybe they'd told her I'd plugged Marshall and she was out for revenge. I stared straight at Cater. She knew exactly what was going through my mind.

"I've been looking over your shoulder for a long time, Malcolm."

I tried to look surprised.

"Am I really *that* interestin'?"

"Some people I've been talking to find you fascinating," she said almost admiringly and began walking back towards us.

"Like who?" I said.

"Like that very rich lady friend of yours in …" she picked up a file on the table "… Notting Hill?"

Now Cat was in the frame. Maybe I'd told her too much. But I was sure I hadn't. It must have been the missus getting her revenge once they'd told her about my extra-curricular activities and the fact I'd done in her old bedmate Marshall. I couldn't really blame her. I'd been playing with fire for years. That family trait of mine, guilt, kicked in then. Maybe I deserved it all.

Then Mr Roote came to my rescue.

"Do you and your officers have any further questions for my client?"

Cater ignored him and looked at Rodney.

"Right, let's get that line-up organised."

I raised my eyebrows at Mr Roote. He smiled. Rodney left the room. Julie Cater then switched off the tape machine and seemed to make a point of unplugging it as slowly as possible.

I got another flash of her thighs in the process. Then she stood up, turned towards me with her hands on hips once again.

"The tape's off, Malcolm. Now you can tell me about it. Get it off your chest …"

"Please, Ms Cater," said Mr Roote, "you've had your interview. This is completely out of order."

"It's all right," I said. "I got nothing to hide."

I found myself looking at her chest at that moment. She smiled at me.

"You're an intelligent man, Malcolm. I can tell you feel bad about what you've done."

That last remark got to me a bit. Cater was reading my mind. It made me very uneasy. Mr Roote looked at me but I shook my head and put my finger up in front of me to tell him not to say anything.

Then she carried on.

"I could tell you I'd get the charges reduced but you know that's bullshit. At least you can clear your conscience and I know that means a lot to you. It's obvious you've had enough of this game."

She waited.

"Well?"

Cater was the brightest and horniest police officer I'd ever encountered. We could have had a fucking ball together in another life.

I paused for another deep breath.

She looked at me triumphantly as if I was about to crack. I squinted up at her seriously.

"Ain't you got more important things to do like solve the racist murders that have plagued this manor for years?"

Cater was clearly lost for words so I moved in for the kill.

"Were you involved in the Stephen Lawrence case?" I asked, knowing full well she *must* have been.

"Yes," replied Cater.

"That's more important than hunting down the killer of a slag like Kenny Marshall."

Cater shrugged her shoulder pads.

"Maybe you're right."

Seconds of silence passed.

Ten.

Twenty.

And then some.

Then it dawned on me. The witness. That old dear Mrs Curran, the lady with the fucking Alsatian. She'd come back to haunt me. I snapped my fingers as I realised it, drawing everyone's attention. Cater looked up immediately. A smile came to her face. Her eyes flared with excitement.

"Just like that, was it?" she asked.

"What?" I said, genuinely baffled.

Then Cater lifted her right hand in the shape of a gun, pulled her middle finger back and snapped the fingers of her beautifully manicured hand.

CLICK.

CLICK.

CLICK.

She then pursed her lips before blowing some imaginary smoke from the top of her imaginary barrel.

"It's that easy, isn't it?" she said with the tip of her finger resting on her bottom lip.

Mrs Curran, everyone's favourite granny, had blown my cover. She'd ID'd me on the street near Marshall's house more than once. That old bird was about to throw me to the dogs. I looked over at DCI Julie Cater who'd gone back to pointing her imaginary gun at me.

Not a word was uttered for at least a minute.

Then I realised I had to tell Mr Roote about the dog lady. I leaned over and whispered in his ear.

"There's one thing," I started, still looking at Cater as I spoke, even though she couldn't hear me. "I forgot to tell you. There's this little old lady …"

I stopped as Rodney re-entered the room. He whispered something in Cater's ear and left again.

I waited for Cater to say something. She pointed that imaginary gun straight at me again. "Last chance," she said.

Was Mrs Curran waiting out in the hall? Would she still have that big mutt on a lead with her? I couldn't picture them any way but together. I shut my eyes for a few seconds and then opened them again.

Julie Cater was still pointing her pretend gun right at me. I knew I had to say *something*.

"My dad always said it was dangerous to point guns at people," I said, reminding myself of the last time I said the same thing to Kenny Marshall.

Suddenly, a vision of Marshall's blown-up pineapple of a head snapped into my brain. I turned off the picture switch as fast as my guilt would let me. Cater nodded slowly at me, a smile curling on to her lips.

She took one long, deep breath and her perfectly formed chest rose by two inches in the process.

"Our witness had to leave so we can't put you in a lineup and we're not going to hold you."

I tried not to look pleased. Then she leaned down next to my right ear. So close it sent a tingle through my body.

"You should be more careful who you fuck," she whispered.

Her tongue almost touched my ear lobe as she spoke.

"What?" I replied.

She leaned even closer. She smelt incredible.

"Was she worth it?" Then she stood up again. "See you soon, Malcolm."

I almost puked my guts up at that moment. I could taste the bile rising up my throat and then expiring in a rancid, bitter odour in my mouth.

That's when I worked it all out.

DCI Julie Cater was the middle-aged black woman Cat said she'd slept with.

I held the legs of the table tightly, swallowed hard and tried to think it through. All Cater could know about were a few horny things I said to get Cat worked up.

But my two worlds had just collided.

I looked straight up at Cater as she stood there, once again, hands on hips. I couldn't help liking her. I ran my tongue across my top lip. We stared at each other. I looked up and down her body and tried to imagine her and Cat slurping at each other like hungry wolves.

That's when I knew Cater knew I did it.

She knew I was guilty but she didn't have a shred of real evidence and there wasn't a fucking thing she could do about it, however many times she jumped into bed with my friend Cat.

Chapter Twenty-Eight

Two, maybe three minutes later, Mr Roote and I walked out of the nick together. "Do you have any idea how they linked you to all this?" he asked.

"Yeah," I said, thinking of Twiggy and all the rest of them, and knowing I wasn't going to do fuck all about it.

Twiggy's time would come, but not over this. He deserved the bullet even if he wasn't to blame.

"Thank you, Mr Roote," I said to my brief. "I'll make sure your bill is taken care of."

"Would you care for a drink?" he asked ever so politely.

I checked my watch. It was past nine o'clock.

" 'Fraid I gotta meet a man about a dog."

"Well, until next time, then."

I didn't disagree. We both knew there would be a next time. I was about to walk away when Mr Roote stopped me.

"You never finished telling me about that little old lady."

I grinned.

"It can wait, Mr Roote."

I moved off towards my motor and started running through my chores for the next few days.

Number one, the cash from the fags and booze and the meeting with my Russian friend, Ludwig.

Number two, my bookie needed a bell by Tuesday. Beyond that I had no plans. I knew something would turn up. A puff run to Holland, whatever. It always did.

The cozzers would be keeping a close eye on me for a bit so I'd have to watch my back. That wasn't so bad. I had plenty of dosh in my pocket which meant more time with the geegees and my well-built, well-spoken she-girl Cat.

Plod were more than welcome to trail me. I'd get an extra big hard-on knowing that DCI Julie Cater had made some poor bastard sit outside Cat's house freezing his bollocks off

279

while I was using Cater's stainless steel loveballs on her bedmate. I remembered how pissed off I'd been when I doorstepped Kenny fucking Marshall as he was having a bunk-up with his bit-on-the-side.

Kenny Marshall. I gave him a brief thought.

I presumed the funeral wouldn't be for a week or two because they'd have to give him a post mortem and all that stuff. Shame really. Must make it tough on the family knowing some nutty professor is slicing his flesh into pieces and then having to wait for so long before burying him. I didn't intend going to the funeral, or even sending flowers. Why take the piss?

Anyway, I got in my motor, loaded up my favourite *Motown Chartbusters Volume IV* and took a long deep relieved breath and smacked the steering wheel hard with the palms of my hands. Then I had one last look back at the copshop.

DCI Cater was coming down the steps.

As my motor warmed up, I sat and watched her strolling through the car park while Marvin Gaye got into his stride with "Heard It Through The Grapevine". I enjoyed watching her swing her hips as she headed towards me. I rolled down the window and Marvin's soul food floated out into the cold air. The game had ended, we both knew it, and she looked more relaxed, more at ease.

I smiled up at her. She put a hand on my car roof and leaned in.

"Marvin Gaye. He was de *real* king of soul."

Cater's voice sounded different – more black.

"Yeah," I said, taken aback that she was talking music rather than crime.

"Shame he got murdered," said Julie Cater, gyrating ever so slightly to the beat.

I knew why Cat couldn't resist her. She had it all.

"His old man did it, didn't he?" I asked.

"Yeah," replied Cater. "Domestic killings are de most tragic."

Her voice was getting more and more West Indian by the second.

"That's what you lot call a point-of-the-circle inquiry, isn't it?" I asked, brimming with confidence.

Cater didn't hesitate to respond.

"Right," she said, shaking her head. "Start at de centre and work yo' way through spouses, lovers, family, friends, coworkers ..." She paused and sighed. "Some ways de're too easy ta solve and ya' end up learnin' tings about people ya wish ya never knew ..."

Cater took a long suck through her perfectly capped teeth and her chest rose.

"On de other hand, cold-blooded murder is more difficult ta solve 'cos dere's no startin' point and no circle. No real connection ta de victim."

We were looking directly into each other's eyes.

"So what happens if a murder seems to have been committed by a stranger but in fact he or she comes from within that same circle?" I asked.

Cater said nothing for about five seconds. Marvin Gaye was still going at full blast.

She smiled and leaned in closer to me.

"Ya did it, right?" she asked.

She knew.

"What d'you reckon?" I asked her, smiling back.

"Ya did it," she said without a flicker of emotion in her voice.

I looked up at her and winked. Then I put the gear stick into D for Drive, whacked up Marvin Gaye and left Julie Cater standing on the pavement.

And that's how Kenny Marshall came to make two paragraphs in the *London Evening Standard*.